Praise for An

Dreams for Stones

Indie Next Generation Book Awards Finalist

...incredibly vivid and emotional tale of love and loyalty, friendship, loss, and faith...*Booklist*

...a lovely story about life changes and love lost and found. *Romantic Times Book Review*

Stunning! Juli Townsend, Author of *Absent Children*

Absence of Grace

...a riveting read of personal struggle, very much recommended. *The Midwest Book Review.*

Both a coming of age and a romance novel, this story is captivating and charming. But be prepared, you may not want to put it down once you start. Karen Bryant Doering, author of *Parents' Little Black Book*

...the writing is perfect. Absolutely smooth and divine. Like the best bar of chocolate. Fran Macilvey, author of *Trapped*

Counterpointe

Endorsed by Compulsion Reads

...a powerful novel of two lovers who face profound challenges. Poignant and insightful...a compelling dramatic evaluation of what it means to love or be loved. *The Midwest Book Review*

...a wonderful exploration of two people from different worlds coming together and finding love and building a lasting, realistic relationship with all the complexities, joys and sorrows that entails. *Long and Short of it Reviews*

Ann's brilliant, well–thought–out prose lifts her stories to a higher literary level than most of today's fare…prepare to be impressed. Pam Berehulke, Bulletproof Editing

Love and Other Acts of Courage

Love and Other Acts of Courage is…beautiful. The plot is engaging and it focused on the development of the characters…and the ending (is) very satisfying. Lorena Sanqui for Readers' Favorite

…a love story woven within an engaging mystery with twists and turns, believable villains, and enough tension to keep you turning pages. Dete Meserve, author of *Good Sam*

…the characterizations of Max, Jake, and Sophie are done so delicately, so perfectly, that each alone would be worthy of a separate story. In short, Love and Other Acts of Courage is so much more than a love story. Kate Moretti, NY Times bestselling author of *Thought I Knew You*

Memory Lessons

…you don't want to miss this inspirational story. David Johnson, author of *The Tucker Series*

…a real treat if you like to read novels that make you feel. Margaret Johnson, author of *The Goddess Workshop*

…high-stakes drama with real characters and an understanding of how women process memory and guilt. Patricia Macauliffe

A lovely and compelling story. Michelle Lam, author of *The Accidental Prophetess*

Look for these titles by

Ann Warner

Absence of Grace
Counterpointe
Doubtful
Love and Other Acts of Courage
Memory Lessons
Vocabulary of Light
Dreams for Stones
Persistence of Dreams
Unexpected Dreams
The Babbling Brook Naked Poker Club Series

absence of grace

Ann Warner

Silky Stone Press

absence of grace
Silky Stone Press
Copyright 2011 Ann Warner
https://www.AnnWarner.net

ISBN 13: 9781720096610

Cover Art by Ann Warner

Published in the United States of America
Library of Congress Registration: TX 7-807-115

Dedication

To my husband, partner, friend.
And to the real Mag who taught me how to cook
and helped me become.

Book Description

The memory of an act committed when she was nineteen weaves a dark thread through Clen McClendon's life. It is a darkness Clen ignores until the discovery of her husband's infidelity sends her on a quest for redemption and forgiveness. However, her journeying is providing few answers and peace remains elusive, even during the time she spends in an abbey. But when Clen makes a decision that is both desperate and random to go to Wrangell, Alaska, she will learn choices are never truly random and they always have consequences.

Former Seattle attorney, Gerrum Kirsey, is of the opinion that most people who end up in Alaska are running from something. Including him. And this appears to be true for the aloof woman who has come to Wrangell as the Bear Lodge's summer cook. When Gerrum learns that Clen applied for the job from an abbey, and that the owner of the Lodge remembers her visiting years ago with a husband, he's intrigued and determined to discover the woman behind the walls.

Chapter One

1962

COLORADO SPRINGS, COLORADO

"Michelle Marie,...we need to talk."

The girl winced at the use of her full name, but that wince gave way to alarm at the sight of both her parents standing in the doorway to her bedroom.

Quickly, she reviewed the past month, searching for a transgression to explain their obvious distress. There was the paper airplane incident during honors English, but she'd already done her penance for that. So...could they have learned she planned to ditch the college wardrobe picked out by her mother with such love and determination? The boys had figured it out, and she'd threatened them with excruciatingly painful deaths if either of them said a word. Still, a clothes contretemps would hardly explain her father's presence

Her mom sat on her bed, while her dad hovered. "You know that fainting episode Josh had?"

Joshua had hit a home run in his last Little League game, but he'd passed out crossing home plate. Very scary. But he was fine after he drank some water and sat in the shade awhile—so what was the problem?

Her father's hand came to rest on her mother's shoulder.

"The doctors did some tests." He drew in a breath. "Joshua has leukemia."

Leukemia? The word made her feel light and floaty, untethered, like that time she rode the roller coaster at Elitch's and couldn't stop shaking for an hour afterward. Joshua and Jason could be real pains. But that, after all, was younger brothers' territory. She yelled at them sometimes. Okay, a lot. They were brats. But this...

Her throat tightened. "He's going to be okay, isn't he?"

"Yes he is." Her mother's words sounded more incantation than certainty, and it didn't help when her eyes filled with tears.

"What about Jase? Is he okay?"

"Of course," her father said.

But there was no 'of course' about it. Joshua and Jason were identical twins.

"They were both tested," her mother said. "Jason is fine."

"I guess I better stay here. Not go to college." They were the hardest words she had ever said. She'd been looking forward to college with a desperation she hadn't admitted to anyone. Had barely admitted to herself. Despite the fact Marymead, like her wardrobe was more her mother's choice than hers.

Her mom straightened and blew her nose. "Of course you're going to college, Michelle. Joshua is going to be just fine."

She should have felt relieved, but somehow she didn't.

~ ~ ~

MARYMEAD COLLEGE MEAD, KANSAS

She left for college on a Greyhound bus. It wasn't the original plan, but her mother had to be in Denver for Joshua's treatment, and her father couldn't give up two days work to drive her. In some ways, though, taking the bus made it easier to leave.

Despite the fact only her father was there to see her off, she still wore one of the outfits her mother had chosen. But at the dinner stop in Limon, she replaced the full-skirted dress with slacks and a tailored shirt. She also cut her hair, something she hadn't had the heart to do before.

Peering into the wavy mirror in the bus stop restroom, she did the best she could, although the result wasn't even close to the pixie cut she'd envisioned. But then, she was no pixie. The boys were the ones who'd inherited their mother's delicate bone structure. She took after her father. In his case, tall and awkward was endearing. On her? Well, suffice it to say she'd made it all the way through high school without anyone asking her for a date.

When she reboarded the bus, the driver frowned and asked to see her ticket. He examined it thoroughly before, still frowning, he waved her aboard. She accepted his lack of recognition as a sign her transformation was a success.

With the bus only partly full, there was nobody in the seat beside her. She turned sideways and curled her feet under her. Bits of snipped hair had slipped down her neck, and they itched, making it difficult to doze off, although that was okay, since she didn't really want to sleep. Instead she wanted to savor this transition from past to future.

She looked around the bus, imprinting it on her memory— the dark interior with only a few reading lights illuminating dozing occupants—as the vibration of the engine settled into a steady rhythm on the flat road.

She ran fingers through her now short hair and looked toward the window, encountering there an image of herself overlaid on the darkness outside. An unexpected vision, that girl, with her straight nose, lips neither thick nor thin, and jaw firmer than most. Her eyes, which appeared darker than they actually were, held in their depths a hint of both excitement and trepidation.

She fluffed what was left of her hair, staring at that girl, beginning to smile. Yes, at last. She looked like herself. Like *Clen.*

Despite the itching, the steady hum of the tires eventually lulled her to sleep, and when the bus arrived in Mead, she stepped into the cool pre-dawn and stretched, savoring a feeling of delicious anticipation.

A man leaning on the door of a yellow cab straightened and ambled over. "You heading for the college, Miss?"

When she said she was, he loaded her suitcases in his trunk. Then he climbed in and looked at her in the rearview mirror. "Wasn't sure you was a Marymead girl at first. Don't look like one, that's for sure." Which was not exactly a ringing endorsement of her new look.

Suddenly nervous, she peered out the window as the taxi began the gradual climb from the downtown to the college. The sun wasn't up yet, but it was light enough for her to see the pale bulk of Marymead's main building, vaguely gothic and definitely churchy, looming over the town. The cab pulled into the sweep of drive in front of that building. "They expecting you this early?" the driver asked as she paid the fare.

"I told them I was arriving on the morning bus."

"Well, I expect you oughta just go ahead and ring the bell then. The good sisters get up early. Likely someone will hear." He unloaded her suitcases then drove off.

When the bell wasn't answered right away, she sat on the steps next to her things, readying herself to appear relaxed and confident to whoever appeared. After several minutes, the door creaked open and a tall slender nun, dressed in garb as medieval in appearance as the building, stepped out. Her face, framed by wimple and veil, was beautiful.

"Michelle McClendon?"

She jumped to her feet and took a quick breath. "Clen. Everyone calls me Clen." There. She'd done it. Finally. Told someone the name she'd chosen for herself.

The nun folded her hands within the flowing black sleeves of her habit and tipped her head. Then she nodded. "Clen. It suits you. Welcome to Marymead. I'm Sister Thomasina."

"Like the cat."

"Ah, a reader. Did you like Gallico's story?"

"It was sad."

"Yes, indeed it was." Thomasina paused as if waiting for more, but Clen was suddenly too tongue-tied to add anything. The nun's eyebrows twitched, giving her a jolly look. "Breakfast is in an hour. Meanwhile, I suggest you unpack and change into something more appropriate." She paused with a flicker of a frown. "You did review the orientation booklet? It gives details about what is acceptable dress."

"Orientation booklet?"

"You didn't receive it?"

She had been a college woman less than two minutes, and already she'd messed up. But with Joshua's illness, none of the McClendon family had exactly been on top of things lately.

Still it should have occurred to her a Catholic women's college would have rules.

~ ~ ~

Lots of rules.

Her roommates got demerits for coming in late from dates or sneaking out at night during the week. Clen got them for leaving books sitting on her bed or for running to get to class on time. But most of her demerits were awarded for her continued flouting of the clothing canon.

Within a breathtakingly short time, she'd amassed a sufficient number to confine her to campus for the rest of the year. That was when Sister Thomasina sent for her.

"Clen." Thomasina gestured toward the chair at the side of her desk. "What are we going to do with you?"

"Wouldn't you rather be a nun than a nanny?" Popping off without thinking, her father called it, but when she saw Thomasina was struggling not to smile, she relaxed.

"Marymead's rules are meant to help us live peacefully together." Thomasina's voice was mild.

"I'm afraid I don't understand how leaving books on my bed or wearing slacks to class interferes with that peace. At least I made the bed and I'm not running around naked." Clen was absolutely certain this time Thomasina was fighting back a smile.

"Well, if you wore a skirt, as the rules require, it would certainly make life more peaceful for Sister Angelica." Thomasina tapped her fingers on the desk and examined Clen. "Do you know why we have rules about dress?"

"We are Christian young women." Clen's voice fell into a singsong chant. "And our bodies are temples of the Holy Spirit, therefore, we must clothe them with dignity and conduct ourselves with propriety."

"I see you've finally read the orientation booklet."

"We aren't nuns in training, you know."

"There's a saying, when in Rome do as the Romans do," Thomasina managed to look stern.

"*Julius Caesar.* Act two. Scene one."

"You're guessing, Clen, and not accurately."

15

Clen knew she needed to cool it, but she was having too much fun. "So...does Sister Demonica's peace trump the majority's legitimate desire for more freedom?"

"Sister Demonica?"

"I think you'll have to agree Angelica is a misnomer. And anyway, isn't peace in the eye of the beholder?"

Thomasina smiled, for real this time, and shook her head. The sharp movement made the starched band of white across her forehead dig in, leaving behind a crease. "We still need rules, Clen. Although I will grant you, lots of things are changing."

Thomasina had to be referring to the Second Vatican Council, currently in full swing in Rome and shaking up the lives of Catholics, both lay and religious.

"Perhaps it is time we reconsidered," Thomasina said. "I don't believe the rules have been updated since I was a student, and I'll grant you, we didn't keep all of them either."

"Yet you became a nun, and now you have even more rules."

That put a thoughtful look on Thomasina's face. It emboldened Clen further. "So why did you do it?" she asked.

"Do what?"

"Become a nun."

Thomasina stared past Clen out the window. "I came to a fork in the road, and this seemed the more...interesting path."

"But are you happy?"

"I'm certainly happy more than I'm unhappy."

"You must have some regrets, though," Clen said. "Didn't you ever want to get married? Have children?"

"Everyone has or will have regrets." Thomasina spoke slowly, and her expression altered to one of such melancholy, Clen regretted her impertinence.

For the first time she saw a nun as a woman rather than as a slightly alien being. Although why *would* someone as beautiful as Thomasina choose a life that required her to wear thick black serge accessorized with bits of white starched to a painful stiffness?

"Did you do it to guarantee you'd get to heaven?" Clen said.

"If I were living this life merely to earn a few gold stars, it's unlikely I'd be happy even some of the time."

"Perhaps you would." Although really, Clen had no idea.

"If that were my reason, I'd likely spend all my time trying to decide if I was being pious enough or doing sufficient good deeds. I'd be living a life ruled by shoulds and musts. I have no doubt I'd be miserable, and likely everyone around me would be as well." Thomasina's sorrowful expression had altered, and her words were once again crisply delivered. "Besides, I very much doubt God is keeping score."

"Then it shouldn't matter what we do."

Thomasina gave her a long, steady look while Clen tried not to squirm. "There is one other thing you should have noted in your reading of the orientation booklet, Clen. Any student exceeding one hundred demerits in a semester is not allowed to return."

At the rate she was acquiring them, one hundred was not going to present a problem—a thought that made Clen's chest feel tight and sore.

"Is that what you want?"

"No."

Thomasina leaned forward as if unable to hear her response.

Close to panic, Clen cleared her throat. "No."

"Well then, let's see if we can agree on something here. If I give you permission to leave campus, do I have your assurance you will buy appropriate clothing? Clothing you *will* wear for classes and meals?"

"Yes."

"Good. I wouldn't want to send you away, Clen. I believe you're going to be good for Marymead, and I hope Marymead will benefit you, as well."

~ ~ ~

Clen left the meeting with Thomasina determined to stop getting demerits. She did want to stay at Marymead, despite her worries about being away from her family while Josh was ill.

She hadn't told anyone about Josh, not wanting that to

color all her interactions. It might not have mattered though, because only one person seemed to be observant enough to remark on Clen's occasional bad days. Maxine.

Maxine had befriended Clen from the beginning and one of her first acts of friendship had been to re-trim Clen's hair, with a far superior result to what Clen had achieved.

And so when Clen needed advice on what to do about her clothing and in particular the formal her mother had insisted she buy to attend Marymead dances, Maxine was the obvious choice of confidant.

"But what if you want to go to a dance sometime?" Maxine said, shaking out folds of pink taffeta and tulle sprinkled with rhinestones.

"Unlikely. But if I do, I am not doing it in that dress," Clen said, grimacing.

"Why didn't you tell your mom you didn't like it?"

"I tried, but she has this idea of me, and that's the dress that fit."

Maxine sighed. "It's a beautiful dress."

"Just not for me."

Maxine held the dress up and peered at Clen. "You may be right about that." She smoothed the tulle and sighed again. "Too bad it won't fit me. I suppose you could sell it. A couple of the seniors are tall enough for it to fit."

"Mom would kill me." But only if she found out, something that was unlikely. Her mother, caught up in dealing with Josh's illness, would hardly notice one missing dress. "Okay," she said, deciding. "Go for it. I'll give you twenty-five percent."

"Done. So...about the meeting tonight. Are you going?" Maxine slipped the dress back into the closet. "Rumor is the student council president wants to find out why we're so dead set against all the rules."

Clen snorted. "Maybe she can explain how she's managed to put up with them for three years."

"What I intend to ask is why they can't set the darn clock to the correct time." Maxine had earned her only demerits for arriving back from a date at the last possible minute, only to discover the grandfather clock that kept official Marymead time was five minutes fast.

"I think Thomasina may be coming over to our side," Clen

said.

"And you think that because?"

"In my last meeting with her, she admitted she didn't keep all the rules when she was a student."

"I'll just bet she didn't." Maxine grinned. "She hides it well, but I believe there's a subversive side to Thomasina."

~ ~ ~

Clen was in the garden studying for midterms when two nuns wearing long striped aprons and carrying pails and trowels emerged from their wing of the main building. As they approached, Clen recognized Thomasina and the sister in charge of the gardens, Sister Gladys, whom Clen had renamed Gladiolus.

It wasn't easy guessing a nun's age, although gray hair sightings helped, but Gladiolus had a face with a comfortable, lived-in look that meant she had to be years older than Thomasina.

The two were chatting as they approached and they didn't greet her, but Clen assumed they'd seen her sitting behind a large lilac that had partially shed its foliage.

Gladiolus gestured with her trowel. "I think the yellow tulips will look good here."

The two settled on their knees on the other side of the bush with their backs to Clen and began to dig, and just as Clen was about to clear her throat to make sure they knew she was there, Thomasina spoke. "So what did you think, Glad. That it would be easy being a nun?"

"A free pass, you mean? I think most of us hoped that would be true, but perhaps it's better we have to struggle so we don't become arrogant or complacent."

"And our sisters. Did you think it would be so difficult to love them?"

"Indeed. And why not? We're all human. Even Eustacia, who no doubt would try the patience of the Good Lord himself. But perhaps that's why she's lived so long. I've often wondered if she really needs that cane or just enjoys having something to shake at people."

Clen muffled a laugh. She and Eustacia had already had several run-ins, and Clen had thought the same thing about the irascible nun.

"And what about Angelica? One of the girls called her Sister Demonica."

Gladiolus chuckled. "Oh my. A girl who sees clearly."

Clen held her breath, knowing it was too late to let them know she was there.

"Yes. Clen McClendon, the unofficial leader of our rebels. Well, actually, the entire class has been causing me no end of difficulty. They're all so...determined to change Marymead. And when I'm not just trying to hold up our side, I must admit they have a point."

"There are too many rules, you know."

"And don't think for a minute that I haven't noticed you keep the trellis on the south quad in excellent repair," Thomasina said.

"Well, we don't want anyone to hurt themselves," Gladiolus replied.

The two laughed softly together then dug silently for several minutes.

Finally Gladioulus spoke. "Do you know what I think as I work in the garden? That we are all God's gardens. Some weedy and overgrown, like Angelica, and some full of prickly cactus, like Eustacia. I see you, my dear, as a spring prairie, filled with silvery grasses and wildflowers of every hue."

Clen took a peek and saw Thomasina sit back on her heels. "What am I doing here, Glad?"

"Ah, Thomas. You're where you're supposed to be."

"Under false pretenses. How can that be right?"

"Pretenses, perhaps. Isn't that true of all of us? But not false ones. Remember, the Good Lord calls each of us in a particular way."

"You won't tell Mother Superior what a fraud I am, will you?" Thomasina said.

"Oh my dear, doubting Thomas, of course I won't. Because you're not."

Thomasina bent over and began digging again, stabbing at the ground with the trowel. "He's been dead fifteen years. When do I stop missing him?"

Clen caught and held her breath in surprise.

"You loved him deeply, Thomas. Do you really want to forget him?"

Once again Thomasina sat back on her heels. Her arm came up to brush her face.. "It happened so suddenly. He was there and then, just...gone, like quicksilver down a crack I couldn't even see."

"There, there, my dear." Gladiolus said. "You have a good heart, but it's been broken. It needs time to heal."

"It hurts so much."

"Shh, I know. I know." Gladiolus put her arms around Thomasina. "You mustn't worry, Thomas. Just as the Father cares for the lilies and the sparrows, he's caring for you, and for him."

"How I wish I had your confidence."

"My dearest one, you may borrow it whenever you wish."

When the two nuns finally went inside, Clen jogged off in the opposite direction, carrying her unstudied book and a radical new view of nuns in general, and Thomasina and Gladiolus in particular.

~ ~ ~

Clen had been looking forward to the fall retreat as a chance to catch up on both her rest and studies, although she planned to skip the talks by the visiting priest. The seats in the chapel were hard and such talks were usually boring. Unfortunately, Eustacia caught her sneaking out the back door and brandished her cane. Resigned, Clen redirected her steps to the chapel.

The priest conducting the retreat was middle-aged and bald with a protruding belly and a penetrating voice. "Outside of the marriage bed, French kissing is an abomination in God's eyes."

Clen thought calling it an abomination was a bit extreme. True, the idea of having some guy stick his tongue in her mouth held no appeal, but she suspected Maxine was doing it, and it was hard to believe God really cared.

As if sensing her thought, Maxine shifted next to her.

"You young women are the ones designated by God to uphold the sanctity of home and family," the priest continued.

If questions were permitted, Clen would have asked what

young men were designated to do, and had they been told they weren't supposed to French kiss anybody except their wives? Most likely not.

Clen closed her eyes, attempting to doze, but Friar Tuck was just warming up, and his voice kept jarring her awake.

"The highest calling is to celibacy. Any of you who feel such a calling should consider yourselves among the blessed ones."

Enough already. Clen slid out of the pew, holding her stomach as if she were in acute pain and went in search of Thomasina.

Retreat not only freed them from classes, it also gave the nuns a rest, and most of them spent part of that free time walking the grounds, filling the crisp fall air with prayers and the clicking of rosaries. Clen looked around and spotted Thomasina, recognizable because of her height and slender build. She was with a stockier nun. Gladiolus, Clen discovered, when she walked up to the two.

"Good afternoon, Clen," Thomasina said. "Out of chapel already?"

"I skipped out early."

"Because?"

"Father was making my stomach hurt. What I want to know is how was he chosen?"

Gladiolus looked on with an interested expression. Thomasina frowned. "Why do you ask?"

"Because whoever suggested this guy should be permanently struck from the list of 'suggestors.'"

"Oh, and why is that?"

"Where to start? Well, for one thing he's got a very loud, grating voice. That seems at odds with the idea of this being a time of peaceful contemplation."

"You mean it's harder to sleep through the talks, don't you?" Thomasina said.

"Sure. That, too."

"Go on."

"He's huge into abominations. French kissing is high on the list—only permitted in marriage it seems. But then he trashed marriage by saying it was a lesser calling than celibacy. All I can say is, if you're hoping to recruit more nuns this is not, in my opinion, the way to go about it."

Gladiolus cocked her head, looking like a bright-eyed sparrow. "How would you do it?"

"Well, for one thing I'd ditch the black serge."

Gladiolus twinkled, there was no other word for it. "As a matter of fact, we're working on it. Anything else?"

"You don't make yourselves more appealing by saying that being nuns elevates you above the rest of us."

"Of course we don't." Gladiolus exchanged a glance with Thomasina. "Thomas, you need to do something about this."

"Perhaps we should sit in on this evening's talk," Thomasina said.

"But he may have already used his best material."

"Well, we'll just see, won't we."

~ ~ ~

Five minutes into the evening's oration, it was clear the good father had a lot more to say, this time about the evils of petting, light or heavy. He was so explicit it was actually kind of interesting. Once again, he ended by saying they could avoid such occasions of sin by answering the higher call to enter the religious life.

Leaving the chapel, Clen didn't see Thomasina or Gladiolus, but perhaps they'd hidden themselves. She doubted the priest would have given quite the same talk had he spotted nuns in the audience.

The next morning, Thomasina sent for Clen after breakfast. "We'll be making the announcement shortly that Father had to leave last night to attend his sick mother. I thought I'd better let you know in case you planned to cut the session."

"Never. After last night I've been waiting with bated breath to see if he could top himself."

"Unfortunately, thanks to you, we'll never know." Thomasina's eyes danced.

"I thought you said he had to leave because his mother was ill."

"I did, didn't I? And now perhaps you could try to remain silent for at least this last day of retreat?"

Clen squeezed her lips together and nodded. Then she ducked out of Thomasina's office before she dissolved in giggles.

For a short time, the episode had muted her worries about Josh—worries that wove like a bass note through the melody of her life.

~ ~ ~

At Christmas, her father met Clen at the bus station. After hugging her, he stood back, holding her hands in his. "Well, well, pretty lady. It surely looks like college agrees with you. You're blooming like a rose."

He used to call her his pretty *little* lady, even when her face was dirty and her knees scabbed up. Then she got her growth spurt and shot up to nearly six feet and he dropped the "little."

He ruffled her hair. "I like this new look. It suits you."

When they arrived home, her mother, who was stirring something on the stove, turned to hug Clen. She arrested halfway into the motion, as if she were playing Statues. Her eyes blinked rapidly. "Oh, Michelle. What happened to your hair?"

"I didn't have time to mess with it, Mom."

"Well, thank goodness it will grow out."

Clen swallowed her disappointment. She'd known it had been optimism of the loftiest sort to expect her mother to accept, let alone compliment, her new hairstyle.

She took off her coat and her mother's nose wrinkled, but Clen was expecting that. "Slacks are more practical for travel, Mom."

"Of course." Her mother smiled, and Clen realized how much older and sadder she looked. "I'm so glad you're home, sweetie. The boys can hardly wait to see you. They're in the den."

Clen went down the hall, her heart rate quickening at the thought of seeing her brothers for the first time in four months. Although her mother had reassured her regularly Josh was doing well, Clen was anxious to verify that.

She stopped in the doorway to the den to find it had been converted into a bedroom. Jason was sitting at a card table in one corner, frowning in concentration as he put together a model airplane. Joshua lay curled in the middle of a hospital bed, apparently sleeping.

She said a soft hello, and Jason looked up with a thoughtful expression. His skin was translucent under its scattering of freckles, and his eyes looked a good deal older than a ten-year-old's had any right to be. She forced a smile. After a beat, he grinned back.

"Hey, Mickey La, you look good. Like a movie star almost."

"Thanks, Jase."

He slipped off the chair and came over for a hug. He'd grown at least two inches since August. His shoulder blades—angel bones, their mother called them—were sharp ridges under her hands.

She let go of Jason and stepped over to the bed. Joshua opened his eyes and gave her a sweet smile. She reached out to smooth his hair, which was wispy and thin. "How are you, Josh?"

"I'm okay. A little tired. I'm glad you're home."

"Yeah. Me, too." No question. Her mother had lied about how well Josh was doing.

~ ~ ~

"I think I need to stay here. Not go back to school," she told her parents after the boys went to bed that night. "I want...I need to be here with all of you."

"Of course you're going back, Michelle." Her mother used her no-ifs-ands-or-buts voice, the one she'd used when picking out Clen's college wardrobe.

"But Josh...he's dying, isn't he."

"No!" Her mother's voice was edged with panic. "You mustn't say that or even think it."

Clen's father moved to put an arm around her mother. "The treatments are hard on him but his doctors are very optimistic," he said.

"If I go back—"

"You're going back," her mother said.

"—you have to tell me the truth about how he's doing. I can come home, be here...help you."

25

"We won't know much until after the next round of treatments," her father said. "Go back to school, Michelle. Finish the year, at least. Then, we'll see."

Her mom started sobbing then, and coward that she was, Clen left her father to comfort her..

~ ~ ~

By the new year, Clen was no longer getting demerits, and that meant no more summonses to Thomasina's office. She'd enjoyed matching wits with Thomasina, and she missed their meetings. On a whim, she stopped by to see the nun.

When she knocked on the door frame, Thomasina looked up from her work. "Clen, how lovely to see you. Do you have a minute? Come, sit down."

Clen took a seat in the chair she'd sat in as a miscreant, still debating whether the impulse to tell Thomasina about Josh was the right one.

"Did you have a good Christmas?" Thomasina asked.

The perfect opening, but still Clen hesitated. "Mom fussed about my hair."

"Well, it's a good thing she didn't see the first version." Thomasina's eyes glinted with amusement. "You looked like you'd been attacked by a demented wombat."

"That could hurt my feelings, you know." Instead, Thomasina's comment had made her smile.

"This second attempt is very becoming. I expect your mom is sad to see you growing up so fast."

Clen shoved the words out. "My brother's sick."

Thomasina's smile immediately faded. "Oh, I'm sorry to hear that."

"Yes. Well. He's getting better. At least Mom and Dad keep saying he is. He has leukemia, and the treatments make him so sick. Sometimes I feel guilty about being here instead of at home, but Mom and Dad insisted I come back."

"Oh, my dear, what a difficult thing to bear."

"I don't know what I should do."

"Nobody can tell you what's best, Clen. Just that whether you choose to stay or go, there will be consequences."

Clen fiddled with a loose thread on her blouse, thinking

about that. Consequences. Always the rub.

"You can come see me anytime," Thomasina said. "And I'll keep you and your family in my prayers. What is your brother's name?"

"Joshua. He's ten."

"Oh my. God will watch over him, Clen. Have no doubt."

But she did.

Chapter Two

1982

ATLANTA, GEORGIA

Entering Melton's office, Clen's gaze was drawn to the large oil painting on the wall behind his desk. From a distance, it was clearly a matador delivering the killing stroke, but up close it was dark swaths of crimson, umber, and black, with an occasional slash of yellow. It was reportedly worth a great deal of money, but Clen was glad she didn't have to spend her days beneath its brooding presence.

Melton, a short, dapper man with a brisk delivery, glanced up from the pages he was marking. "Ah, Clen. Excellent. I need you to substitute for me at the Prism shareholder meeting in New York tomorrow morning. You don't have to speak, just show the flag, take good notes. My secretary has the tickets and itinerary. Flight leaves this afternoon at three thirty."

"That doesn't give me much time." Clen, who had recently been promoted to Melton's department, had been warned he had a habit of dumping assignments on associates at the last minute, but this was the first time he'd done it to her.

His manicured hand dismissed her with what she'd dubbed his pope wave. "It's only overnight. Still, I know you women always need time to pack."

Right. As if he didn't.

"You can leave now. If you feel you must." He waved again, dismissing her.

So generous of him to give her four hours' notice, and without even a token effort to explain why he was unable to attend.

~ ~ ~

Three hours later, hot and out of breath, Clen sank into a seat in the Delta Crown Room at the Atlanta airport. She drew in a slow, careful breath and let it out, glancing around the room.

Paul? What was he doing here? And sitting with a woman wearing a tight red sundress, no less. If she was a business associate, she was way overdue for the dress-for-success chat. As for Paul, he'd supposedly left for Chicago this morning.

Mesmerized, Clen watched as the woman lifted a straw tote onto her lap. It was decorated with brightly colored flowers and a large "Virgin Islands" label stitched across the top. It was the twin of the bag Paul discouraged Clen from buying on their honeymoon by labeling it "tourist-tacky."

White earrings banged against the woman's jaw as she dug in the bag. When her hand emerged, it held a dark blue ticket folder that matched her long fingernails.

Before Clen could react, Paul and the woman gathered their belongings and walked out. Clen got unstuck and followed. The concourse was crowded, and Clen kept track of the two by watching Paul's head bob along. Finally his head bobbed to the right and, when she reached that spot, she was just in time to see the two walking through a boarding doorway.

Paul had the woman's straw tote on his shoulder and his hand planted in a proprietary fashion in the middle of her bare back. Clen looked from the now empty doorway to the flight information posted behind the desk.

The flight was to St. Thomas. Not Chicago.

That meant...this was exactly what it first appeared to be. Her husband was having an affair.

Clen groped her way to an empty seat where nausea and dizziness held her in place as she struggled to accept this shift in her world. Paul going off, not to Chicago with a business associate, but to St. Thomas with a woman.

If she had just accepted the evidence when she first spotted the two, maybe she could have done...something, although it was her nature to hesitate. In fact, her customary pause-to-consider strategy underpinned most of her professional success. Always, always she looked before she leaped, but if there had ever been a time to simply leap, this was it. Maybe she should have walked up to the woman and given one of those gaudy earrings a sharp yank. Although no telling what might have happened next.

FINANCIAL ANALYST ARRESTED FOR ASSAULTING HUSBAND
AND WOMAN COMPANION AT AIRPORT

Except...Paul wasn't worth it. That much was blindingly clear.

Her mind spun, tossing up bizarre images. Of herself splashing Paul on their honeymoon in St. Thomas, the two of them laughing as they played together in the warm water. And how did that lead to this...this duplicity of Paul's with a squatty, heavily-bosomed blonde? A woman so dissimilar to Clen, she might as well have come from another planet. A woman he was taking to St. Thomas, where he would kiss those bright, overdrawn lips, unzip that too-tight dress, and reach out to fondle those...mammaries. God, they couldn't possibly be real, could they?

Another wave of nausea hit, and Clen clamped a hand over her mouth until it abated. She may not have deserved Paul's unconditional love, but she surely didn't deserve such a graceless betrayal. She looked around, struggling to remember which direction she'd come from, trying to figure out where she now needed to go.

Crowds of people strode purposefully past. Men in suits carrying briefcases and looking harried. Women, most wearing colorful dresses except for the few like her in business attire. Everything so unbearably normal. She took a deep breath, stood, and stepped into that flow, leaving it again when she reached a restroom. With shaking hands, she scooped water into her mouth and then onto her face. She didn't look in either the mirror or at the women who bustled around her. Just moments earlier, she, too, had been bustling, with somewhere to go. Then, just like that, her bustle was...gone.

She reclaimed her carry-on from the Crown Room and drove home to the large, formal house that was more Paul's taste than hers. She left her suitcase by the back door and leaned on the kitchen counter, staring out at the perfectly groomed backyard.

Now what?

She needed to call Melton, of course, although, at the moment, it was difficult to give a flying fig about him, the trip to New York, or her job. Still, better not to burn too many bridges until she had time to think things through.

So...Melton first. And her excuse? Bad traffic, an accident? Definitely not the truth—that she was undone by the discovery her husband was taking another woman to St. Thomas.

At the thought, a wave of emotion swamped her—anger, hurt, but perhaps not much surprise and, floating on top, the hopelessness she thought she'd left behind long ago.

She lifted the phone, and without further debate about what she was going to say, dialed Melton's number. "Is he there?"

"Clen?" The voice of Melton's secretary, usually so cool and efficient, held a hint of raised eyebrows. "Aren't you supposed to be on your way to New York?"

"That was the plan. I missed the flight."

"Oh. Do you have a cold? You sound stuffed up."

"Something like that." For sure, she felt miserable.

"Well, it serves him right," the secretary said. "He's always doing that. Palming stuff off because he's decided he'd rather squeeze in a round of golf or something. I'll call New York and tell them he can't make it, and I'll tell him you were hit with a stomach virus. Just be sure you take a couple of days off."

~ ~ ~

Hard to believe it could be that easy. If only everything was—like deciding what to do about Paul.

The option that first came to mind was to go upstairs and tear apart his closet of meticulously organized suits and ties. But although a demolished wardrobe would upset him, it wouldn't rock his world the way hers had been rocked.

Another possibility was to flee, taking nothing, not even extra underwear or a toothbrush. But if she did that, Paul would contact the authorities.

No. There had to be other more dignified, more creative...more useful ways of handling this.

31

Suddenly, she knew exactly where to begin.

~ ~ ~

The night Paul returned from St. Thomas, Clen waited until he changed clothes and came back downstairs.

"We need to talk," she said.

"Can't it wait? I'm tired, and I have a report to go over before tomorrow morning." He poured a cup of coffee, put it in the microwave, and set the timer.

"Sorry. It can't." The car was packed, and she was ready to drive to the Peachtree Plaza where she'd already registered.

"Can you keep it short, then?"

"Sure. Can do. I'm leaving you." The unexpected rhyme pleased her.

The microwave pinged, but she'd managed to pull his attention away from both coffee and report. "What? What on earth are you talking about?"

"I...Am...Leaving...You."

He looked so shocked, she felt, briefly, like laughing.

"You can't mean it."

"Oh, but I do, Paul." She pushed away the memory of his lips on hers, his hands touching her with easy familiarity as they made love. No. Not love. Sex. But those lips had lied and those hands...

"Is it another man?"

Wild laughter tickled the back of her throat. "No, Paul. It's a woman."

Laughter continued to threaten as his expression segued into shock. "You can't be serious."

"Dead serious. I've transferred my share of our assets into a separate account. I'm leaving you the equity in the house and its furnishings. Here are the figures." She handed him the sheet of paper with the details of what she'd done.

"Who's the woman?" he said, taking the paper from her.

She shook her head. "I don't know her name, actually. But does St. Thomas ring any bells?"

"What? Of course it does. We went there on our honeymoon."

"In June, nineteen seventy. So, how many times have you been back? And before you answer, don't forget this week."

He looked discomfited but for only a moment. "What do you expect? A man has needs."

"I never refused you, Paul."

"But you made sure I knew what a martyr you were."

His anger coming at her in waves began to distort the fragile internal harmony she'd managed to recover in the days he'd been gone. Further, the blatant dishonesty of his words took her breath away. When she got it back, she almost said, *you sure never worried if you were meeting my needs.* But she didn't want to get into a nuclear exchange with him. Nothing to be gained. Not anymore.

"You plan to marry her?" she said.

"Who?"

"The lady in red."

They stared at each other, until Paul looked away.

"So, what's her name?"

He cleared his throat. "Amber."

The line, *amber waves of grain*, from *America the Beautiful* popped into Clen's head. Once again, she struggled not to laugh.

Paul scrubbed a hand through his hair. "I don't know. She can't cook." His face reddened, so perhaps he realized how self-centered that sounded.

He shifted his feet, then he began to read the paper she'd handed him. "Whoa. You've appropriated more than your share." Only five minutes in, and he already had the aggrieved spouse act down pat.

"Actually, I've been extremely generous."

"Oh, come on, Clen. There's no need for this." A wheedling note distorted his rich baritone. "We make a good team."

Not only unfaithful, but delusional. "You do realize you didn't say, 'Don't leave me because I love you.'"

"That goes without saying, babe."

"Yes, it's pretty much gone without saying for thirteen years."

"I don't recall hearing it all that often myself."

"You may be right." She paused, gazing at him with more

attention than she had in a while.

He glanced away.

"So tell me. Why *did* you marry me, Paul?"

"What?"

"Did you love me?"

"Of course."

"And now you don't."

He rubbed his forehead then glared at her. "What is love, anyway?"

"You must have some idea if you claim to have felt it."

"Hell's bells, Clen, stop being so analytical. That's the problem, you know. Love is...excitement, spontaneity, the thrill of the chase."

"And then you caught me, and the thrill was gone."

"I didn't say that."

"Is that why you didn't want children?"

He looked away from her. "I thought you didn't want them. And I was good with that."

"No, you didn't think that at all."

He shifted, turning sideways, as if to leave, and yet he stayed.

"I think love is unselfish, intimate, honest," Clen said.

"There," he said. "That's it in a nutshell. We see the world in fundamentally different ways."

"How odd we never noticed." Possibly, it was the most honest they'd ever been with each other. Too bad they'd left it until it no longer mattered.

Paul pulled in a breath, then sighed and dropped his gaze from hers. "What are your plans?" He asked the question in the same offhand way he often asked how her day had been.

She'd always suspected he didn't care about her answers, and so this last time she didn't try to give him one. There was no longer any point. They'd become that couple in the Audrey Hepburn movie, *Two for the Road.*

Question: What kind of people don't even try to talk to each other?

Answer: Married people.

Chapter Three

1981

SEATTLE, WASHINGTON

Pam greeted him with a kiss, then led him over to where the guest of honor was seated. "Grannie, this is Gerrum Kirsey. Gerrum, my great-grannie Adelaide."

He accepted the hand Adelaide offered, to find her grip was surprisingly robust for an elderly woman.

She smiled up at him with eyes alive with intelligence and mischief. "It's a relief to finally meet you, Gerrum Kirsey, and to see you're human, after all."

"Grannie!"

"Well, the way you described him, I wouldn't have been a bit surprised if he'd shown up wearing a toga and toting a lightning bolt."

"I had strict orders," Gerrum said. "No lightning bolts and definitely no togas."

"Oh, well. I suppose Pam told you I'm much too old for such excitements."

"She did happen to mention something about a ninetieth birthday?"

Adelaide sighed. "Oh my, that sounds old, doesn't it." She cocked her head, smiling at him. "Pam tells me you've asked

35

her to marry you."

He hesitated, and Grannie Adelaide pounced. "Ah, I see perhaps my granddaughter was the one who popped the question. Well, she always seems to know exactly what she wants and is prepared to go after it. An admirable quality, I suppose. So tell me, Gerrum, do you always know what you want?"

"No. Not always." In fact lately, uncertainty had been causing him a great deal of difficulty.

"You mustn't let Pam bully you while you make up your mind."

"Grannie, what a thing to say."

Adelaide reached for her great-granddaughter's hand, the one with the diamond ring he'd so recently placed there, and she rubbed her thumb across the stone. "Dearest Pam, you remind me so much of your grandfather. That's why you're my favorite. But constant certainty can sometimes be difficult to live with."

"Indecision can be every bit as annoying." Pam's tone held that sharp note Gerrum had learned to be wary of.

"Yes, of course it can." Adelaide nodded at him with what looked like collaboration. Thick as thieves, the two of them. No question, he was going to enjoy being related to this woman.

Adelaide released Pam's hand and sat back, smiling. "I suppose I'd best speak to the other guests, otherwise your mother will be annoyed with me. Come back and see me later, Gerrum. There are things you need to know about this young woman that only I can tell you." Once again, the eyes were twinkling.

Pam laughed, but to his ears, it sounded a touch off. Or perhaps he was projecting the unease he'd been feeling since his arrival in the Palmer family home.

He'd known Pam's family was, to put it in the vernacular, filthy rich. But full comprehension had eluded him until he walked into this gigantic room with its angles and curves of white, chrome, and glass.

Random color was provided by two huge paintings that looked like framed drop cloths that bookended the room. No doubt they were worth more money than he could hope to make in three lifetimes, but they overlooked a room that had not even one cozy nook where a person could flop onto a slightly rumpled chair and dip into a book.

"I like your grandmother," he told Pam as they walked over to the bar set up next to a fireplace large enough to roast a cow.

"She likes you, too, but she was teasing, you know. About having things she could tell you. About me."

"Oh, is that so. And here I thought you two were close."

"We are, and she would never tattle on me."

"I may have to take Grannie Adelaide to lunch sometime."

"Don't you dare." She punched him lightly on the arm, but she was smiling. So maybe he'd misread that slight hint of annoyance earlier. Usually, he had the opposite problem—that of missing Pam's storm warnings.

The bartender handed a glass of champagne to Pam and a rum and tonic to him, and they stood for a moment, out of the flow of guests, sipping their drinks. It was rather like standing on the sidelines of a Cary Grant movie, Gerrum thought, watching as uniformed maids passed trays of intricate hors d'oeuvres and champagne flutes to women in elegant gowns and glittering jewels and men in formal black and white.

In a flurry of peach silk, Pam's sister came over and leaned in to whisper dramatically, "Mother wants us."

With a look of apology and a brief touch on his arm, Pam left him. He continued to sip his drink, watching Adelaide receiving birthday greetings and thinking about what one of his colleagues said when he learned of the engagement. *If you want to know how a girl will turn out, look at her mother.*

What he hoped was that Pam would turn out like Grannie Adelaide with her twinkly eyes, good humor, and forthright manner. If that happened, he'd be a lucky man indeed.

He finished the drink and turned to the bartender. "Tonic and a twist, please."

"No rum?"

"Not this time. Thanks." Not that he wouldn't enjoy another drink. But one was his normal limit even when he wasn't just off-center of everyone's attention as Pam's newly intended.

Pam still hadn't returned, and he was about to mingle on his own, when her brother approached and gestured with his glass toward the door to the terrace. "Shall we?"

Gerrum followed Winston Palmer the Third into the cool of the Seattle evening. Below the terrace, a perfect swath of lawn stretched to the water's edge where an elegant yacht lay twinned by its reflection in the still waters of Lake Washington. The onset of twilight had turned the overarching sky a deep and lovely rose, and the distant peaks of the Cascades floated like clouds in the clear air.

"You looked like you needed rescuing." Winston's tone was patronizing, his gaze assessing.

"Not at all. I was perfectly content in my corner."

Winston raised an eyebrow and fished out a pack of cigarettes and a gold lighter. "Pamela tells us your father was a commercial fisherman."

"That's right." Gerrum declined the proffered cigarette.

Winston lit up, inhaled, and blew a cloud of smoke he waved away from his face. "Good money in it?"

"It rather depends on your definition of good." And no doubt Winston's definition would vary considerably from Gerrum's.

"Is that why you chose the law?"

He chose the law after a day spent in his underwear on the Seattle docks shivering his way through an Army physical. Which he'd passed with flying colors. A no-brainer after that. Maintaining his student deferment as long as possible was vastly preferable to becoming intimately acquainted with a Vietnamese rice paddy. "Commercial fishing's a hard life. Uncertain," he said, instead.

"I understand why you'd prefer the law," Winston said.

And Gerrum had, in the beginning.

After he graduated from law school, Vietnam was still looming, so he signed on with the Air Force. The four years of trial work as a judge advocate had been interesting, although he'd ended up mostly prosecuting kids who'd gotten smashed and done some smashing. After his discharge, he returned to Seattle to the position Pierson and Potter had held for him.

The first years there had been good. Only lately had the constant pressure to increase billable hours and the demands of clients who needed a will changed the day before yesterday begun to wear on his spirit.

He still found the logic of the law satisfying, but when he did look up from yet another trust document or will, it was to stare out at Puget Sound and miss the other thing he'd stayed in school to avoid—following in his father's footsteps as a commercial fisherman.

A sudden image of the *Ever Joyful* tied alongside the Palmers' sleek yacht made him smile, although that coupling was no more incongruous than his with Pam—her blonde delicacy contrasted by his dark coloring and solid build.

"Pamela tells us you're doing extremely well at Pierson and Potter. That you were named partner in record time." Winston blew a smoke ring. "Of course, it works to your advantage they're taking a modern attitude about race."

Gerrum's gut tightened. He took a sip of tonic, making a conscious effort to relax or at least to appear that way.

"I met your sister," Winston continued. "Attractive girl. Adopted, is she?"

"No. Actually, not."

"Odd. She doesn't look like an Eskimo."

"We're Tlingits." And he and Jeannie had faced thoughtless comments about their dissimilarities for as long as either of them could remember.

"Excuse me?"

"Our mother is a member of the Tlingit people." And when his mom learned he was marrying into a wealthy Seattle family, she'd had reservations. Not without reason, it now appeared.

"Is she joining us today?"

"No. She's not." She'd been invited, but despite his pleading the case, she had declined.

"Well, I don't have to tell you, I suppose, we're concerned about the age difference. But we're more concerned about the mixed marriage aspect."

Gerrum took a gulp of tonic, wishing for the first time it contained the absent rum.

"The parents hoped this was a passing fancy of Pamela's, but given that rock on her finger, I'm guessing it's a done deal. Although, seeing your sister...perhaps they'll feel reassured."

A good thing Gerrum's glass wasn't a delicate champagne flute. Carefully, he loosened his grip. He knew how to deal with this. Had been dealing with it since he was six. But he sure didn't expect to get hit with it today. And did Grannie Adelaide share the primitive views of her family? He'd hate to think that of her.

"Jeannie will be pleased she's served as a reassurance for you." A struggle, but he managed to keep his tone civil.

Winston blew another smoke ring and squinted through the haze, not even having the grace to look uncomfortable. "I love Pamela. A mixed marriage is a risk. Not sure society is quite ready for it."

"Not to mention present company?"

Winston shrugged. "I want what's best for my little sister."

"Last time I checked, she gets to choose, not you."

Winston took a deep drag of his cigarette and eyed Gerrum as he let the smoke trickle out. "Guess you're right." He stubbed the cigarette out in an urn of sand provided for that purpose—as if this were the hotel it resembled rather than a private home. "No hard feelings, I hope?"

"Absolutely." Gerrum kept his voice even, his expression bland, and Winston nodded, accepting the ambiguity of Gerrum's response, before going inside.

Gerrum remained on the terrace, feeling the same tightness in his chest he always felt when someone displayed their prejudice. It was a feeling he'd first encountered the day the older kids cut him away from the other first graders and surrounded him chanting, *Gerrum the Jap. Gerrum the Jap.*

As the chant had risen louder and faster, others ran to join in, until his sister pushed through the crowd, grabbed his hand, and pulled him out of the circle, kicking the shins of the ones stupid enough to stand in her way. As Jeannie stomped away with him bobbing in her wake, a blast from a teacher's whistle ended recess.

He'd pulled on her hand, to make her stop. "Jeannie, why are they calling me a Jap?"

She turned and glared at him. "Don't use that word. It isn't nice. You're Tlingit."

The teacher blew another blast, waving her arm to urge on stragglers as the afternoon drizzle settled into a steady beat of rain. He lifted his face, letting the rain disguise the tears that had filled his eyes without permission.

With an annoyed click of her tongue, the teacher ushered them inside. "Quickly now, Jeannie, Gerrum. You should have come as soon as I whistled."

His throat burned with the unfairness of it. Was she both blind and deaf?

After that first time, the chant picked up whenever Jeannie wasn't around. Its singsong cadence, accompanied by unpleasant laughter, was the discordant music of that year, trapping him in misery. The chanters too many and too big for him to fight. *Sticks and stones...* He'd always thought they would have hurt less than the words.

Eventually, he came to understand the teasing was prompted by his darker skin and vaguely Asiatic features— Tlingit gifts—while Jeannie, who took after their father, was exempt.

When he was once again calm, Gerrum returned to the party. Pam was still missing, so he looked for Jeannie. He found his sister in a corner, a familial trait it seemed. She, at least, was being social, conversing with an elderly man parked next to her in a wheelchair. It was Jeannie's gift. To seek out the strays everyone else ignored and to discover what made them unique. Then some of that would find its way into one of her novels.

Jeannie had been writing for years, and had a devoted fan base, but whether the story he'd recently begun to write was any good, he had no idea. He just knew the writing of it was providing him with more satisfaction than the endless drafting of legal documents that filled his other hours.

He made his way to Jeannie's side, thinking about how to discuss that with Pam. Whenever he'd attempted to bring up concerns about his career, she'd put him off, but after his encounter with Winston, he knew he and Pam must talk, as soon as possible. And his future as an attorney was only one of the topics they needed to address.

~ ~ ~

Gerrum put his arm around Pam and pulled her tight against his body. He loved holding her like this after they'd made love. Loved touching her skin, which was as smooth and soft as fine suede.

She sighed. "It was a terrific party, wasn't it."

Well, he certainly could have skipped the revelation his soon-to-be in-laws were bigots, but why dim Pam's pleasure in the day. "A wee bit of a blather and a folderol."

Pam giggled. "Maureen O'Hara in *The Quiet Man*."

He nipped her neck. "Not even close."

"Guess I'll have to pay the penalty." She twisted around to kiss him then snuggled back in his arms.

"Pam...we need to talk."

She yawned. "About?"

He should probably let it go until morning, except he'd already let it go too long. Besides, Pam was nicely relaxed. He pulled in a breath and took the leap. "I'm planning to ask for a leave this summer."

Pam pulled out of his arms and turned to face him. "You have got to be kidding me. You are kidding, aren't you?"

"No. I'm not."

"You've just decided this. Without discussing it with me?"

"I am discussing it with you."

"It sounds to me like you've decided."

"You know I've been trying to figure out what to do about my career."

"Oh, that again. Surely, it's a momentary blip. It happens to everyone. You'll get over it." She reached out and smoothed the hair off his forehead.

She'd used similar words to derail this subject before, but if he continued to let her brush him off, he'd end up a forty-year man at Pierson and Potter. The thought made him shiver, the shiver accompanied by the vision of a cold white world–gray sky, bare trees, and in the foreground, an animal caught in a trap, gnawing at its leg.

His chest tightened. "It's not a blip."

"A phase, then. You're a successful man, Gerrum, and now is hardly the time to make changes."

"I've been saving, and I've paid down this house, so we'll do fine with a decrease in sala—"

"But this house is inadequate. You can't possibly think I'd live here long term."

"As a matter of fact, I did." Obviously, wishful thinking on his part.

She moved further away. "So what do you expect me to do? Be the breadwinner? Or perhaps you think Daddy will support us? Marry a rich girl, live a life of leisure."

Pam, who'd been interning at Pierson and Potter, planned to join her father's firm in the legal department after she graduated this spring, and she'd always sounded excited and pleased about her chosen career path.

"Of course not. I intend to support you. Support us. But I make a lot less than your father. We'll have to live more simply. I thought you understood that."

"What do you plan to do with this leave, anyway?"

"I want to take the *Joyful* up the inland waterway. Do some writing. See how I get on with it." He pictured himself floating on quiet blue waters, surrounded by mountains, working on a story, the image so vivid it was difficult to pull away from.

"But writing's just a hobby."

"If I can figure out a way to combine it with the law, I think I'll be a happier person. A better husband."

"And while you're gallivanting around Alaska, I'll be...?" She sat up covering herself with the sheet and flapped her free hand.

"Since you're taking the summer off, you can come along." Although that vision of a moment ago hadn't included her. A thought he immediately banished.

"I'm taking it off to plan the wedding."

"Surely the wedding can't take all your time. You'll like Alaska, and we'll be together."

"I'm sorry, Gerrum. I have no interest in spending the summer living on a smelly old fishing boat, and it isn't fair of you to just spring this on me." She swung her legs over the side of the bed and reached for her clothes.

He sat up, disturbed by the distress in her tone, then turned to watch her. "I'm not springing it on you." At least not exactly. "I told you before I wasn't completely satisfied with the law. That I intended to make some changes."

She located her underwear and proceeded to put it on with quick, jerky motions. "Not completely satisfied? Who is? But adults make the best of things." After delivering that barb, she moved to the end of the bed and collected the rest of her clothes. Then she made a wide berth around him as she headed for the bathroom.

"Well, I think making the best of things for me includes an annual leave. I'll still make good money."

"Oh, come on, Gerrum. If you think Pierson and Potter will go along with you taking an annual leave, you're dreaming." She disappeared into the bathroom, closing the door with a snap.

She might well be correct, but it didn't change his mind.

While she was in the bathroom, he got dressed. She came back out wearing the outfit she'd arrived in before the party and carrying her formal gown shrouded in a garment bag. Anger was brewing in those crystal eyes, but her next words were still soft.

"Gerrum Kirsey, just so we're perfectly clear. If you think I have any intention of marrying someone who toys for one minute with the idea of giving up an excellent career to go off to Alaska to write, you're insane." She paused for his response, but he stood motionless and silent, a rabbit frozen in the shadow of a hawk.

She shook her head, finally letting go of her icy control. "For God's sake, Gerrum. You're thirty-seven years old. You're engaged to be married. It's time you settled down, not time to go off chasing an impossible dream."

She was right, but if one gave up dreams at any age, what was left?

She glared at him, obviously waiting for him to back down. To say he'd been kidding. That no way would he do something so antiestablishment and ill-advised, not to mention downright bizarre, as take time off from his real career to go to Alaska and write.

But that image of himself as a rabbit stilled his words and slowed the very pulsing of blood in his veins. If he backed off now, gave in, their relationship would never again be one of equals.

Her eyes glittered. "Dammit, Gerrum. It's enough already that you're an Eskimo."

"Tlingit."

"Whatever. My family's been giving me grief over that, you know."

"So Winston informed me."

She tossed her head. "At least you're a Tlingit in a three-piece suit. No. This isn't happening. I won't let it happen."

The light from the bathroom spun gold in her hair and turned her eyes that lovely clear-water color. Seeing that, his heart felt like it was breaking. But in the silence that now lay between them, her words continued to resonate, overlaying her beauty with ugliness and reminding him of the puzzlement he'd felt when he first discovered having a mother who was an Alaskan Native made him different, and somehow not the equal, of paler-skinned classmates.

"So...what's it going to be, Gerrum? Alaska. Or me?"

What happened to 'I love you?' Such simple words but, in this moment, impossible to say. Equally impossible to continue the attempt to convince her it didn't need to be the one thing and not the other. He let the silence stretch a millennium before clearing his throat to speak.

In the end, it was easier than he expected. "Alaska."

That shocked Pam into immobility, then her head began to shake. "No. No. You cannot do this."

When he didn't respond, she turned and stalked to the doorway where she stopped and hooked the dress on the door frame. For an instant, relief lightened his heart. But then she pulled her ring off and slapped it on the dresser, snatched up the gown, and left without looking back.

How had it come to this?

He'd loved that Pam was decisive. Feisty. That she was a woman who would be both a worthy opponent in court and his equal in the bedroom. But despite her never failing to express her opinion, before this they'd never had more than a mild disagreement. Although, in light of what had just happened, that may have been because he'd never truly opposed her.

He started after her, arriving at the back door as she pulled out of the driveway. He watched which direction she went before returning to the bedroom to dress and grab his wallet and keys. But as he slipped the key into the ignition, her words replayed in his mind—*at least you're a Tlingit in a three-piece suit*—and his hand stilled.

Funny how they each, with a single word, had changed the shape of the future.

Eskimo.

Alaska.

"Words have power," his mom would say. "They must be used with care."

He pulled the key out of the ignition and, shaking off any remaining indecision, went back inside his no longer inadequate house.

~ ~ ~

Jeannie stood silently beside Gerrum in the *Joyful*'s cockpit. He'd called his sister shortly after dawn to invite her to spend the day on the water, and without hesitation, she'd said yes.

"The engagement's off." He didn't expect to speak so bluntly, but once the words were out, a weight lifted.

"Oh, Gerrum, I'm sorry to hear that. What happened? You both seemed so happy yesterday."

"Yeah." They were, and then, abruptly, they weren't. "I told her I want to take a leave this summer."

"Your timing could have been better." Her tone was mild and held no reproof, one of the many qualities he loved about her.

"She was going to be upset no matter when I told her."

Jeannie placed a hand on his arm. Fierce as a child, she had matured into a serene woman. "Perhaps with good reason. You are changing the rules."

But what happened with Pam was more than bad timing or rule-changing. If that were the whole of it, he'd right now be seeking her out, trying to reconcile. "Winston took me aside yesterday. He wanted to make sure I knew the Palmers were concerned about me taking a dip in their genetic pool. He said seeing you reassured them."

"But surely Pam didn't—"

"Yes, she did, although she was willing to overlook my ancestry, as long as I kept my job."

"Can't you work it out?"

That was the dilemma. After all, how could a single quarrel be enough to end a relationship that twenty-four hours ago he'd expected to last the rest of his life? Except, unfortunately, or fortunately, that single quarrel revealed something so essential, so divisive, something he'd never even suspected...

The *Joyful*'s bow dipped, then came up as they bounced across the spreading wake of a container ship headed toward the Port of Seattle. Spray slapped against the windscreen.

That wake...rather like what happened last night. Starting out small and focused, but growing and spreading until it rocked and shook everything in its vicinity.

He'd labeled what he felt for Pam, love. But it must have been less than that, because today, with the ocean sparkling and a brisk breeze to push against, he wasn't grieving her loss the way he expected to. There was pain, of course. Pain it was difficult to pin down to its exact geography, but he was beginning to suspect it wasn't a broken heart.

~ ~ ~

Given his engagement was off, and therefore Pam's opinion was no longer an issue, Gerrum decided to go all the way and resign his position..

"This is a surprise, Gerrum." Walter Pierson leaned forward with a frown. "I thought you were happy here. What can I do to change your mind?"

"Nothing, I'm afraid. I do appreciate all the opportunities you've given me."

"It's Rhinehard, isn't it. I heard he was sniffing around. We'll match his offer."

"It's not Rhinehard, and I'm not trying to hold you up for more money. I'm going to Alaska."

"Alaska?" Pierson's frown deepened.

"I want to spend time there. See what develops."

"Oh, I get it. A connecting with your roots thing, eh?"

His roots were mostly a cause of discomfort. His parents' unconventional union leading to unpleasant experiences for both them and their offspring. But while connecting to roots was not exactly his goal, it was close enough, he supposed.

"Well, if that's it, take a leave," Pierson said, his tone gruff. "Get it out of your system. Then you can come back refreshed. Ready to redouble your efforts."

If Pierson had stopped with the first part of that statement, Gerrum might have been tempted. It was his original plan, after all. But the reminder that any concession granted now would require payback later, firmed his resolve.

"I appreciate the offer, but no thank you."

Pierson sat for a moment, then pulled out a cigar and worked at lighting it. "Could be a bust, you know. What then?"

"I won't know until, or if, it happens."

"Well, if it does, check with me first. Can I get your agreement on that?"

"If I ever return to Seattle with the intention of practicing family law, I'll let you know."

"Humph. Don't think I'm not aware of the disclaimers in that statement." The cigar was finally drawing, and Pierson took a couple of puffs, examining Gerrum as he did it. "When I turned forty, I had a midlife crisis, you know."

"How did you handle it?" Gerrum said.

"Not well. Almost got divorced over it, as a matter of fact. Then I came to my senses. No doubt you will, too. When you do, we'll be glad to take you back."

Although it was comforting to have a fall-back position, in this instance Gerrum preferred not to have the temptation to return to the easy and familiar.

Chapter Four

1963

MARYMEAD COLLEGE MEAD, KANSAS

"Clen, Maxine, welcome back." Thomasina was doing her usual rounds, greeting all of them as they unpacked and settled into their dorm rooms for the new year. "How were your summers?"

"Good."

They'd answered in unison, with Maxine following up with a giggle while Clen bent over her suitcase to hide her face. No way was she telling anyone the truth about her summer.

"Glad to hear it. Would you come see me, Clen? Soon. I need to talk to you about something."

Thomasina moved on to greet other arrivals, and Maxine nudged Clen's arm. "You're her favorite."

"Am not." But the comment pleased her.

When she went to see Thomasina, the nun told the secretary to hold her calls then asked Clen to close the door. It all felt a bit ominous.

"I wanted to show you something, Clen." Thomasina handed over several typed pages.

"What is it?"

"A proposed revision to our rules."

"I thought the issue was dead." Thomasina had tried to get a rule revision through the previous year. The debate raged most of second semester but, in the end, the only changes were a verb tense or two and a couple of commas.

"I think last year I requested changes that were too minor," Thomasina said. "This year, I'm going for a complete overhaul. After all, it's working for the pope." She smiled. "One rule will be of particular interest to you, but keep it to yourself for now. I don't want everyone's hopes up. I'm sharing them with you because you were the major catalyst." Thomasina sat back and folded her hands. "And now, the truth about your summer."

"It was fine."

"How is Joshua?"

"He's better." So was she lying because she felt guilty to be here, not home, or because she bought into her mother's insistence they must be positive? "Thanks for sharing this with me. I need to go, or I'll be late for class." Another lie. Something she seemed to be getting good at.

~ ~ ~

A month into the school year, Thomasina's proposed rule changes were passed by a special board that included both student and faculty representatives. The sophomore class representative stopped by Clen and Maxine's room with the good news.

The next morning, Clen was commemorating the first day of the new order when she encountered Sister Angelica. The nun stepped in front of Clen, forcing her to a halt. "Michelle McClendon.. And here I thought you'd reformed."

"Oh, you mean the slacks? Haven't you heard? The rules have changed."

"Those changes do not go into effect until next semester."

Clen shrugged. "I've been moved by the spirit to celebrate."

The nun glared at her. "You, young woman, are incorrigible. I simply do not understand why Thomasina continues to defend you. I expect if I give you demerits, she'll simply wipe the slate clean again."

"She makes me do penance first."

"Good. Glad to hear it. I'll put you down for five. I hope it's an unpleasant penance."

"Awful. She forces me to think."

The nun's eyes narrowed. "Are you laughing at me,

50

missy?"

It was yet another mark against Angelica—that she steadfastly refused to call her Clen. "Absolutely not. Thinking is difficult work."

Angelica humphed in dismissal. Clen wanted to skip away but restrained herself. They were her first demerits in almost a year.

~ ~ ~

"Clen? Could you come here for a minute?" Thomasina gestured from her doorway.

With the hallway nearly empty, Clen couldn't pretend she hadn't heard the summons. She sidled into the office. "I'm going to be late for class."

"How odd that would worry you. Sister Mark tells me you've missed several classes recently."

"I bet the academic dean at Princeton doesn't go searching out students who cut classes."

"I'm sure you're correct." Thomasina lifted an eyebrow and motioned for Clen to take a seat. "However, the last time I checked, this wasn't Princeton."

"Nope, men are definitely thin on the ground around here."

"I want to know why you're skipping Sister Mark's classes?"

Clen sighed. "Have you ever taken a class from Sister Mark?"

"As a matter of fact, I have."

"Then you should understand why I prefer to read the book on my own."

Thomasina gave her a steady look, and Clen tried not to squirm.

"You might keep in mind, class discussions are part of the educational experience. I also notice you've jumped the gun on the new dress code."

"I figure all I have to do is avoid Sister Demonica. She's the only one who still cares."

Thomasina's mouth twitched. "It's Sister Angelica, and she is correct. You are in violation of the current rules. I suggest you not retire the skirt quite yet."

"I told her you always exact an awful penance when I get demerits."

"Did you. And that penance is?"

"You force me to think."

"Indeed. Then let me pose you a question. What is freedom?"

"It's everyone being able to make their own decisions about what to think, do, wear."

"And yet, if you were completely free to do whatever you wanted, you might do something that limited my freedom. Correct?"

"I suppose so. Yes."

Thomasina sat waiting.

"I get it. Without limits, there'd be chaos."

"And civilized societies negotiate those limits. Now, while I'll concede what you wear is not a major issue for most of Marymead society, it is a sore point for Sister Angelica. By the way, it might interest you to know she voted in favor of the new rules."

Clen did squirm then. "I'm sorry. I'll go change."

"After class. Now go."

~ ~ ~

Clen walked out of a history exam on November twenty-second to find clumps of girls in the hall crying.

"Kennedy." "Shot." "Dealey Plaza." "Dallas." The words drifted in the air, oddly disconnected.

She skirted the groups and ran downstairs to Thomasina's office. The door was open, and Thomasina and her secretary were standing by the secretary's desk listening to a radio. Thomasina nodded at Clen without speaking. Together, the three of them stood listening to the ebb and flow of the story.

Kennedy had been seriously wounded...he'd been rushed to Parkland Hospital...he was in surgery. Until finally, "At one p.m. this afternoon, President John Fitzgerald Kennedy, the thirty-fifth president of the United States, died from an assassin's bullet in Dallas."

Thomasina gripped Clen's hand so hard it hurt. "Walk

with me, Clen."

They hurried through deserted corridors to a side door to the outside. It was chilly, but Thomasina's habit would keep her warm, and Clen was wearing a sweater.

"I couldn't stand being inside," Thomasina said. She pulled in a deep breath. "The river?"

When Clen nodded, the nun set off at a brisk pace down the hill past the picnic area and onto the path along the river. The path was narrow, forcing them to walk single file. A sharp gust caught Thomasina's veil and flung it out in an arc. She turned her head and caught the veil, then twisted and tucked it into the cinch around her waist.

After a fast mile, they stopped and leaned hands on their thighs, gulping in deep breaths of air.

Thomasina straightened, facing the river. "Thank you for coming with me, Clen, and for not nattering."

That silent walk with Thomasina was the only grace note in the somber days that followed.

~ ~ ~

Winter that year seemed particularly dark and dreary, not only because of Kennedy's assassination, but because of a more personal loss the Marymead community suffered in late February.

First came whispers at breakfast that an ambulance had been called and a nun was removed on a stretcher. Most were guessing Eustacia had finally succumbed. She had to be at least a hundred and ten. But then a black edged announcement was posted on the main bulletin board. Sister Gladys was the one who had died.

"A brain aneurysm is what I heard," said the woman who ran the switchboard.

"What's that?" Clen asked.

The woman shrugged. "Whatever it is, it's quick."

Clen looked up aneurysm in the dictionary. A blood vessel had burst in Gladiolus's brain—something every bit as cruel, in Clen's mind, as God letting Joshua get leukemia.

Knowing Thomasina and Gladiolus were friends, Clen wanted to tell Thomasina how sorry she was, but she hesitated, remembering how Thomasina hadn't wanted words when Kennedy died.

After the Mass of Remembrance, Clen went for a walk in the winter-bare garden. In the corner next to the trellis that Gladiolus had kept in good repair for girls who stayed out too late, she found a rose bush, and although spring was still weeks away, the bush held a bloom.

She picked it and took it to Thomasina's room, where she left it on the pillow.

~ ~ ~

After Sister Gladiolus's death, Thomasina changed. When Clen stopped by to chat, the nun would give her a distracted look and cut the conversation short. When Thomasina walked down the hall, she barely acknowledged anyone she passed. And when classes ended that year, Thomasina was missing from her usual station by the door.

~ ~ ~

Clen spent the summer reading to Joshua, who found it hard to hold a book for very long. As she turned a page, he interrupted. "Mickey La, am I going to die?"

She sucked in a quick breath. "We all die sometime, Josh."

"That's not what I mean."

"I know." She leaned over and touched his hand where it was lying on the covers.

"Mom won't let me talk about it. She says I have to be positive so the cancer cells will go away. But they aren't going." He sounded matter-of-fact, as if they were discussing something ordinary like which pair of pajamas to wear or what book to read next. It made Clen's heart clench with pain.

"What do you think it's like?" he asked. "Dying."

She tried to swallow the lump in her throat. "I think it's like going to sleep and having a wonderful dream. In that dream you can do anything you want, go anywhere." Actually, she had no idea what death might be like, but Joshua didn't need to hear that.

"What if I just want to be here with Mom and Dad and you and Jase and go to school, play Little League? Just...be a regular kid with an ordinary, boring life? Instead, all I get to do is lie here, and the only choices I have are which channel to put on the stupid TV and what to eat. Except, most of the time I'm too sick to eat."

"The treatments make you sick, but they'll also make you better so you can do all that." Clen bit her lip to stop any more of her mom's Pollyanna phrases from emerging.

"I don't want to do anymore treatments, Mickey La. You've got to help me. Make it stop."

"I can't, Josh. I wish I could. I'd do anything—"

"Then tell Mom for me. I don't want to go back to Denver. Please?"

"If you don't get the treatments, you won't get better."

"I'm not getting better. Don't you get it? I can't make the cancer go away. I tried. Promise me you'll talk to Mom. And don't leave me. Promise me you'll stay with me. That you won't go away."

"I promise, Josh."

Chapter Five

1982

"Do you have any idea where you're going or what you're doing yet?" Maxine asked as she buttered a roll.

"I guess I'll just get in the car and start driving," Clen said.

"Hey, we were going to do that. Remember?"

Clen did. The summer after they graduated from college, she and Maxine had planned to travel before they settled down to look for jobs in the fall. Then Maxine met a guy, and travel plans turned into wedding preparations.

"I'm still kind of sorry we didn't take that trip," Maxine said.

"You did okay."

Maxine ended up with four cute kids and a doting husband, and now Clen had been handed another chance to indulge her old dream of wanderlust. Thanks to Paul and their joint investing acumen.

"Ever since you called, I've been thinking about where I'd go if I were you." Maxine set her knife down and rummaged in her purse. "I decided it would be nice to spend time in a place like this."

She pushed a brochure across the table with the tip of a fingernail that matched her lipstick. It always amused Clen that, although Maxine would go home to a chaotic household

56

filled with kids and dogs, she always dressed more formally for their lunches than did Clen, who would return to an office.

"Their retreat program has a terrific reputation."

Clen glanced at the brochure. It was from an abbey, for Pete's sake. She pushed it back. "You know I'm more a fan of advancing than retreating."

Maxine rolled her eyes. "When was the last time you went to church?"

"Mass was still in Latin."

Maxine shook her head. "You're always making jokes, but I doubt God will find that one amusing."

Which was only one of the bones Clen had to pick with the creator of the universe. "Come on, Maxie. You know God and I aren't on speaking terms, and it's working for both of us."

"You may think it's working, but when something bad happens you'll want to have God on your side."

"God takes sides?"

"What? No...of course not. Well, maybe."

It just showed Maxine knew as little about God as Clen did. Besides, the worst had happened, and God didn't lift a finger, if God had fingers. And Clen could easily guess Maxine's response if she started a debate about that.

Hoping to cut off further God discussions, she waved her hand with its short, unpolished fingernails at Maxine, then slipped the brochure into her briefcase. "I'll read it later." She wouldn't, but since Maxine had to suspect that, it wasn't precisely a lie.

"I heard from Sister Thomasina last week." Maxine delved into her purse again, then held out an envelope that Clen declined to accept. "Don't you want to read it? She asked about you."

Clen shook her head, wishing she hadn't put the brochure away. Wishing she had something with which to deflect any discussion of Sister Thomasina.

"I thought you two were such great friends," Maxine said, frowning.

Clen had long ago given up trying to figure out what she and Thomasina were—her feelings for the nun a confused mix of love, anger, and puzzlement accompanied by a dull ache. "That's so far in the past. Nearly twenty years."

"Seventeen." As their fortieth birthdays approached, Maxine had become a stickler on the mathematics of such statements.

"Let's just say, it's another circumstance where moving on works better than looking back," Clen said. "Remember what happened to Lot's wife."

Maxine sat fiddling with the pages of the letter. It was a continuing mystery to Clen how Maxine, who'd had only casual interactions with Thomasina during their years at Marymead, had established such a steady correspondence with the nun. But perhaps Thomasina was simply being courteous, responding whenever Maxine wrote, and Maxine wrote to everyone she knew, constantly.

The thought of all that writing made Clen tired.

"Fine." Maxine put the letter away. "I'll tell her you're peachy."

"Thanks, Maxie. You're a peach, yourself."

"So, about the abbey?"

"I expect the reason it appeals to you is because you live with teenagers."

Maxine tried to look stern, but her lips betrayed her. "You're probably right." Then her expression turned serious. "You know you don't need to put on your tough girl act with me, Clen."

"Better to laugh than to cry."

"She really had a triple-D bust?"

"They were the most humongous breasts I've ever seen. In fact, when she leaned, I fully expected her to tip over."

Maxine giggled. "You are so bad."

"Obviously."

"Oh, Clen, he's a louse and you don't deserve what he did to you."

"Actually..."

"What?"

"It's just...I always felt deep down it was too good to be true. You know. A man like Paul, falling for someone like me? The first time he asked me out, I figured he'd misdialed and decided to be nice about it."

"Oh, stop it. You're funny and smart and great-looking,

and you deserve someone so much better."

"I'm not petite, not blonde, and most definitely not endowed."

"He married you."

"And I don't know why. Neither does he. I asked him. He couldn't answer."

"Well, he was lucky to have you, and dumb as a Brussels sprout to mess it up."

"I doubt he'd appreciate being compared to a Brussels sprout." And if she could focus on the image of Paul rendered rotund and green, she might be able to make it through not only this lunch but whatever came next.

"At least think about the abbey?" Maxine said.

Clen nodded because that was easier than saying "no" and having Maxine continue to push the idea. Besides, Maxie was right. There were probably few places more peaceful than an abbey.

~ ~ ~

After Clen told Maxine about her separation from Paul, she finally called her parents. "Mom." She managed only the one word, but that was okay, because Stella McClendon was never one to let a pause go to waste.

"Michelle. I was just telling your dad we should give you a call. It's been awhile." It was her mom's way of letting Clen know she'd once again failed the dutiful daughter test.

Clen pulled in a breath and spoke quickly. "I've left Paul."

"What? But why?"

"Short answer? He cheated on me."

"Are you sure?"

"Of course I'm sure."

"Oh, Michelle, I'm so sorry to hear that. I thought he was perfect for you."

"Well, he's certainly made it clear I'm not perfect for him, which makes him being perfect for me a bit of a problem."

"Now, there's no need to be sarcastic. From everything you've told us, I think I can be excused for assuming you were happy."

Clen rested her elbows on the hotel desk with the phone

receiver tucked into her ear. Was she ever happy with Paul? Although, her mother was right that she'd painted rosy pictures. Probably because it was harder to admit to parents you'd made a mistake then it was to admit it to yourself.

"So where are you, hon?"

"I'm still in Atlanta. At the Peachtree Plaza." She recited the phone number. "I won't be here long, though. I turned in my notice. I'm just finishing out the week."

"Then what?"

That was *The Question.* There was Maxine's suggestion of the abbey. Not that it had any appeal. Probably best if Clen stuck with the driving-at-random plan. Or maybe she could book a trip to somewhere exotic. The Great Barrier Reef, Machu Pichu, Mount Fuji. Have adventures.

Anything was possible, which was perhaps why she was having such a hard time making a decision.

"Hon, are you still there?"

"I was thinking about your question." Although thinking about it made her feel panicky.

"Why not come home for a visit? We'd love to see you. You and I can go shopping, get our hair done."

"I'll go shopping with you, but only if you agree to call me Clen."

"Oh, Michelle, you are such a kidder. We'll drive to Denver and ask Nancy join us. We'll have a good time."

"Nancy?"

"Jason's girlfriend. She's a sweetie. You're going to love her. We're expecting Jason to pop the question any day now."

"Don't you think I'd put a crimp in things?"

"Of course you won't. It's times like this you need your family."

But did they need her? Standing around casting a pall because of a Paul? The unexpected pun made her glad she hadn't spoken the thought aloud since her mother never did seem to get her sense of humor.

"Just come home, sweetie."

The mere thought of that brought on the usual restlessness that became her constant companion within twenty-four hours of proximity to her mother. Sticking to small doses of each other's company was best for both of them. But if she wasn't going home, where was she going?

Before she saw Paul at the airport with the Lady in Red, Clen had thought her life settled, stable. Now she knew her life, like a complex pattern of carefully stacked dominos, had just been waiting for a nudge to topple it.

And after the collapse, there'd been the rush of activities— the cleaning up and clearing away, the legal documents, the stilted conversations—until now, finally, everything was finished and all that remained was the decision of what to do next.

That question had been poking at her, turning food into something she had to force herself to chew and swallow, and sleep into a place she could no longer locate.

After talking to her mother, she grabbed a piece of hotel stationery and a pen, ready to write any thought that came to mind.

Nothing.

Okay, McClendon. Focus.

All she needed was a first step. Something simple. How about—which direction would she drive when she left Atlanta? She opened the atlas she'd recently bought. Clearly, the direction that offered the greatest scope was northwest. She shrugged. It was as good a plan as any.

~ ~ ~

She purchased a compass, attached it to the car's dash, and as Atlanta receded in her rearview mirror, refined her plan further. She'd stick to back roads and drive no more than four hours a day, stopping at the nearest town, no matter the size, to stay the night.

Joseph-and-Marying, her father had called that approach on a family vacation. That time, they'd been hoping for adventures. But what she mostly hoped for now was that wherever she laid her head each night sleep would find her.

~ ~ ~

The first day, following the prompts of the compass, Clen took a series of roads that meandered north and west. She passed near or through a litany of small towns with intriguing names—Cedartown, Mudslide, Hokes Bluff, Arab, Tooks

Corner. At the end of the four hours, she reached Ethel Green, Alabama.

The town was small, but large enough to have a gas station, a diner, and a motel with a vacancy sign— a weathered strip of clapboard, that looked like it had been hung the day the motel opened a hundred years ago and not moved since. The proprietor, a heavyset woman with tired eyes, showed little curiosity as she collected the night's rent and turned over the key. Clen suspected a lack of curiosity wouldn't always be the case in a town this size.

After eating in the diner, she strolled the downtown, eventually turning onto a side street to explore what kind of houses the people of Ethel Green had built. Most were of modest size and shaded by large trees, but two blocks from the main street, she encountered a row of shacks with clotheslines strung in straggly yards. In one yard, clothes hung limp in the quiet air like pages of a book picked out of a puddle. A door banged, and a black girl came out carrying a basket on her hip. She set the basket down, lifted her arms, and began unpinning a row of diapers and tiny shirts.

Transfixed, Clen stood watching, wishing she'd thought to bring along her sketchbook. The girl suddenly noticed her and stopped moving. Clen smiled and raised a hand in greeting, but the girl turned away, grabbed the basket, and hurried into the house. Feeling uncomfortable, Clen walked back to the motel. There she pulled out her sketchbook and began to draw the girl from memory.

Slowly the picture expanded. The side of the shack with its ramshackle porch, the rows of washing—not just tiny garments, but larger shirts as well—the girl's slender arms raised to unpin the wash, the basket at her feet.

When Clen lifted her pencil from the page, she was surprised to discover it was nearly midnight. Even better, she was sleepy.

~ ~ ~

In succeeding days, Clen often ended up in towns too small to have motels. She discovered that asking about a night's lodging at a nearby gas station or diner always yielded information about someone who had a room they were willing to rent. In a tiny hamlet in Tennessee, that room was in the house of an elderly woman named Mag.

When Clen asked Mag for suggestions of where to eat, her hostess chuckled. "Not much of that sort of thing hereabouts. But if you won't turn your nose up at home cooking, I'd be happy to fix us both something."

"I don't want you to go to any trouble."

"It's no trouble. Kind of nice to have someone to feed. Not much fun cooking for just myself. You can help if you like."

With Mag directing, Clen chased down a chicken, and Mag chopped off its head. Grimacing and trying not to sneeze, Clen plucked it, then Mag showed her how to cut it up. By that point, Clen wasn't altogether certain she'd be able to eat the thing, but she didn't share the thought with the old woman.

Mag hauled out an ancient electric frying pan and plunked a cube of butter, a cube of margarine, and a large dollop of shortening into it. She set the heat on low, and while the grease warmed, she dredged the chicken pieces in flour.

After she added them to the gently bubbling grease, a delicious smell began to fill the air.

"Now, we let it cook nice and slow while we sit," Mag said, pouring two glasses of iced tea and leading the way to a small front porch shaded by white clematis. As she rocked, Mag began to talk. Clen listened, alternately sipping tea and sketching.

"Started out in Pennsylvania, my family did. Granddad was a farmer but my father was a shopkeeper. After he married my mother, they moved west, looking for better opportunities, I suppose. I was their second child. My mother always had a preference for my older sister, Helen. Real pretty, Helen was. Blonde curls, blue eyes. Delicate looking."

Although Mag was short and dumpy with eyes a pale washed-out blue, Clen found her so appealing, it was hard to believe the mother could have preferred the beautiful sister.

"One Christmas we both got dolls," Mag continued. "I'd been wanting a doll for as long as I could remember. And oh my, how I loved that doll. I named her Annie, and I took her everywhere I went. Helen mostly ignored her doll. Didn't even give her a name. One day she left it out in the yard, and the neighbor's dog got hold of it. And my, did that old dog go to town. Shook that doll something fierce. When Helen discovered it, she went crying to our mother, and Mother made me give Annie to Helen. Helen never even played with her, but she wouldn't let me touch her.

"Never forgot that. Funny how something that happens when you're six can stick with you your whole life." Mag stopped talking and Clen's hand moved quickly, trying to transfer to the page what she was seeing in Mag's face—an ancient sorrow that was still causing pain even though it happened some eighty years ago.

Mag shook herself and stood abruptly. "Time I checked on that chicken."

"You need help?"

"No. No need for you to get up."

After a minute Mag returned. "How's that picture coming along?"

"Good. If you keep telling me stories, I'll finish in no time."

"Where was I?"

Clen was too angry with Mag's mother to answer.

"Well, let's see. Suppose I tell you about the cooking. I started cooking when I was twelve, after Mother died in childbirth. Helen was older, but she was useless in the kitchen. At first, there were only six of us, but then Father remarried. That meant more babies. Ended up we added three half brothers and two half sisters. An even dozen for dinner every night.

"I liked it well enough, cooking for a crowd. Made for a change when I married Lou. We only had three children, so I never did cook for a crowd again. Lou was a good eater, though. He always said I was the best cook he ever met. That it was why he married me." Mag rocked and chuckled, then went silent.

Looking at the old woman, Clen held her breath.

"He's been gone five years now, but sometimes I still forget. Think he's just in the other room, reading his paper, and when I remember he isn't, I don't feel much like eating." Mag shook her head as if dislodging a pesky fly, then gave Clen a wry look. "Well now. Didn't mean to get into all that. Nothing ever gets accomplished with whining. My stepmother was fond of saying that. Mostly to those of us weren't hers, but true for all of that."

Mag returned to the kitchen, with Clen following. She removed the chicken from the skillet, then she poured most of the pan drippings into a jar. "We'll use this when we make bread tomorrow."

She added flour to the remaining drippings and then milk and cream, making a thick gravy that was one of the best things Clen had ever eaten.

The next day Mag showed her how to bake bread and to cook ribs so they left behind crisp brown bits to flavor the potato dumplings she also taught Clen how to make.

Clen stayed a week with Mag. When she left, she took with her a fresh-baked loaf of bread, a jar of homemade plum jelly, and notes about how to make the delicious dinners Mag had cooked for the two of them. She also carried a sketchbook filled with drawings—Mag cooking, the old house in its frame of flowers with two shadowy figures sitting on the porch, the apple tree in the backyard with an old-fashioned wooden swing hanging from one of the branches.

"Looks like it's just waiting for the next time a little one comes to visit," Mag said, sounding pensive, when Clen showed her the sketches.

After leaving Mag, Clen continued driving, stopping only for a single night each place. And wherever she stopped, she sketched. Some subjects posed for her. Other times she captured a quick study of someone who was unaware—an old man reading his paper at the counter of the local diner, a small boy petting his dog in the park.

In the diners where she ate along the way, Clen chatted with cooks and waitresses, collecting recipes and cooking tips although she had no idea why she was doing it. But it, like the sketching, gave some structure to her days.

Her best days were the ones when she didn't think about the past, as if that quick turn she'd taken a couple of days before had left the past wondering where she'd gone.

But it always found her, eventually. And when it did, the bits and pieces she'd managed to avoid thinking about during the years in Atlanta buzzed around her, as relentless and irritating as flies—dive-bombing or sliding into the edge of her vision just when she'd begun to relax.

She'd been on the road swiping at those memories for five months on the night she found herself in a small Montana town with a monastery. Walking back to the motel after dinner, she passed near the monastery walls and heard the monks chanting. The deep, rich voices wove together in a simple repetitive melody that was so muted and softened that it seemed like something she was dreaming.

The last note faded into a moment of stillness before the voices began the next chant.

Shaken, but uncertain why, Clen walked back to that night's lodging, her thoughts turning to the dilemma of where she would spend the winter. There was already snow in the mountains, and that meant the cold weather would soon reach the plains as well. She didn't want to be caught by it, not with her tolerance for cold lessened by the years in Atlanta's warmth.

The best solution was to head south, and on the way she could stop in Colorado Springs for that visit home she kept putting off.

~ ~ ~

The time Clen spent with her parents was every bit as difficult as she expected it might be. Jason and Nancy, who were planning a summer wedding, came to Colorado Springs for Thanksgiving, but they spent Christmas with Nancy's family in Boulder. That left Clen to carry the burden of her mother's expectations for the holiday.

"You need to settle down, Michelle. Is it even safe? Your going from place to place the way you do? Why not stay here. You don't have to live at home, you know. You could get an apartment."

"I'm not ready for that."

"Do you know when you will be?"

"Sorry, I wish I did." She knew her mother pushed because she was worried, but that didn't make the relentless questions any easier to tolerate.

A Christmas card arrived from Maxine, adding another dollop of guilt. Clen had promised to stay in touch but hadn't. Her only regular contacts since leaving Atlanta were her parents and the attorney who was handling her divorce.

When she told the attorney she'd be in one place for at least four weeks, he promised to finalize everything for her to sign. The paperwork would be easy to get together, he told Clen, since, Paul, who had initially blustered about his share of their joint accounts, had, in the end, decided not to contest.

So when the postman rang the bell right before Christmas and handed over the large envelope, Clen knew what it was without looking at the return address. She took it to her room and pulled out the contents. As she read through the pages, tears began to run down her cheeks.

If her mother had seen her crying and asked why, she wouldn't have been able to answer. Perhaps the tears were a sign she'd been fooling herself about how little she cared for Paul, or maybe she was grieving the loss of what might have been—the stability of loving someone. The possibility of family.

~ ~ ~

Clen left Colorado Springs the day after Christmas and spent the winter months wandering the southwest. By the time spring arrived, she was desperate for stability. But her future continued to have clarity only in her dreams, a lucidity that always slipped away when she awakened.

But one morning, part of a dream memory remained behind—a chapel with ornate marble carvings turned rosy by light slanting through colored windows. That image flowed into one of a garden surrounded by walls, with robed figures pacing its perimeter in silence. That was all. Or all she could remember.

Marymead. The chapel part, at least, but she had no idea what it meant.

Chapter Six

1981 - 1984

WRANGELL, ALASKA

Two weeks after leaving Seattle, Gerrum entered Wrangell's Reliance Harbor and checked in with the harbormaster. He was directed to a temporary berth amidst a cluster of boats—everything from a sleek white yacht to an ancient tug.

The day was warm for early April, and the clear skies and calm seas had made the run from Petersburg a pleasant one. He'd almost decided to stay longer in Petersburg, where he'd spent the morning writing, but he wanted to visit more of the small communities dotted along the inland waterway between Ketchikan and Juneau before deciding where to anchor for the summer.

Although, it wasn't only a summer anchorage he was considering. He'd also begun thinking about the possibility of finding someplace where he could start a small business of guiding fisherman. That would provide a modest but somewhat steady income while he waited to see if writing panned out. He knew from Jeannie's experience making money as a writer took time. Better then to do something that would stretch out his resources.

After securing a berth for the *Joyful*, he walked downtown, making note of amenities like cafés, shops, and grocery stores. Wrangell's downtown was larger than either Petersburg's or Haines'. Unlike Ketchikan, the buildings comprising the Wrangell community curved around the base of the mountain instead of climbing the sides.. And unlike Petersburg, there were no sloughs that at high tide were deep enough to handle a good-size boat, but at low tide emptied out to roughly the depth of a wading pool.

He headed back to the marina, pleased with what he'd seen. When he reached Bear Lodge, located near the marina, the idea of spending the night in a bed that didn't move, and bathing in abundant hot water was suddenly appealing.

After showing Gerrum a room, the innkeeper, one John Jeffers, offered him a cup of coffee, and Marian Jeffers joined them in the inn's dining room.

"We've got lots of nice places around Wrangell," John said when Gerrum asked about area attractions.

"There's the garnet reef. It was willed to the Boy Scouts, but anyone can buy a permit and do their own digging. Even without digging, it's an interesting place to walk around. Then there's Anan Observatory where you can watch bears going after salmon."

"And don't forget the Stikine River," Marian added.

"Yep. That's a good one. East of here, on the mainland. Navigable all the way into Canada. There are hot springs about twenty miles in, glaciers, waterfalls, lakes. Makes for a nice day if you've got a fast boat and the tides cooperate."

"Why the tides?"

"The Stikine delta empties out real good at low tide," John said. "Means, you don't time it right, you can get stuck getting back to Wrangell."

"A time-honored Wrangell romantic tradition," Marian said with a chuckle.

~ ~ ~

In the morning, Gerrum, well-rested, showered, and shaved, walked back downtown to the Visitors' Center.

"You the one with the pretty green boat, ain't you?" said the middle-aged woman behind the counter.

Taken aback at how fast that information had made the rounds, he smiled. "Guilty as charged. I'm Gerrum Kirsey."

"Pleased to meet you." She reached out a hand. "Doreen Matthews." She squinted at him. "You're Native, ain't you."

"My mother's Tlingit. From this area, originally."

"Well, how about that. Welcome home, Gerrum Kirsey."

"Thank you."

"What can I do for you?"

"Are you free for a cup of coffee?"

"Anytime."

She grabbed a sweater, put up a sign and, chatting all the way, walked with him to Maude's Café. Garrulous and friendly, Doreen was clearly an excellent choice for the Visitors' Center. She was also direct and inquisitive.

After he let her pry into his background as much as he cared to allow, he finally got her to reciprocate with information about Wrangell. She was able to tell him the approximate number of visitors coming through each season, the number that stayed overnight, the number booking guided trips, and the most popular type of trips.

While she talked, he made notes on one of the café's paper placemats. The information dovetailed with what the Jeffers told him, but now he had figures he could use to run some numbers.

"If you get your paperwork in order, I'd be happy to start referring visitors to you for sports fishing, and later in the season you could offer Anan trips," Doreen said.

"I'm also interested in the viability of offering Stikine trips."

"Doubt that would work for you. You need a smaller, faster boat to make a go of it on the Stikine."

Essentially the same thing the Jeffers had told him. "Is anyone doing Stikine trips?"

"A few tried it. Never seems to take."

"Do you know why?"

"Trip to the hot springs takes most of a day. Means you're always going to hit a low tide either going or coming. The boats what can get across best are too small to be comfortable for, say a party of four to six. That's what's needed to make a go of it."

He walked Doreen back to the Visitors' Center and returned to the *Joyful* with the placemat of figures and an idea beginning to form.

~ ~ ~

"Only thing worse than a Native acting like he's good as you is a Native who's a goldarned lawyer." The man who spoke was standing at the bar dressed in the typical Wrangell attire of flannel shirt and jeans held up by suspenders.

Gerrum knew the remarks were aimed at him, and they triggered a familiar spurt of adrenaline. Trying to appear calm, he turned to John Jeffers with a questioning look.

John tipped his chin toward the man. "That's Elmer Cantrell. Convinced there's a conspiracy behind every bush, even if it looks like a bull moose."

"They ain't going to be satisfied till they get it all," Cantrell countered, turning around and leaning back on his elbows. "That there Native Claims Settlement Act." He hawked, the sound every bit as disgusting as the disgust it was seeking to convey. "Don't make no difference. They want it all. And what makes them think they're special anyway. Wasn't I born here? Seems to me, that makes me as native as some half-assed Tlingit lawyer from Seattle."

Gerrum bit down on a reply. It never paid to engage a bigot in a debate. John tossed money on the table and motioned for Gerrum to follow him outside.

"Are Native claims still an issue?" he asked John, as they walked away from the bar. "I thought that was settled in the seventies."

John shrugged. "Always seems to be a loose end or two. Enough to keep your garden-variety racist like Cantrell stirred up."

"Does he have company?"

"What? You mean in Wrangell?"

Gerrum nodded, hoping for a negative. Until the encounter with Elmer, he'd had a good feeling about Wrangell.

"Folks around here are mostly tolerant, though they do like to gossip. Hell, it's a form of recreation. But there's no malice in it."

"Except when someone like Cantrell gets hold of it."

"That's a man loves the sound of his own voice. No guts to back it up, though. Only picked on you because you were with me, and he knew I wouldn't let you clean his clock."

~ ~ ~

After a week in Wrangell, time Gerrum spent both writing his novel and checking further on the information he'd been given, he left the *Joyful* in John and Marian's care and took the ferry back to Bellingham to follow up on his idea.

In Bellingham, he commissioned the building of a boat based on a New Zealand design he'd read about, and he paid for it with the money he'd gotten from selling his Seattle house. The boat would be powered by an engine lying flush with the keel and would have a draft of less than a foot, making it fast, maneuverable, and perfect for the Stikine trips he hoped to offer.

The boat would be ready the following spring, at which point, he'd have two boats to offer trips with. That meant he'd need a partner. After he returned to Wrangell for the remainder of the summer and mentioned his plan to John, Terry Borges ambled down the dock and introduced himself. Lanky and relaxed, Terry stepped aboard the *Joyful*, his open, sunny countenance a direct contrast to one particular Wrangell resident.

His handshake was firm. "Don't make 'em like this no more," he said, thumping the rail.

As they chatted, Gerrum could see Terry was engaged in a casual but thorough perusal of the *Joyful*. Although the troller might look a bit ragged, she was sound.

"John told me you was looking for someone to run one of your boats. Take visitors and fishermen out and about. But I only see one boat."

"The other one's being built. It will be here next spring."

"Another troller?"

"No." Gerrum invited Terry to sit in the galley and handed him a cup of coffee, then he outlined his plans. When he finished, Terry agreed to join him the following year, and they shook hands on it.

Watching Terry amble back down the dock, Gerrum thought how funny it was that life often seemed to turn out that way—that the thing you thought you were running from was what saved you.

It was something he and his sister talked about when he visited her in Seattle that winter.

"You always insisted you didn't want to depend on a boat for a living," Jeannie said, picking up her knitting and bending her head over it, as the needles began to move in a slow rhythm.

"I know, but I think I'll enjoy it. For sure it means less stress, more leisure than I had at Pierpont and Potter. Time to write." He stretched his legs to soak up the warmth from the wood-burning stove. It was a typical Seattle winter day, damp and overcast, but this room was like a warm, beating heart.

Jeannie looked up with a smile. "How about Pam? Are you still glad you called it off?"

"Good lord, yes. Would have been the biggest mistake of my life."

"It might get lonely up there, though."

"Are you lonely, Jeannie?"

"Sometimes." She gave him a quick glance. "Better off lonely than with the wrong person, I suppose."

"Amen to that." They sat in companionable silence, while he tried to think of something he could say to make his sister feel better about either her situation or his. "Maybe we're better off alone, we two. Getting too old to change, maybe."

Jeannie snorted. "Since when is thirty-seven and forty old?"

"You have to admit, it's getting there."

For a time she knitted in silence while he let his current plotline simmer.

"I have a friend who told me when it's the right person, you just know," she said.

"Reassuring." It hadn't happened that way with Pam, although, of course, that might be a case in point.

"I'd like to feel that way about someone," she said. "Certain. No doubts."

Yeah. He'd like it, too. Didn't seem like either he or his sister had a talent for it, however.

The needles stopped moving, but Jeannie didn't look up. "I asked Mom once how she knew Dad was the one."

"What did she say?"

"He had the prettiest boat."

He smiled at Jeannie, wishing he had more comfort than

that to offer her.

Jeannie set her knitting down and stood. "Guess I better do something about dinner. It surely won't cook itself."

~ ~ ~

The spring of his third year in Wrangell, Gerrum attended the Kiwanis salmon bake at Marian Jeffers' insistence. Plate in hand, he looked for John and Marian among the people sitting at the picnic tables scattered under tarps to hold off the inevitable rain. He spotted them and walked over to take the empty spot across from John.

"Have you two met?" Marian gestured to the woman seated next to him.

"Hailey Connelly, isn't it?" He hadn't met her, but he'd heard the commentary. She'd arrived early in the spring and opened an art gallery on Wrangell's main street.

She nodded, her eyes narrowing as she examined him. "You know, I don't believe I recall you being among the lure-the-city-girl-up-the-Stikine crowd."

He chuckled. "Nope. Gerrum Kirsey. And I wasn't going to attempt it. Not after you told Del you were so allergic to hot springs he'd better be able to do a tracheotomy if he planned to get you near one."

"Does Del have black, brown, or blonde hair?" Hailey asked with a bright smile that was so insincere it made Gerrum grin. Marian stifled a chuckle.

"Del's as bald as a cue ball," he said.

"Well, I didn't want to hurt his feelings." She lowered her eyes.

Was it an attempt to be demure? If so it was doomed. That ship had already sailed. "Del had to ask around to find out what a tracheotomy was," he told her.

"Don't doubt that one bit," John said.

Hailey and Marian resumed their conversation, and John asked Gerrum how the jet boat was doing.

"Last year was good, and I'm hoping to top it this year."

While Gerrum continued to talk to John, he remained aware of Hailey. Her voice had a touch of a Southern lilt, and although he couldn't examine her closely from his position next to her, he'd seen enough to be able to vouch for one part of Rog Remington's statement: "Girl's pretty as a movie star." He had yet to check out the second part: "But up close she's too damn snippy for a man to take any joy in the view."

Hailey didn't strike him as snippy so much as a woman who didn't suffer fools without remarking on it. An unusual trait in someone as young as she appeared to be. Early to mid-twenties was his guess. Pam's age. Pam had also been assertive to the point where some might have considered her snippy. Perhaps it was a trend among younger women.

~ ~ ~

Following the salmon bake, Gerrum didn't see Hailey again until two weeks later when he treated himself to dinner at the lodge and found she was doing the same. After he greeted the locals, Gerrum walked over to Hailey and, with a lift of his eyebrows, asked permission to take the bench seat across from her.

She shrugged, which he counted as an assent.

"I heard you're a writer," she said after he sat down.

"That's right. My first book comes out this fall."

"Bet it feels good."

"You better believe it. Took three years to write and sell. Marian's planning a big do as soon as the publisher ships us copies. If you're around, you'll have to come."

"I'd like that. What kind of book is it?"

"A mystery."

"Oh, good. I like mysteries. So how did you come up with your plot?"

"Umm. Bits and pieces from stories I've heard, read. Personal experiences, observations. I watch people all the time. Listen in on their conversations."

"Most of which are, you know, like rainy-day dull, like, you know."

"Too true. But every once in a while, I pick up a gem, like your 'rainy-day dull.'"

He could see the compliment pleased her.

The cook, a young man who'd just graduated from cooking school, carried plates of food over to the counter. Tonight's offering was spareribs, baked potatoes, green salad, and cornmeal muffins. Gerrum picked up plates for himself and for Hailey, and while they ate, they continued to chat.

He found her pleasant to talk to, although pleasant was not precisely the right word for what he felt watching her cut and delicately eat her food. That same delicacy applied to stirring her coffee, her mouth curving into a smile at something he said.

Too bad she reminded him of Pam. And that she was so young. Although, her presence did have the potential to add an interesting dimension to the season.

Chapter Seven

1965

MARYMEAD COLLEGE MEAD, KANSAS

The autumn of her junior year, Clen struggled with bouts of nausea accompanied by tremors and a feeling of deep foreboding.

When she was little, she'd been afraid of the dark, and these incidents reminded her of that, except the fear was stronger and lasted longer.

Whenever she felt an attack coming on, she would look for somewhere to hide until it passed. As a result, she'd become familiar with the location of all the janitors' closets, the least visited parts of the library, and a storage room in the basement.

If anyone did see her and asked if she was having a problem, she said she had cramps. And that worked for a time, until the spells came more frequently and lasted longer.

"Clen, nobody has cramps four times a month," Maxine said. "You need to do something about it."

"I'm okay."

Maxine didn't argue. She simply told Thomasina, who came to their room where Clen was shivering under the covers.

Thomasina sat on the edge of the bed and laid a hand on Clen's forehead. "You don't seem to have a fever."

"No. I'm c-cold."

"How often does this happen, Clen?"

"It's n-nothing. Just cramps."

"How often?"

"M-maybe once, twice a week."

"And you've lost weight."

"I don't feel like eating."

"I'm going to insist you see a doctor."

A spasm caused her to roll into a ball.

"Clen, what is it?"

"He died. Josh did. This summer."

"Oh, Clen. My dear. I am so, so sorry." Thomasina smoothed her hair.

"A priest came. He said Josh's illness was God's will. I wanted to scratch his eyes out."

"Of course you did. What a stupid, stupid man."

"You don't think it was God's will?"

"In one sense I suppose we can say that everything that happens is God's will. But do I believe God sits in heaven picking out who will get cancer or have an accident or die young? No. Of course, I don't."

"What good is God then? If he doesn't stop bad things from happening."

Thomasina was silent so long, Clen finally turned to look at her.

"I'm sorry, Clen. I'm afraid I don't have an answer for that."

"Maybe there is no God."

Thomasina straightened her veil and stood without answering.

When Clen saw she was preparing to leave, she spoke quickly. "Please, don't tell anybody. About Josh?"

"If that's your wish, of course I won't. But you go see a doctor."

Clen did see a doctor, who asked a lot of questions about symptoms. She didn't tell him about Josh, so he could be forgiven for thinking her problem was merely physical. He gave her a tonic to drink before meals.

Gradually, the spells abated.

~ ~ ~

Six weeks after Thomasina's house-call, Maxine came into their room and dumped her books on the bed. "Hey, did you hear the news about Thomasina?"

"What news is that?"

"She's leaving."

"What? Why?"

"All I know is the where. She's going to spend time in an inner city parish in Chicago."

"When does she go?"

"Actually, I misspoke. I think she's already gone."

"You're kidding me."

"Nope." Maxine already had her head stuck in her closet. It was Friday afternoon. That meant she'd be spending the next couple of hours trying on outfits and experimenting with makeup as she got ready for a date.

"I'm going to spend some quality time in the library," Clen said, trying to sound casual.

Maxine waved a hand. "Yeah. Sure. Study some for me."

Clen walked over to the Administration Building and sauntered by Thomasina's office. The door, as usual, was open. She stuck her head in, and the secretary looked up. "Can I help you?"

"I was hoping to speak to Sister Thomasina?"

"Sister left for Chicago this morning."

"H-how long is she going to be gone?"

"I believe she's planning on at least six months, perhaps longer. We'll be posting her address on the bulletin board if you'd like to write to her."

"Thanks." Blindly, Clen stepped out of the office and walked down the hall and back outside. There she took the path leading to the picnic area by the river.

How could Thomasina leave without one word? They were friends, weren't they? Clen sat on one of the picnic tables and stared at the river. There had been rain over the last couple of days and the water rushing by was opaque and brown.

Staring at it, she felt like smashing something or crying like a baby. Instead, she sat for a long time, staring at that ugly water.

~ ~ ~

Clen's salvation after Thomasina's departure was the drawing class she took second semester to fulfill part of the fine arts requirement. She signed up only after being assured by Mr Howard, one of the few laymen teaching at Marymead, that he would be grading more on her dedication than on her talent. He also told her he could teach anyone to draw, a claim she expected him to have to withdraw after trying to teach her.

The first time the class met, he handed out copies of a line drawing of a man sitting in a chair. He told them to turn the drawing upside down and copy it.

Clen went to work, determined to earn a decent grade for effort if not for execution, but when she turned her paper around, she found herself staring with delight at a more than competent copy of the original drawing. Around the room, others were having a similar experience.

"What's happened here," MrMr Howard said, "is that usually your creative efforts are immediately critiqued by the left, analytical side of your brains. A real busybody, the left is. 'That doesn't look a bit like a hand,' it will say. Or, 'No, you've made it too big, too little, too dark, too light.' That flow of commentary makes you uncertain about your ability to create, and that uncertainty restrains your natural talent.

"But today, when you turned the picture upside down, nothing looked exactly the way the left brain expected it to. Eventually it became confused and fell silent, and that allowed your right, creative side to take over and guide your pencils.

"Now that you've exposed the left brain, your job will be to get it to leave you alone to create. One way to do that is to promise it an opportunity to comment once you've finished."

The course hooked Clen on drawing—the only thing in her life that was no longer tinged with darkness.

~ ~ ~

The notice on the bulletin board announced there would be a Civil Rights march Sunday afternoon in downtown Mead.

Although there was only one television for the entire dormitory, located in the area where smokers congregated, Clen had a radio, and she'd regularly listened to reports about the Civil Rights Movement. As well, in a literature class, they'd been assigned to read *Black Like Me*. The author of the book had dyed his skin and then spent time traveling around the South discovering how differently he was treated when he was no longer viewed as white.

Personally, Clen had never had much contact with black people, and until she began listening to the news and reading the book, she had no idea how badly they were treated in the South.

"Are you going?" asked the senior girl standing next to Clen, also reading the notice.

"I doubt a march in Mead, Kansas, is going to have much impact on Alabama or Mississippi, do you?" Clen said. She had an advanced calculus exam on Monday and she planned to spend the weekend studying for it.

"Probably not, but it's the right thing to do," the other girl said. "Hope to see you there."

Clen decided the girl was right. When she joined the march she found she was one of roughly one hundred people, many of them Marymead students. They walked from one end of Mead's downtown to the park at the other end. In the park, a black pastor from a church in Alabama stepped onto the temporary platform and spoke about church members who had been killed in the struggle. He described the horrific deaths so graphically, Clen had difficulty joining in the singing of "We Shall Overcome" that followed. It was only the Methodist minister's long, meandering closing prayer that gave her time to regain her composure.

The march had been unsettling, but it had also been safe and peaceful with no worries about tear gas, fire hoses, or police dogs. Clen was glad she'd taken the time to stand up for something she believed in, but she very much doubted she would have had the courage to do it were she living in the South.

~ ~ ~

Thomasina returned to Marymead by the time Clen's senior year began. Clen managed to avoid the nun for the first two weeks, but then Thomasina summoned her. "Clen, we need to talk."

God, she hated those words. "Sure. Talk. Fine."

"You didn't answer my letter."

"You sent the letter to Betty Knox, not me." Betty had come to the cafeteria to pass out the notes Thomasina had written.

"You're angry with me."

Clen tightened her lips.

"Are you willing to listen to an explanation?"

"I'm going to be late for class."

"You don't have a class this hour."

"Okay. Explain." Clen knew she was acting like a five year-old brat, but she couldn't seem to help herself.

Thomasina walked over to the window and stood staring out. "This last year and a half I let myself get overwhelmed. With the work. With..." She paused, apparently searching for words. "Sister Gladys was a very dear friend. When she died...it depleted me. I think you may understand what I mean."

Depleted. A good word for what Clen felt, as well.

"I want to apologize to you for my behavior. I knew it was a difficult time for you, with your brother's death, but I had nothing left to offer you, or anyone else."

"You could at least have said goodbye."

"You're right, of course. I should have."

Damn it, Thomasina wasn't giving her anything to vent her anger on. "So did it work? Going away?"

"Not entirely."

"Did you at least figure out what good God is?" Clen said.

"I think the gift of life comes from God with the possibility for both joy and pain. None of us escapes without drinking a full measure of both."

"Well, we don't all seem to get the same measure of good stuff."

"No. It's hard being human," Thomasina said, her tone soft.

"I need to go..."

"Come see me again, Clen."

But she didn't, and whenever she encountered Thomasina, she hurried through the interaction, escaping before the need to confess overwhelmed her.

~ ~ ~

"If you won't go to a mixer, how do you expect to meet someone?" Maxine asked.

"I tried it once. You saw what happened. Or maybe you didn't. You were so busy dancing while guys were practically falling over themselves to beat a path around me."

"That is a huge exaggeration. I saw you dancing."

"Did you happen to get a look at the guy?"

"Well, he was a little short."

"You think?" Clen sighed. The man's stature hadn't been the problem. He'd even been a halfway decent dancer. "Would you believe? He's a bodybuilder."

"Really?"

"Really. I now know more details about building up pecs than I can bear to think about."

"We're girls. We don't do pecs."

"Yeah. You know that, and I know that, but it seems to have escaped Mr Bodybuilder's attention."

"There were lots of other guys."

"None of whom gave me a second look."

"You need to give it another chance."

"No thanks. I have a philosophy paper due Monday. I think working on that is a much better use of my time."

~ ~ ~

A week later, Maxine went downstairs to meet the soldier from the nearby base who'd made a date with her at the mixer. In five minutes, she was back.

"Come on." She grabbed Clen's arm and pulled. "You've got to help me out. He brought a couple of extra guys. We're going bowling."

"I need to change."

"Into what?"

"Well, at least let me comb my hair."

83

"It's fine. Come on."

Clen gave in. It was bowling, after all, and she liked to bowl. With six of them, how bad could it be?

The guy designated as her date, Samuel Saint Burke, was good-looking enough he didn't need to be fixed up with someone like her. She liked him for being a good sport about it.

Several days later, he dropped by and invited her to a movie. After that, he came by every few days to take her for a walk or for pizza. Eventually, she asked if she could draw his portrait. When he arrived for the session, she had him sit on a stool at the front of the empty art classroom, and she set up her drawing board a few feet away.

She worked laboriously, trying to get the proportions right. Trying as well to capture her sense of him—masculine and strong, but tempered by something softer.

"It's nice getting away from the barracks," he said. "Always something going on. Banging doors, loud music. People yelling down the hall. Wears a person down, but I expect you know what I mean."

She gave him a questioning look.

"Living in a dormitory," he said. "It can't be a whole lot different from a barracks."

"Oh, you've got that wrong. We have rules. We bang a door, yell, or play music too loud, we get demerits."

"Then what?"

"We can't leave campus. Or have visitors."

"Exactly like the military."

Did he realize how appealing he was when he grinned? Clen looked back at her paper and erased yet another line. "It's not so bad. Guess I'm used to it. I've been on my best behavior for, oh, a couple of years now."

He shifted, and she waited for him to settle before she continued to draw.

"There's something you need to know about me," he said. "Don't want you to go getting the wrong idea or anything. You see...I'm engaged."

She steadied her pencil and continued making random marks on the page in front of her. Marks that no longer had anything to do with capturing the planes and angles of his face, the suppleness of his mouth, the humor in his eyes.

"I joined the group because my buddies gave me a really hard time." He clenched and unclenched his hands. "But I like you. Being with you. It's peaceful. A break. I thought we could just be friends. You know, nothing romantic or anything."

Of course he wasn't interested in a romantic relationship. How could she have thought he was? It would take a lot more than a name change and a haircut to transform the awkward girl nobody ever asked out.

"Is that okay with you?" he asked. "Because I know it's kind of weird, and I'll understand if you don't think we should."

"No." The word croaked out.

At the one syllable, his face fell.

"No, I mean, no problem. It's okay. Sure. Friends. Works for me." A practice boyfriend. She would have laughed except it got caught in her throat.

That night she had a shaking spell. The first in months.

~ ~ ~

She began calling him Saint as a reminder of how they needed to behave, and the friendship worked. At least for him. Clen, though, was quickly in way over her head, and she was barely managing to hide that from him when he learned about the Marymead ball.

"How about it? Would you like me to take you?" he asked.

"Absolutely not."

"Because you don't know how to dance?"

"Of course, I know how to dance. I'll have you know I spent years being pushed around dance classes like I was a large cardboard carton."

He grinned. "You must let me take you, then. To see what dancing's supposed to be like. After all, that's what a friend is for."

"I don't have a dress."

"Rumor has it Mead has stores. Come on, Clen. Please? I love to dance. It's no different from going for a walk or to a movie with me."

She suspected that was a lie, but she gave in anyway.

She made Maxine go shopping with her although likely it would have been impossible to keep Maxie away. When she pulled the slim, dark green dress that reminded her of a Chinese cheongsam off the rack, Maxine made a face. "I get that you don't want pastel, but that dress is too...plain."

But plain was her goal. The dresses Maxine was pushing, although conservative by Maxine's standards, would still make Clen feel like an over-decorated cake.

She came out of the changing room in the green dress, and Maxine caught her breath and bit her lip. "Oh. Well, it's not as bad as I thought, but you won't get past the dress police with that." Maxine pointed at the deep slit up the side of the narrow skirt.

"They check bosoms, Maxie, and I don't have any." Clen knew she was going to buy the dress as soon as she saw the look on her friend's face.

On the big night, when she walked toward Saint, he got a similar look. And that set something roughly the size of a kangaroo bounding around Clen's stomach.

He took her hand. "C-Clen?" He cleared his throat. "You look...amazing."

What was most amazing was that he seemed to mean it, although he was the beautiful one—in dress blues that matched his eyes. He continued to stare at her with that new look that was admiring. And something more. A something that made whatever was lurching around inside Clen's stomach land with a thump.

They walked over to the Fine Arts Building and she introduced Saint to Thomasina, who, if she noticed the slit, refrained from commenting on it. Then they entered the dimly lit ballroom, and Saint took her in his arms. Clen laid her cheek against his, breathing in the good scent of soap, aftershave, and warm skin as he began to guide her around the room, moving with an ease and competent authority that made her feel delicate and graceful for the first time in her life. For a brief, magical time, she allowed herself to forget he was engaged.

On the way back to the dorm after the dance, he led her off the path into the shadows and took her once again into his arms, holding her even closer than when they were dancing. She knew she should pull away. Should stop him before she knew what it felt like to kiss him.

Such a simple thing, a kiss. The touch of his lips on hers. Causing such upheaval. Such a yearning to press against him, until there was no more Clen separate from Saint.

No longer did the idea, nor indeed the reality, of his tongue in her mouth seem the least bit disgusting.

After that night, every time she saw him, there were more kisses. In the car after they'd sat without touching in a movie. In a dark corner of the lounge where nobody could see them. Behind a tree along the river. Neither of them either willing or able to stop.

What stopped them was Vietnam. After Saint shipped out, they wrote to each other, but when he returned to the States, it was to his fiancée.

Clen didn't hear from him again.

Chapter Eight

1985

RESURRECTION ABBEY STOWE, VERMONT

Midway through the second year of her nomadic existence, Clen finally decided she had nothing to lose, and perhaps something to gain, if she took Maxine's advice and visited an abbey. Still, it took her until November to make her way to a small abbey in Vermont.

As a visitor, Clen could attend services in the chapel up to seven times a day, starting with Vigils at 3:15 a.m. and ending with Compline at 7:30 p.m. That was something she chose not to do. Instead, outside of the three simple meals in the visitors' dining room, the rest of the time she slept or walked the expansive grounds, soaking up the peace, stopping occasionally to sketch a tree, a bird.

After she'd been at Resurrection a week, she was summoned to an interview with Mother Abbess. The nun gestured to a chair in the small interview room, then gave Clen a soul-fingering look. "I am told you've requested a longer stay with us."

Although not stated as such, it was clearly a question—one Clen struggled to answer. "I've changed my life. Ended my marriage. Left my career."

"Are you questioning those choices?"

"No. They were the right decisions. I'm just not sure what comes next."

"Perhaps it would be useful for you to have a regular companion as you seek that answer. I believe Sister Mary John would be a good choice. She has a great deal of insight into such difficulties."

Clen had arrived at Resurrection wound tight, her body brittle with the stress of her journeying, and she had no interest in Mary John's insights. Instead, she preferred to be left alone to relax in the peace that seemed to be part of the very walls here. But if the price for remaining was to meet with this Mary John person, she would do it.

~ ~ ~

Sister Mary John turned out to be a short, dark-browed nun with shrewd eyes. She and Clen walked in the garden each Tuesday and Thursday in the hour after breakfast. At first, they spoke only of trivial things, until Mary John's willingness to let her set the pace led Clen to share some of her history—a history she was still guarding the most intimate parts of when the Abbess sent for her again.

The nun inclined her head, her fingers steepled, examining Clen. "You have stayed considerably longer than most of our visitors, and yet I do not believe you have a calling to join us."

A certainty Clen shared. After all, becoming a nun was hardly the typical career path taken by a person furious with God. She'd kept her anger hidden, of course, although she suspected if she admitted it to Mary John, the nun would respond with a sniff and a quick reassurance: "It doesn't matter so much how you feel about God, Clen. What's important is that God loves you."

As the Abbess continued to examine her, Clen struggled to meet that serene gaze without squirming.

"I believe it will soon be time, Clen, for you to take the next step to discover what God has waiting for you. And have no doubt, my dear, the Lord will be with you."

Clen bowed her head and completed the formula. "And also with you, Mother."

She managed to leave the interview parlor without stumbling—a minor miracle given how badly she was shaking. In her room, she sat on the edge of the narrow bed and wrapped her arms tight around herself in a vain attempt to still her trembling.

Despite the Abbess's reassurance, Clen wasn't yet ready to strike off into an unknown future down a road with signposts she didn't recognize.

She'd already made one stab at that and ended up at Resurrection.

~ ~ ~

In the days following the Abbess's pronouncement, Clen spent mornings in the garden. The recent snow had melted, leaving behind a tangle of winter-bare branches. Here and there, tiny green shoots were beginning to appear. She closed her eyes, listening to the sounds of birds singing and squirrels scampering through the crisp leaf litter. Then she opened her eyes and sketched her surroundings—a bird sitting on the bare branch of a maple tree, a squirrel drinking from a birdbath, a nun bent over a cold frame tending seedlings. As her pencil moved across the page, she tried to picture her future, but it remained a blank.

"I'm stuck," she finally told Mary John. "When I leave Resurrection, I have no idea where to go or what I'm going to do when I get there."

"Well, do you at least know where you *don't* want to go?"

"Atlanta, for sure. Probably any big city."

"Quickly. Name a place that appeals to you."

"Alaska."

"Do you know why?"

She might just as easily have said Kathmandu, or Timbuktu, for that matter. Alaska was just another word, but then that word gifted her with a memory—deep blue chunks of glacial ice in the most improbable shapes, floating in water that reflected the sky. "I visited there once. It's an amazing place. I'm sure the winters are brutal, but in the summer...it's beautiful." She shook her head to disperse all that blue. "It isn't the answer, though."

"Don't be too quick to discount the gifts of the subconscious, my dear. Play with it a bit. Pretend you're going there. Exactly where would you go? Then think about a job. Do you want one? If so, what kind?"

After that conversation, Mary John's words kept nudging at Clen whenever she sat down to sketch. Distracting her as well from making any sense of the spiritual readings that accompanied their meals. Not that she usually paid attention to them, but still.

Resurrection observed the rule of silence. Since she'd been there, the only people Clen had spoken with were Mary John and Mother Abbess. Now the silence that in the beginning had been so soothing had become oppressive. A space filled with thoughts that had no coherence or resolution. Even her most reliable companion, her drawing, changed. Instead of sketching what was in front of her, she found herself doodling spruce trees and mountains. The doodles were puny things but with sufficient power to distract and nag.

Clarity about her future remained elusive, however, and time was running out.

She finally examined the idea of going to Alaska more closely and remembered the time she and Paul spent in a lodge in Wrangell. In particular, she remembered her conversations with the cook, a recent graduate who was using the summer position in Wrangell to enhance his resume. Without much expectation, she wrote a letter to the owner of the lodge asking if that position had been filled for the coming summer.

~ ~ ~

WRANGELL, ALASKA

The ferry slid north at a placid pace, parting the quiet waters of the inland waterway which reflected shorelines dense with the growth of spruce, fir, and cedar. Clen stood near the bow, her hands clenched on the railing, bracing herself against the steady push of cold air and memories. Memories evoked most vividly by the smell—a ripe, tangy mix of seaweed, bird guano, and saltwater—all borne by the chill April breeze. That breeze swirled amongst rocks and evergreens, tossing her hair about and pulling tears from her eyes. Although, if she were honest, she would have to admit it wasn't just the cold causing the tears.

They were also in remembrance of the woman she'd been the last time she came to this place—with Paul. Married only a year and not yet knowing how unhappy they were going to make each other.

"Let me look, Daddy."

Startled out of her bleak thoughts by the piping voice, Clen turned to find a small boy, standing on his toes to look over the railing. He pulled on the sleeve of a man with a matching crop of unruly brown curls who was peering through binoculars at the shore.

"Is it a bear? Is it?" the child demanded.

Clen looked where the father had the binoculars aimed but saw nothing that appeared to be a bear on the narrow rock ledge they were approaching. Then a slight movement caught her eye, right there—a black animal the size of a dog.

The child continued to chatter excitedly. The man handed him the binoculars, then lifted the boy so he could see.

She and Paul had talked about children on that trip to Alaska. He'd said he wanted Clen all to himself awhile longer, but then the unhappiness started, and neither one of them mentioned having a child again.

After the man set the boy down, the child held the binoculars out to Clen. "D'you want to take a look?"

"Thank you. I would."

"He's right over there. He looks tiny, but it's a bear all right."

Glad of the distraction, Clen moved the glasses slowly across the ledge until, with a suddenness that startled her, she found herself looking into the close-set eyes of a large bear. For several seconds the animal seemed to inspect her, then it lowered its head and appeared to be grazing on the thick thatch of green covering the rocks.

"Do you see him?" the boy asked.

"Indeed. He looked right at me."

"Oh, bears don't see good. They hear good though." His words held the authority of a much older child.

"Is he really eating that green stuff?" she asked.

"Yep. He's awful hungry."

She handed the glasses back and smiled her thanks, hoping he and his father would leave her alone again.

No such luck. With the ice broken, the man settled against the rail for a chat. "Where you headed?" he asked.

"Wrangell." She kept her tone neutral and her eyes on the shoreline, regretting the fact she'd accepted the binoculars, although she had enjoyed seeing the bear.

"Hey. That's where we're going, aren't we, son?" The man rubbed the boy's head, further disordering the curls. "We're staying a week, visiting my sister. How about you?"

"I'm there for the summer."

"Wow. Lucky you. This your first time in Alaska?"

"Second." They'd taken the ferry that first time too, she and Paul, disembarking wherever the ferry stopped: Juneau, Ketchikan, Haines, for a day, or two, or three. And here she was again, in Alaska. Alone this time, except for memories breathed in along with chilled air. Memories of herself, a thick white scarf around her neck, laughing and posing with Paul when some stranger offered to take their picture. In those pictures, they stood frozen in time—a glacier behind; the future, gleaming with promise, ahead. Carefree and happy.

Clueless.

At least she had been.

"This is our fourth visit," the man said, pulling her back to the present. "We've been coming every year since my sister moved here."

So where was the mother? Easier to struggle with memories of Paul than to deal with this talkative man.

"Daddy, I'm cold."

Finally.

"How about hot chocolate?"

"Super." The boy turned an eager look toward Clen. "You could come with us."

Her thoughts tumbled uselessly for a moment before she was able to string words together, thanking the child but turning him down. He gave her a disappointed look.

She angled away from him, biting her lip to keep from giving in and saying, on second thought, hot chocolate sounded perfect. And if it had been only the child, she could have managed it, but she wasn't yet ready for the other. More questions and chat from the father, that ordinary back and forth lobbing of words. Something she seemed to have lost the knack for.

The two left, and in their wake grief ballooned in Clen's

chest. She gripped the railing and bit down on a sob. What had she been thinking, returning here? On the basis of what? Those few days all those years ago when she'd managed for a brief time to believe happiness was possible? Although even then, she'd suspected happiness was a figment of fairy tales, and the best one could expect from life was contentment, something she no longer expected to find.

She stared at the calm waters they were passing through. Only the muted vibration from the engines and an occasional screech of a gull disturbed the stillness.

Quiet.

That was the real reason she'd chosen Alaska when she left the abbey.

~ ~ ~

For the remainder of the trip, Clen avoided the boy and his father—not difficult to do given the size of the ferry. When they docked in Wrangell, she watched from the upper deck as the two went ashore and were greeted by a woman who loaded their duffels into a small car. Only then did she collect her own luggage and disembark.

John Jeffers, the owner of Bear Lodge, was easy to spot, although it helped that he was leaning against the side of a van decorated with a picture of a bear and the lodge's name. She walked toward him, past the hopeful kids who met every ferry with TV trays and cardboard boxes piled with the deep red garnets they'd dug up from a nearby garnet reef. She'd bought Paul a particularly fine specimen to use as a paperweight.

"Mr Jeffers?"

"Ms McClendon?"

"Please, call me Clen."

"And I prefer John. You call me mister, makes me feel old. I might be getting there, but I surely don't want to be reminded of the fact." Teeth flashed amid the bush of a short brown beard. He eyed her two suitcases. "That all you brought?"

"Figured I could leave the suits, high heels, and formals behind," and what a relief that was.

"Hey, you got that right. Still, seems like most women can't pass up a chance to cart around a bit of everything." He grinned and swung her luggage into the back of the van, then opened the door for her before getting in himself and starting the engine. A relief he didn't remember her—not that she expected him to—thus sparing her any discussion of her previous visit or questions about her companion on that visit.

Driving away from the ferry dock, John pointed out the sights, and she attempted to match this Wrangell with the one in her memory.

"We've got a bit south of three thousand people on the island. Means we're big enough you can mostly avoid those you don't like, but small enough you better watch what you say in public." He glanced at her, and she managed a smile.

"May be hard to believe today, but this was the busiest place in Alaska back during the gold rush. Downtown there burned in the fifties. When we rebuilt, we made sure there were spaces between all the buildings, and it seems to be working."

Next, he pointed toward the harbor. "That's Shakes Island and the building on it is a traditional Tlingit tribal house."

The road curved past the small island and on toward the marina with its tangle of masts, antennas, and gear. Bear Lodge, a gray clapboard building of indeterminate pedigree, sprawled on a piece of flat ground abutting the marina, and it looked exactly as she remembered.

John pulled up near the back door where two wooden barrels containing red geraniums flanked the porch and provided a tiny patch of splendor. A husky lying on the porch raised its head to examine Clen. Delighted, she knelt and extended knuckles for a sniff. Once she knew there would be no child, she'd suggested a dog, but Paul rebuffed that as well. "Too much trouble," he'd said.

"His name is Kody," John said. "He was one hell of a sled dog in his day. Weren't you, boy?" He set the suitcases down and gave the dog's head a brisk rub. "Now, all he does is eat and sleep."

Inside, John led the way through the dining area, with its open kitchen and long communal tables, and turned into a narrow hall. At the end of the hall he opened a door and stood aside. "I hope this is okay?"

She stepped past him and took in a quick, relieved breath. The room was bright and airy with walls painted a soft green. A window framed with gauzy curtains spanned most of one wall, and a small side window was open, letting in a fresh, clean smell—a mix of wet earth and spruce with a faint undertone of sea. "It's more than okay."

"Glad to hear it." John set her suitcases by the door and backed from the room. "I'll leave you to settle in. Whenever you're ready, give us a holler. Marian will want to go over everything with you."

Clen sank into the easy chair feeling a welcome release of tension. She'd put a brave face on it, but she'd been nervous— no, make that terrified—at leaving Resurrection Abbey and coming to Alaska.

After a time she stood and began to unpack, putting clothes, books, and painting and drawing materials into their proper places, not yet thinking about the rest—the fact that in a day or so she would begin her tenure as Bear Lodge's summer cook.

She closed her eyes and pulled in a deep breath of earth and sea-scented air. It wasn't going to be easy, but this room, the Jeffers, and Wrangell itself...maybe everything would be all right.

Chapter Nine

The scuttlebutt about the Jeffers' new cook took all of fifteen minutes to make the rounds that spring, the fourth since Gerrum had moved to Wrangell. The information included the particulars that instead of the usual male cooking school graduate, the Jeffers had hired a woman. And while the woman was no spring chicken and a bit too tall to make most men comfortable, she was still worth looking at. Not to mention, her cooking wasn't half bad. Since this constituted high praise, Gerrum finally went to the lodge for dinner to see for himself.

John Jeffers was setting salads on the counter. "Gerrum, about time you came in."

"Heard you have a good cook this year."

"Yeah. You want to meet her? Hey, Clen, come on over here. Say hello to Gerrum Kirsey."

The woman was standing at the stove, with her back to them but he could see the scuttlebutt certainly got the tall part right. The straight posture indicated she was someone who, as a child, either didn't give a damn she'd towered over the boys or whose mother had been relentless on the subject.

"Sorry. Can't leave this gravy on its own quite yet." The voice was a good one, low-pitched and firm.

"Hell, let me stir that." John walked over and took the spoon away from her. "Shake hands with Gerrum. Lady's name is Clen McClendon, Ger."

With obvious reluctance, she stepped toward him and extended a hand. "Gerrum?"

"Like Jeremy without the y and spelled with a G," he said.

"A result of some really bad penmanship. I was supposed to be Gerald." Usually that line got a smile. Not this time.

Despite her solemnity, she had a good face, one free of artifice. Clearly, Avon calling got no answer there. Not that it was needed. And the lack of feminine fussing extended to her hair, which was almost as short as his, and her clothing— jeans, a tailored shirt, and a chef's jacket. The only complexity in her appearance was the expression on her face. It held an odd mix of wariness and determination along with a faint, mysterious hint of what appeared to be desperation.

After the briefest of greetings, she retrieved her hand and turned back to the stove. John handed over the spoon and raised his eyebrows at Gerrum, communicating as clearly as if he'd spoken aloud, *Women. Who can figure?*

Gerrum turned to check who else was at dinner. The Jeffers limited the number to fifteen, and the lodge's guests took precedence over Wrangell residents. But this early in the season it was easy for locals to get a reservation.

Tonight, there were five tourists sitting together at one of the communal tables while four Wrangell fishermen, all of whom greeted Gerrum with varying degrees of enthusiasm, sat at a second table. Sitting by herself at the third table was Hailey Connelly, another woman who wasn't easy to figure. One most of Wrangell's bachelors had quickly decided the previous summer it was wise to give a wide berth.

"Hey, I didn't realize you were back." He took the seat across from her, surprised at the burst of pleasure he felt on seeing her.

"Then it's a major gossip breakdown. I could have sworn Maude saw me arrive. She isn't sick, is she?"

Maude, who had the café of the same name on the main street, considered herself Wrangell's one-stop shopping mecca for coffee and gossip. Precious little that happened in Wrangell escaped her attention.

"I had a trip today. Likely made it difficult for her to track me down."

Hailey nodded toward the kitchen. "So, what do you think of our new addition?"

"Just met her. What about you? What do you think of her?"

Hailey shrugged. "I think she'd prefer the kitchen to be

behind a closed door."

Gerrum glanced over at John's cook. It was his theory that most people who ended up in Alaska were running from something, regardless of what they had to say about the matter. And he'd be willing to bet his next royalty check John's cook wasn't here following her dreams. He'd also be interested in her real reasons for coming to Wrangell, if she ever wanted to talk.

At the moment, however, the conversational ball was being kept in play by Rog Remington, five foot nothing and sixty if he was a day. "Well, we know she can cook but can she dance?" Rog raised his voice, directing the comment at Clen who was standing at the stove, dishing food onto a plate.

Her back stiffened slightly in response.

"How about it, Miz McClendon?" Rog persisted. "Bet you do a mean two-step."

Clen turned and carried the plate over to the counter and gave Rog a look that would have shut down a lesser man. "I'm sorry. Were you speaking to me?"

Rog was undeterred. "Two-step, waltz, tango." He lifted his arms. "You know, dance?"

Clen focused on the plate as she set it down. "Rumba, mamba. I can probably name a few others, if you give me a minute."

"To heck with naming the dadburn things. Do you know how to do them?"

"Sorry. I don't dance." With that she turned decisively back to the stove. It was a bravura performance, and Rog and his cronies exchanged chuckles. Clen rubbed at her forehead as if it hurt.

When Rog opened his mouth, prepared to make even more of an idiot of himself, Gerrum spoke quickly. "Ran into Swerdlap today. Said he expected there to be an opening the next day or so."

"Better be," Rog said. "Goddam chickenshit rangers. By the time they decide we can drop a hook, the kings'll all be upriver."

"My, aren't we the gallant one," Hailey murmured, as Rog's rant about Alaskan fishing regulations continued.

Clen delivered two more plates to the counter, giving Gerrum a quick nod of gratitude. Or that was his interpretation. "Just helping out," he told Hailey, his gaze still on Clen. "Until she gets all the assholes properly categorized."

"Trust me, that's a woman who can spot an asshole at fifty paces."

"Doesn't mean she might not appreciate a helping hand."

Hailey raised her eyebrows with delicate precision. "Just so that's all you're offering."

The proprietary tone unsettled him. He'd enjoyed talking to Hailey last year whenever they happened to meet, but he was still uncertain he wanted more than that. And so he ignored the nuances lurking in her comment and made a mundane inquiry about her winter.

"It was good. There's always lots to do in Seattle, and I found several new artists whose work I'm adding to the gallery this year. How about you? Overheard any good conversations lately?"

"Nope. Not a single rainy-day dull gem, but I did finish another novel this winter. Now I'm waiting to see what my editor thinks of it."

"I hope she likes it. I'm definitely ready for another Gabe Skyler adventure."

"You read my book?"

"I'll have you know I was first in line at the bookstore the day it came out. I expect you to sign my copy."

"Be happy to," although, he did dodge her invitation to come back to her place to do just that as they finished dinner, a response he could readily explain.

Chapter Ten

Clen's first days in Wrangell were filled with talk. For a start, there were the Jeffers. John and Marian were hospitable people, and they wanted to make sure she was settling in and learning her way around. That meant whenever they encountered her, they stopped to chat.

And they weren't the only ones. Clen was watching a pair of bald eagles flying around the back of the grocery store, when the butcher came out. "Getting acquainted with Ike and Tina are you?" he asked.

"Ike and Tina?"

"Those two." He nodded toward the eagles. "They help me get rid of scraps. Say, ain't I seen you around? Yeah. I know. You're the new cook at the lodge, ain't you?"

She admitted she was and was relieved when the eagles swooped in and distracted him, allowing her to escape.

~ ~ ~

Everybody in town seemed to know who she was. As she checked the produce section in the grocery store, the manager came over and introduced himself. A woman planting petunias gave her a tour of the salmon cannery tucked into what would otherwise be the house's garage. And an elderly man pottering among the roses surrounding the tiny Catholic church introduced himself and invited her to Mass.

But it wasn't the butcher, the produce manager, or the priest who made her feel so beleaguered she considered never leaving her room except when absolutely necessary. No, that honor went to the single men of Wrangell who assumed she was there looking for a man.

She'd laughed when Marian said the odds of a woman finding a man in Alaska were good, but the goods were mostly odd. Now, having discovered the truth of that statement, she was no longer smiling. One by one, the odd goods had stopped her on the street or come to the lodge with offers to show her around. In three days, she'd met six men, all of whom suggested a trip to the Stikine hot springs that Marian had warned her about.

The friendly chattiness of the Wrangell residents was a striking change from the serene silence of the nuns at Resurrection, but it was the hearty teasing of the men that was an escalation she was ill-prepared to deal with.

She went to bed every night exhausted.

~ ~ ~

At the sound of the back door opening, Clen looked up from the onions and carrots she was chopping for that night's dinner to see the visitor was yet another fisherman wearing the Wrangell uniform of work boots, flannel shirt, and jeans.

"How'd you do, Miss." The man's head jerked a bit as he glanced around. "Thought I'd be neighborly, welcome you, like. Elmer Cantrell?"

If he wasn't sure of his name, how did he expect her to be? She nodded without speaking and continued to chop.

"You had a chance to see some of our sights yet?"

She shook her head, her eyes on her chopping. "I've been really busy."

"You can't work all the time. You name the day, I'll be happy to show you round. Maybe take us a trip to see them Stikine hot springs. You heard about them?"

"As a matter of fact, I have." *Six times and counting.* And the thought of going there with this latest entry to the dating game—this Elmer Cantrell?—made her feel queasy. His hair was greasy, his clothes not quite clean, and something distinctly unpleasant lurked in those muddy eyes.

"I'm afraid I get seasick on anything smaller than a ferry."

She transferred the carrots and onions into a large roasting pan and walked over to get the meat out of the refrigerator. "That's why I make it a rule to avoid small boats."

He shifted from foot to foot, apparently trying to decide whether she was having him on. She ignored him, rubbing salt and spices into the meat before adding it to the roasting pan along with a half bottle of red wine.

After more indecisive shuffling, Cantrell finally took his leave, and she breathed a sigh of relief. She hoped she wouldn't encounter him again.

~ ~ ~

The only local man who'd received the imprimatur of a personal introduction from John Jeffers was the one with the odd name. Gerrum Kirsey. He had the dark coloring, stocky build, and slightly exotic appearance she had learned to associate with Native blood, although when he spoke, his accent held none of the local flavor.

After meeting him, she seemed to see him everywhere she went. One morning as she was picking out meat at Rusty's, she heard his voice. Looking up, she saw him reflected in the glass window behind the meat case. A woman, plump and middle-aged, was gripping his arm.

"Gerrum. Am I glad I ran into you. Wanted to let you know we tried your suggestion and it worked a treat."

"Glad to hear it."

"Not as glad as we are to have them Mooneys off our backs. You'll have to come to dinner so's we can thank you proper."

"You don't have to do that, Myra. I'm just pleased the idea was a success."

"Now, none of that, Gerrum. You're coming. Tomorrow? Joe'll be happy for the excuse to break out the Glenlivet."

"Well, I surely don't want to turn down either your good cooking or Joe's whiskey."

"Six suit you?"

He nodded and Myra gave his arm a pat before she released him. Then she pushed her cart on down the aisle while he turned the corner and disappeared down the adjacent one.

When Clen got back to the lodge, she asked Marian about the interaction.

"Oh, the Mooneys have been fussing about Myra and Joe driving on their side of the property line for at least five years. Always keeping it simmering. My personal opinion? They all enjoy it too much to settle it. But it took an ugly turn this spring when the Mooneys started digging potholes in the disputed strip."

"So what did Gerrum suggest?"

"I didn't realize Gerrum was involved, but if it was his idea, it was a good one. Joe and Myra planted shrubs in the holes. Plants don't care who owns that strip. Heard it took the wind right out of Sharon Mooney's sails when she saw it. Even said 'good morning' to Myra the other day."

Clen considered the story amusing, and so she made a point of finding out where they all lived and walked by on one of her evening strolls. The shrubs were thriving and the driveway ruts were now reestablished five feet closer to Myra and Joe's house. She wondered at the stubbornness that had kept the four from such an obvious solution.

Another time she saw Gerrum was when she'd just come out of a shop on the main street. Gerrum was on the opposite side, walking with, and listening attentively to, the young woman he'd sat with at dinner the night Clen met him. Elmer Cantrell approached the two, and as he got close, he made a big show of crossing to Clen's side of the street.

"Asshole." The woman had turned and flung the word at Elmer.

Gerrum bent his head and said something to her. After a moment her posture softened, and he took her arm and walked her into Maude's Café. Clen stepped back inside the shop she'd just exited in order to avoid her own encounter with Elmer.

~ ~ ~

Gerrum and the young woman were once again at dinner. They made a striking couple. Dark versus light, solid versus graceful. Later, Clen asked Marian about the woman.

"That's Hailey Connelly. She owns ZimoviArt," Marian said.

"She's so beautiful. I don't understand why the men aren't falling all over themselves to sit with her."

"Well, maybe because she made it abundantly clear last year they were wasting their time. Except for Gerrum, of course."

"Yeah." John scraped the food off the last plate and placed it in the dishwasher. "The rest need to count their fingers after they shake hands with her."

Marian chuckled. "Hailey's too smart for them, that's the real trouble, but she and Gerrum are a good match."

"I saw them downtown, and Elmer Cantrell made this big show of crossing to the other side of the street to avoid them."

"Well, that's Cantrell for you," John said. "Our resident bigot. Doesn't like Gerrum. I suspect, in part, because Hailey does. He's always trying to get Gerrum's goat."

"It didn't look like it worked with Gerrum, but Hailey called him an asshole loud enough for half of Wrangell to hear," Clen said.

John chuckled. "Good for Hailey."

"The impetuosity of youth," Marian said.

"She does look young," Clen said. "So she and Gerrum are a couple?"

"I'm not exactly sure what they are," Marian said, looking thoughtful. "Friends for sure, but he's got to have nearly fifteen years on her."

"Hell, woman. Are you saying Gerrum's an old coot? Because, if so, that means you think I am too."

Marian gave him a saucy look and flipped him with a dishtowel. "That's not a trap you're going to catch me in, John Jeffers."

Clen left the two of them chuckling together.

~ ~ ~

Curious about Hailey, Clen walked downtown the next morning to check out ZimoviArt. The display window for the gallery was on the side street leading to the dock where cruise ships came in, which was probably why Clen hadn't noticed the gallery before.

The window contained an attractive arrangement of children's fur parkas, lacy knitted scarves the color of chocolate milk, and carvings of bears and eagles. All of it was pretty *de rigueur* Alaskan stuff. What wasn't *de rigueur* were the framed quilt squares suspended from hooks in the ceiling. Unlike most quilt patterns, with their careful geometric arrangements and often conservative color choices, these pieces glowed like a drift of flowers. One appeared to be channeling Gauguin—a free-form pattern with swirls of purple and green interwoven with magenta hexagons that looked like flowers. Clen could also see that the gallery walls were covered with paintings. Intrigued, she stepped inside to discover that many of the paintings were watercolors, a medium she loved and was working to master.

Hailey was on the phone behind the small counter. She lifted a hand in a brief greeting that invited Clen to meander on her own, something Clen preferred.

She wandered over to look at a painting of young women with flowing, translucent dresses. Although the fashion was from an earlier time, it reminded Clen of nights when there was a dance at Marymead and the halls were full of giggling girls in pale dresses. The next pieces to catch her eye were a series of small canvases of wildflowers rendered in clear, bright acrylics.

Finally, she stopped in front of the largest painting in the gallery. At first, she saw only the way the colors flowed, with no one color dominating; but then, all at once, the shape of a woman mounted on a unicorn emerged.

Hailey completed her call and stepped out from behind the counter. "You're Clen, from the lodge. I've been rude. I should have introduced myself earlier. Sorry. I'm Hailey Connelly." In spite of her youth, she looked so elegant and poised, that the rushed, awkwardly phrased greeting was a surprise.

"That's okay. I could have done the same." Clen swiveled, her hand gesturing. "You have some wonderful paintings, and the quilt squares are amazing."

"Oh, I'm so glad you like them. I found them lying on an old barrel in a country store in Missouri, and I just had a feeling. Tess, the girl who does them told me, 'Momma and my aunts make big quilts, but I'd rather do a picture 'stead of repeating the same old pattern over and over. But Momma's probably right, they ain't good for much. Still, I think they're some pretty.'" Hailey's voice had fallen into a soft Southern cadence as she quoted Tess.

"She sounds like a sweetheart."

"She is," Hailey said, smiling.

"Are you from Missouri?"

Hailey's expression immediately sobered, and she shook her head. "Not anymore. How about you? Is there someplace you're not from anymore?"

"Atlanta."

"And now that we know each other's darkest secret, is there something I can help you with?" Hailey asked, with a smile.

"I just came in to look, but that one quilt square is begging me to take it home."

"Which one?"

"The Gauguin."

"Ah, I thought the same thing when I saw it." Hailey walked over and unhooked the green and purple square and brought it to the counter. "It's a hundred dollars. Do you still want it?"

"I do."

"How would you like to pay?"

"Since I'm being totally spontaneous, I don't have any money with me. Could you hold it for me, until I get you a check?"

"Oh, you can take it with you now, if you like. Just bring me the check whenever it's convenient."

Hailey wrapped the quilt square, and Clen walked out carrying it, glad she had an excuse to return.

Chapter Eleven

A couple of weeks into the season, Gerrum stopped by Maude's Café for an early supper and found Hailey doing the same.

"It's such a lovely evening," Hailey said as they finished eating. "Why don't we go for a walk?"

It was an appealing idea since he'd been bent over an engine most of the day. "Sounds good. How about Mount Dewey? The view ought to be good tonight." He made the suggestion knowing that although it was steep, the trail to the top of Mount Dewey was wide and smooth—a requirement given that Hailey was wearing a gauzy dress and sandals.

As they began walking, Gerrum kept the pace leisurely, although Hailey seemed to be managing the climb easily. When they reached the top, he walked over to the drop-off to take in the view.

The strait below glittered with sun sparkles, and a boat out in the channel cut a glassy swath through the shimmer. He turned his head to discover that Hailey was standing twenty feet back, one hand over her mouth.

"Are you okay?" he said.

"I...I don't like heights."

"You should have said something. We could have walked somewhere else." As he stepped toward her, she flung herself into his arms, and her mouth collided with his.

Startled, he stepped back, his hands resting on her shoulders, and tried for a teasing tone. "Hailey. This *is* a shock. I thought all you wanted to do was check the view."

"View, shmew." The tone was fierce, but the look on her

face was one he'd label vulnerable.

"Come here." He put an arm around her shoulder, seeking a way to back them out of this situation as gently as he could. "You are one beautiful woman, and if I were ten years younger, I'd jump at what you're offering."

"Oh no, you don't. You don't get away with a lame excuse like that." She stepped away from him, her hands clenching at her sides. "Either you like me or you don't."

"I do. I like you very much."

The vulnerable look returned. "So why don't you want to kiss me?"

"I'm not sure that's true. You just surprised me."

She studied him for a moment, her head cocked. "Well, I don't think I want to kiss you, after all."

"Okay. I like our being friends, Hailey." He hoped that would cement the deal, although, why he didn't view Hailey, who was both beautiful and intelligent, in a romantic light was an interesting question. *Indeed. And do you know the answer?* his psyche needled.

Hailey shook her head looking exasperated, an improvement over her earlier look.

"You gay, Gerrum Kirsey?"

"Rarely."

"The inscrutable savage, huh?"

"One of my best roles."

"So...you're saying coffee without commitment."

"Friendship has its own requirements."

"Sure," she said. "So why don't you walk me home, already."

He breathed a sigh of relief.

~ ~ ~

Later, seeking a way to continue as Hailey's friend, Gerrum stopped by ZimoviArt and invited her for morning coffee at Maude's Café.

After he and Hailey picked a booth, Maude bustled over with mugs and a pot. She slapped the mugs on the table, poured, then stood, her hip cocked, the coffeepot in one hand, the other hand resting on his shoulder. He fought the urge to shrug it off.

"Say, what I want to know," Maude said, in a voice that could easily chop rocks, "is when're the most eligible couple in Wrangell going to provide us with the social event of the season?" She followed the comment with a titter that shook her considerable bulk.

Before Gerrum could come up with a response, Hailey smiled sweetly and fluttered her eyelashes at Maude. "You know, I was just now saying that exact thing to Gerrum." Her voice settled into a full-bore Southern drawl. "'That Ike and Tina,' I said, 'it's plain thoughtless they ain't letting us in on their plans.'" Ike and Tina, not the Turners, but the pair of eagles that hung out at the IGA.

Maude looked startled, and two locals having a late breakfast at the counter choked back laughs. One of them with more courage than brains offered, "Girl got you good, Maudie."

Maude sniffed and straightened, finally removing that unwelcome hand. "My, aren't we just the kidder, though." The tone was jocular but her eyes were cold. She gave the man who'd spoken a taste of that malevolent look, and he promptly shifted his attention back to his plate of eggs.

Maude moved away, and Hailey shuddered. "Lord, Gerrum, can you believe that woman?"

"It's her major talent."

"What? Embarrassing people?"

"She's a master at startling people into telling her what she wants to know, and if she gets more than she expected, all the better." Personally, he'd found Maude's Café to be an excellent place to brush up on the body language of discomfort, something that was useful for his writing. Today, however, he'd been the one squirming.

"She's a horrible old biddy." Hailey spoke almost loud enough for Maude to hear.

"But a Wrangell original." He toasted Hailey with his mug, breathing a sigh of relief that she seemed more annoyed than embarrassed by the scene. Relieved too, that she'd deflected Maude so effectively.

~ ~ ~

The first time Gerrum encountered the Jeffers' new cook

outside the lodge, he was carrying boxes down the dock and didn't see her until he almost knocked into her. When she yelped, he stopped, peered around the stack, and found himself gazing into a pair of hazel eyes that made him feel as uneasy as the time he'd had an up-close-and-personal encounter with a black bear and her cubs the previous spring. "Sorry. Didn't see you."

Clen's irritation, or perhaps it was merely startlement, was replaced with a skeptical look. "You also missed Kody, and you'll note he's no Chihuahua."

"Too true. How about a cup of coffee? To make up for me almost knocking you two off the dock. Or tea." He spoke quickly, hoping to stop her from walking off, which was clearly her intention.

After a brief consultation with Kody, Clen said a cup of tea sounded good and followed him to his boat. He stepped aboard and set the boxes down, then turned to offer Clen a hand. Kody remained on the dock, flopping in a patch of sun.

Clen stepped aboard and looked around. "I wondered whose boat this was. I like the color. It's the only one like it."

"You've never been to Nova Scotia, then."

She gave him a quizzical look.

"It's a common boat color there. It was a bit of a memory of home for my dad's fishing partner." But outside of the teal-colored hull with its black trim, esthetics weren't his father's strong point, and when Gerrum inherited it, the boat's cabin had been rudimentary and minimally equipped. He'd spent his first winter in Wrangell fixing it up to better support overnight sports fishing trips, but he'd still tended toward the practical rather than the beautiful. No doubt, from a woman's point of view, it was still uncomfortably basic.

"And her name," Clen said. "*Ever Joyful.* I like it."

"My father's pet name for my mother." The reminder made him smile as he put a kettle on to heat. "She's Tlingit. Her clan is from this area."

Clen took a seat and placed the sketchbook and pencil box she was carrying on the table. "You were born here?"

"Nope. Born and raised in the State of Washington. How about you, where are you from?" He placed mugs and the tin of tea bags on the table in front of her.

"Colorado. So, have you lived in Wrangell long?"

111

"This is my fourth year." He poured the water into cups then pointed at the sketchbook. "You're an artist?"

Her hand moved to rest on the book as if to prevent any inadvertent glimpses of what was inside. "Scribbles. For my own pleasure." She looked around as if searching for another topic, her gaze coming to rest on the jet boat. "So is that boat yours too?" she asked, pointing.

He nodded.

"I think I saw you off the petroglyph beach one day," she said. "It looked like fun."

"It is. Would you like a ride?"

She frowned, chose a tea bag, and dipped it into her cup. Finally, she looked up and said yes, she would, and he decided it was a lucky thing after all that his party for the day had canceled—not his first response to that news by any means.

They finished their tea and then transferred to the jet boat. As soon as they were clear of the harbor, he threw the boat into a spin, an impossible move with any other kind of watercraft, and rather like one of those twirling rides at an amusement park. As they whirled, Clen, who was seated near the bow, turned and smiled, and it was as if another woman peeked at him from behind that sober facade.

She already intrigued him with her restraint and obvious self-assurance. That smile added layers to his interest.

Back at the dock, she graced him with another smile before reverting to her usual solemnity. He watched her walk away, tall, straight, and self-contained, wishing he could have gotten her to stay longer and to smile again.

Chapter Twelve

"Did you enjoy your jet boat ride?" Marian asked that afternoon as Clen was finishing dinner preparations.

"How did you know about that?"

"Honey, everybody in Wrangell knows."

"Big mistake, huh?"

"Not necessarily. You just need to brace yourself for the commentary."

Commentary was a pleasant, unassuming word that clearly had no relationship to the thorough ribbing Clen endured over the next several days. It seemed like every man who'd invited her onto his boat, along with a few who hadn't, made it a point to come to dinner, sometimes in groups. "Hey, heard you liked that there jet boat. But it kind of makes it hard to appreciate the scenery going so fast, don't it?" Rog Remington said. "Now my boat, she's a bit on the slow side, but she gives a real comfortable ride."

"How nice for you," Clen said, turning away as he and the other locals shared a chuckle. It was enough to immunize her against speaking to any Wrangell male ever again.

~ ~ ~

Gerrum was walking back from the marina when John Jeffers hailed him. "Hey, Gerr. Glad I spotted you. Marian's off to a church meeting and the Mariners are playing, if you're interested."

Gerrum followed John upstairs, and the two of them settled with beers in front of the television.

"You found a good cook this year," Gerrum said.

"Yep," John said, grinning. "We're nearing capacity most

113

nights, what with all the local traffic she's pulling in. Not sure if it's the cooking or the cook." He gave Gerrum a questioning look that Gerrum ignored.

"You'll have to give her a bonus."

"It keeps up, you may be right."

With John settled into a comfortable back and forth, Gerrum judged it time to try more probing questions. "How'd you happen to find her?"

"Didn't. She found us. Wrote out of the clear blue, asking about the job. Claimed a friend mentioned it to her. But after she got here, I recognized her. Came a few years back, right after we opened. Had a husband with her. Doubt I'd recognize him again, but she's not an easy woman to forget."

Gerrum agreed. Clen was memorable although that was odd given she presented herself in such a simple, unadorned way. Not to mention, she never took part in conversations unless forced to. Usually a person who did that was easy to overlook. Instead, he found himself more intrigued by her unexpressed thoughts than by anything others said aloud.

"Did you mention her being here before?" he asked.

"Nope. Figured she'd a said something if she wanted to talk about it."

The sound of a sharp crack as a Boston hitter connected with a pitch pulled their attention back to the game. The camera followed the arc of the ball, which floated through the lights and then right into the glove of the Mariners' left fielder. Side out.

John sat back with a sigh of relief. "The funny thing is, she wrote about the job from an abbey. It's the main reason we hired her, matter a fact. From her letter, Marian figured she was an ex-nun taking a first step back into the world."

Gerrum's imagination leapt into high gear. He could easily picture Clen in an abbey. Much more difficult to imagine her married. Although, given she didn't wear a wedding ring, it seemed likely the husband was out of the picture. Either ex or dead. Gerrum's money was on ex since Clen's attitude toward the bachelors of Wrangell had more misanthropy about it than grief.

"Do abbeys take someone who's been married?" he asked John.

"Damned if I know. You'll have to ask Marian. You ready

for another beer?"

~ ~ ~

When Clen returned to ZimoviArt with a check to pay for the quilt square, she brought her portfolio along. "I hoped you might be willing to tell me what you think of these."

Hailey accepted the check and raised her eyebrows in a questioning look.

"You have a good eye." Clen gestured at the paintings on the gallery walls. "I just thought you might be willing to offer me...I don't know. Suggestions, maybe?"

"Sure. I can do that."

While Hailey looked through the pictures, Clen wandered around the gallery. For several minutes, the only sound was of pages turning.

"Your portraits convey a distinct sense of personality," Hailey said.

Clen gave up trying to pretend she was examining the carving of a bear and walked over to the counter.

"However, to make them more commercial you need to consider adding touches more evocative of the area. You know, maybe frame a face with a fur parka or place an evergreen or the outline of a mountain in the background?"

Hailey divided the pictures into three piles. One pile contained the sketch Clen had made of the black girl in Ethel Green and the ones she made at Mag's. Hailey gestured toward that pile. "I like these very much, but I already have enough non-Alaskan pictures. These, though," her hand floated over the pile of sketches and watercolors Clen had done of Wrangell, "they should do very well. The harbor scenes, in particular. You've managed a sort of dreamy quality that pulls me beneath the surface realism of the scene. I can definitely sell them for you."

"Oh, I don't want to sell anything."

"Why not?"

"You really think you can sell them?"

Hailey glanced at Clen, then went through the Wrangell pictures a second time. She picked out three harbor scenes. "If you get these framed, I'll be happy to put them on display." Then she looked at the third pile, a collection of portraits. "I'd even be willing to hang one of these. This one I think." She pulled out the portrait Clen had done of Thomasina. "The Wrangell Picture Gallery can do the framing for you."

~ ~ ~

"Bet you'll never guess what John's cook does in her spare time," Hailey said the next time she and Gerrum had morning coffee together.

"Maude has been uncharacteristically silent on the subject."

"She's an artist. She brought in some work to ask my opinion."

"And?" Gerrum prompted.

"I'm going to hang several of her paintings as soon as she gets them framed." Hailey fiddled with the multiple rings on her fingers, her gaze focused somewhere in the middle distance. "Marian told me she wrote asking about the job from an abbey, but personally, I find that hard to believe. She doesn't strike me as the ex-nun type. What do you think?"

"Can't say I'm acquainted with any nuns," Gerrum said. "Makes me a poor judge."

"Well, I have known a few, and I think Clen would send a mother superior into fits in no time flat."

"What makes you say that?"

"Well, can you imagine her casting her eyes down in humility?" Hailey snorted. "And if someone told her to do something she thought was stupid, I think she'd tell them to go fry ice."

As would Hailey, for that matter. The thought brought a smile to Gerrum's face.

~ ~ ~

It took a week for Clen to get the framed pictures back. As soon as she did, she carried them into ZimoviArt. Hailey propped the harbor scenes against the wall and stood back. "See? I knew these would look good."

"They don't feel like they're mine anymore," Clen said. The framing made the pictures look more polished but also more foreign.

"Well, that is the plan, after all. By the end of the summer, a number of these better belong to someone else, or several someone elses, or I need to find another calling."

"I'm not exactly sure I'm ready to part with this one." Clen's hands moved to rest on Thomasina's portrait, still lying on the counter.

"She looks like she could be a nun," Hailey said, walking over.

Clen looked down at Thomasina's face, which she'd drawn surrounded by dark shadows. "You must have a nun or two in your background to spot that."

"I'm the only person I know who's lived in a convent but wasn't a nun and never had any intention of being one."

"Oh, I'm quite sure you have company." Herself for instance, although Clen had no intention of being that open with anyone in Wrangell.

"Yes. Well, we need to talk about your bottom line," Hailey said. "I can price these where they'll sell easily, or I can price them for the more discriminating shopper. I'd like to know your thoughts, so you won't be disappointed." Hailey slid the portrait of Thomasina out from under Clen's hands and walked over to hang it next to the wildflower paintings.

"Definitely price them for the discriminating shopper," Clen said, still debating whether to let Hailey display Thomasina's portrait. "Actually, I have no idea what would be reasonable. I'd like my framing costs covered, of course. Beyond that, you're the expert. Why don't you price them and see how it goes, and we'll talk again *if* you manage to sell one."

"Oh, I'll manage. *If* I get anyone in here who knows art from shinola."

"Isn't the expression something else from shinola?"

Hailey grinned. "Umm. Tell you what, when the first one sells, I'll take you to lunch to celebrate."

Clen walked out leaving the portrait of Thomasina behind, still uncertain it was the right thing to do. But otherwise, the visit with Hailey had left her with a pleasant feeling of possibility.

~ ~ ~

Gerrum was at the Visitors' Center checking with Doreen on his bookings, when she mentioned seeing Clen enter ZimoviArt that morning carrying a large package.

When he finished with Doreen, he walked next door. "Are Clen's paintings hung yet?"

Hailey pointed, and he moved slowly from picture to picture. The harbor scenes were good, but it was the portrait that snagged his attention. The woman in the portrait had an air of serene melancholy that was only slightly leavened by the promise of humor in the shape of the mouth.

He lifted it off the wall and brought it over to the counter. "I think this one is priced too low. I'd say it's worth at least two hundred."

"Are you interested in buying it, or do you just want to criticize my pricing?" Hailey said.

"I want to buy it. I'd never try to tell you how to conduct your business."

"What a relief." Her lips curved into a totally fake smile. "It would surely be a pain if I had to answer to a grubby Alaskan fisherman every time I did something."

"Yep. I can see that. In your shoes, I wouldn't even want Elmer in my store."

It was the kind of sally he expected her to laugh at and return. Instead she looked startled. He handed over his credit card, and she made an imprint.

Then she gave him a sharp look. "Two hundred, right?"

He shrugged. He'd been teasing, but he didn't mind paying the extra fifty. He could afford it, and he suspected neither Clen nor Hailey, into whose pockets the money would go, were all that prosperous. But the way Hailey was acting...he tried to recall if she'd looked as strained when he first walked into the gallery. He didn't think so.

Shaking off his discomfort, he carried the portrait home where he hung it in his writing room. Over the next few days as he wrote, he began to imagine the woman in the portrait reading over his shoulder. Eventually, he found himself writing what he thought might please her.

It was an odd fancy. And not one he planned to share.

~ ~ ~

After two days of off-and-on rain, the sun was back out, and the water was clear and still. Clen went to the harbor to sketch. She picked a vantage point, and Kody turned in a circle or two before settling to sleep beside her—his nose almost touching her thigh—the most peaceful and undemanding companionship in all of Wrangell.

The boat she'd chosen to draw was a grizzled one with scabrous paintwork and a superstructure dark orange with decay. Rather like an old man startled awake and not given enough time to wash and dress properly. It rubbed gently against the dock as if responding to her attention.

As she began to draw, her thoughts were pulled back to the question she'd been debating the last two days—was she going to retrieve the portrait of Thomasina from Hailey's gallery or not.

"Most people sure wouldn't see that boat as a potential work of art."

She peered up at the man who had spoken, shading her eyes against the glare, but she'd already recognized the voice. "It's the awfulness that makes it interesting."

Gerrum crouched next to her and rubbed Kody's ears. "You just might find old Rolf even more interesting than his boat."

"Is he the one with the beard?"

Gerrum nodded, still patting Kody who pushed against his hand with obvious pleasure. Gerrum was the only person besides the Jeffers and her that Kody seemed to like.

"Beard is an understatement. I suspect he has a Sikh or two in his gene pool."

Clen smiled and flipped to a fresh page, deciding to give in to the impulse that had nudged at her since she'd met this man. "Can you hold that pose for a minute?"

When he nodded in agreement, she began to sketch. With quick, minimal strokes, she drew an outline of him squatting next to Kody. Then, with that blocked in, she switched her attention to his face. His gaze was lowered watching the sketch progress.

She drew the shape of his face then focused on his eyes, trying to capture their half-closed shape along with the smile lines at the corners that hinted at good humor and an underlying steadiness. The next time she glanced at him, it was to find he'd shifted from watching the progress of his portrait to examining her.

"That's amazing." He nodded toward the sketch. "I knew you were talented because I've seen your work in Hailey's gallery. I just didn't know you could draw that fast."

She shook her head, continuing to add to the rough sketch. "This is only preliminary. I'm just trying to lock down some details so I can work on it later. For one thing, you're not going to want to hold that pose for long."

"Too true. As a matter of fact..."

"Sure, go ahead. Take a break." She continued to add to the sketch as he stood and stretched. Then he dropped down again. She wasn't expecting that, but she wasn't going to quibble. If he was willing to continue to pose, she'd push it as long as she could. She narrowed her eyes, noticing how the light slid off his hair—hair straight and shiny as the fur of a wet otter. Black, but in the bright sunlight, there was a faint sheen of something lighter. Not red, though. Umber, maybe.

Usually she stuck to graphite or charcoal for portraits, but it might be interesting to do a watercolor of him, if she could just get the mouth right. Frowning, she rubbed out a line and redrew it.

He stood. "Sorry, but I need to get going. I've got clients to pick up. I wouldn't mind doing this again sometime, though. Unless once was enough?" He gestured toward the drawing with a question in his eyes.

It wasn't. She'd caught him in profile, but she wanted to draw him straight on, as well as from the other side. It always fascinated her how much asymmetry was present in every face. She'd once experimented with drawing half faces and then making the second halves exact mirror images, and what resulted was always off.

"If you're willing, I'd like to do more."

"Tell you what, you let me show you around and I'll sit for you. We can even combine the two."

Her head started shaking before she'd consciously decided. "Oh, I don't think that's a good idea." Kody picked up on her agitation and whined softly.

Gerrum leaned over to pat Kody. "You mean because you'll

get teased about it afterward."

That wasn't exactly what she was worried about, but it would do. "It's a blood sport around here."

He grinned. "Second only to gossip. If there isn't something juicy to chew on already, teasing's a way to develop new material. But you've been holding your own."

Because she'd been careful since the jet boat ride not to give them anything further to work with. So, was it worth another bout of teasing for an opportunity to do more sketches of him? "What were you thinking?" The words slipped out before her usual caution could stop them.

"Tomorrow's your day off, right?"

Everyone in Wrangell seemed to know she had Thursdays off.

"It so happens, I'm free, too. We could make a day of it. Take the jet boat. Leave at ten, be back around four. Hit all the highlights. The Stikine, the hot springs, the garnet reef. How does that sound?"

Like a date. No. She needed to say no. But she did want more sketches of him, and it would be nice to see the Stikine. When she and Paul were here before there had been no jet boat to make the trip possible. But there was also the unresolved issue of his and Hailey's possible 'coupleness.'

"O...kay." She was going to regret it. She was sure of it.

"Bring a bathing suit. For the hot springs."

A bathing suit. Right. As if that was happening. Although, it might be kind of fun. She'd have to think about it. The suit had been lurking in the bottom of her one suitcase for more than a year. Maybe she would take it along and just see how things went.

"See you tomorrow at ten." He smiled, and when he did, his eyes almost disappeared into the fans of sun-touched lines at each corner. She wished she could draw fast enough to capture the way he looked in that moment.

He left, and after working for a time on the sketch of Gerrum, she switched back to the one of the boat, remembering as she did so her interaction with Hailey.

How could she have forgotten how good it felt to receive praise for her work? Of course, it hadn't happened in a very long time. Probably not since she graduated from college. Paul had always discouraged her sketching, and he particularly disliked her drawing him. Perhaps because he sensed it was her way of searching for the real man beneath the polished surface.

She shrugged off the memory of Paul, but what was harder to dislodge were the memories of Thomasina set loose by seeing the portrait framed and hung in Hailey's shop. That had brought a flood of remembrance both positive and painful.

She missed Thomasina, although she was the one who had failed to keep in touch. At graduation, Thomasina had held onto her hand and asked her to write. She'd said she would, but she hadn't. And now, so many years had passed, it was too late to do anything about it.

But there was one thing she could do. Retrieve the portrait.

~ ~ ~

"Do you have radar or something?" Hailey asked when Clen walked into ZimoviArt.

"What do you mean?"

"I sold one of your pictures." Hailey frowned.

Clen thought that odd, since the news made her feel buoyant. "Which painting and who bought it?"

"The portrait." Hailey turned away to fiddle with something. "A pleasant, middle-aged man bought it."

Puzzlement at Hailey's odd lack of enthusiasm was replaced by a sinking feeling in Clen's gut. "You didn't. Please...you didn't. I...I came back to tell you I decided I didn't want to sell it. Where did he go? What did he look like? Maybe I can catch him, get it back."

The deep bellow of the ferry's departure horn interrupted them.

"I'm so sorry, Clen." Hailey looked as sick as Clen was feeling.

Well, Clen had wanted to exorcise Thomasina from her life. Now, it seemed, she'd succeeded.

Chapter Thirteen

"In the Tlingit language, Stikine means great river," Gerrum told Clen as they prepared to cast off. "And, in case you're wondering, that's about the extent of my bilingualism."

"You mean to tell me you don't know how to say please, thank you, and where's the restroom?"

"I doubt the Tlingit have a word for restroom." It pleased him Clen was willing to be playful. A good omen for the day.

They left the harbor, and he opened the throttle. Clen, who was sitting in the bow, faced forward to enjoy the ride across the shallow delta. When they entered the river itself, it was wide and deep, its swift currents gray with glacial runoff.

Gerrum ran up the main channel at high speed for several miles before turning into a small tributary where he nosed into the bank and dropped anchor. Without the engine's roar, the chuckle of the river and occasional birdsong were audible.

The water here was clear and shallow, and together, yet apart, they watched it dapple over rocks and small fish.

"Too bad you weren't here to see the eagles gathering for the hooligan run," he said.

"Hooligan?"

"You'd probably call them smelt. The champagne and caviar of the eagles' diet."

"Do you ever get tired of all this?" Clen asked.

He shook his head. "Each time is different. Different skies, different weather, a new group of people. A bear, snow geese heading north, eagles, a moose."

"What's your favorite thing about it?"

He paused for a moment then pointed to his ear. "The quiet."

Clen nodded toward the sky. "Except for that." A plane, an ancient DC-3, was lumbering toward them from the east, flying low and following the course of the river.

"That's the second so far," she said.

"They're gold planes. Flying out the ore. There's a mine upriver."

She picked up her sketch pad and began to draw. While she sketched, he thought about what to show her next. Perhaps the waterfall he'd discovered this spring, up a shallow tributary most boats would be unable to navigate. He'd been saving it, for what he was not altogether certain.

When Clen closed her sketch pad, he pulled in the short length of anchor chain, restarted the engine, and returned to the main channel. After several minutes at top speed, he slowed and turned into the creek.

The engine note dropped to a low-pitched burble as he maneuvered through the narrow defile. Then they rounded a curve, and the stream widened into a deep pool—a dead end of sorts, since the pool was fed by a waterfall cascading down thirty feet of rocky cliff.

Clen's mouth curved, and her eyes softened. "Oh, how lovely."

No question, that was the reason he'd waited. In order to share it with someone who would savor its beauty and inaccessibility as much as he did. He shut down the engine and secured the boat. The water at the base of the cliff was churned into white foam, but where he'd anchored, the water was deep and dark.

Once again Clen picked up her sketchbook and began to draw with quick, sure movements. Judging by the direction of her glance when she looked up, he thought she was focusing on a spruce bent over the falls.

He looked away, giving his attention to their surroundings. A few minutes later, Clen turned the sketchbook around to show she'd captured him in profile looking up at an eagle, with the waterfall and tree behind him. Although his face tended to look round and soft in photographs, Clen had sketched hollows and angles in cheek and jaw that made him look more like himself. It pleased him.

"Are you ready to move on?" he asked.

Clen closed the sketchbook and lifted a hand to encompass the pool, trees, and waterfall. "You have my full confidence in deciding where we go next."

He counted her acquiescence a victory in what he viewed as a personal challenge to get this woman to smile more often and to bend those arms she used to keep everyone at a distance.

Back in the main channel, the jet boat skimmed the opaque surface of the river, making short work of the rapid current. As he watched for debris, he thought about what to suggest if there were visitors at the hot springs. They'd become a popular destination since the forest service built a soaking tub, and often, particularly on weekends, the tub filled with guys who didn't bring swimsuits but did bring an ample supply of six-packs.

Whenever he found a boat tied to the small dock, he tended to give the place a pass, but today his luck held. No boats, no people.

After a leisurely lunch, he suggested a soak in the hot water. Clen looked around at the arrangement of deck, tub, and changing cubicles before agreeing. Her agreement was especially pleasing, since he'd fully expected her to say she'd forgotten her suit or didn't have one. Another small victory in a day filled with them, if one were keeping score—which, it seemed, he was.

Clen came out of the cubicle wrapped in a towel. She set it aside as she slid into the tub, giving him only a brief glimpse of the figure she'd been hiding with bulky sweaters and chef coats. Her swimsuit was a navy one piece, utilitarian rather than provocative, but Clen looked good in it. More substantial than a girl but still long-legged, slim-hipped, and sleek as a seal.

"So tell me," she said. "Before you moved to Wrangell, where did you live and what did you do?"

He was beginning to suspect she asked questions not out of true curiosity but rather to maintain her distance. This time, he wasn't letting her get away with it.

"I was an attorney. In Seattle." He anticipated her next question, which he could almost see forming on her lips. "I left because I was bored. So what did you do, before Wrangell?"

A brief shadow of something, possibly annoyance, crossed her face. "Financial analyst, Atlanta."

"That's quite a leap. From financial analyst to cook."

"So's attorney to fishing guide."

"Good point. What's your story?" he said.

"Oh, the usual, I suppose."

When he remained silent, she glanced at him. He raised his eyebrows in inquiry.

After a moment, she shrugged. "I don't know. Tired of being in a rut, I guess. I decided to do some of the things I dreamed about when I was younger."

"You dreamed of working as a cook?"

She snorted softly. "Hardly. But I wanted to go somewhere new and not just visit, but be part of the community."

"Where did you learn to cook?"

"The basics from my mother. Then I met this elderly woman who shared some of her secrets." A smile played on Clen's lips. "The sort of meals we serve at the lodge aren't fancy. The biggest challenge is figuring out quantities, and John helps with that."

Her gaze drifted to the meadow, and he grabbed the opportunity to examine her. Like the woman in the portrait he'd just bought, her eyes seemed sad. She lifted a hand out of the water and brushed a strand of hair behind her ear, leaving droplets on her cheek that looked like tears. He tried to memorize it all so he could write it down later. The pale glimmer of water on skin, the way her mouth curved when she was silent, the dark feathering of hair framing her face, the faint lines beginning to form in the corners of mouth and eyes. If he were a painter, he'd call it *Portrait of a Woman at the Threshold.*

"Why did you pick Wrangell?" he asked.

She shook her head, as if gathering her thoughts from a distance. "I don't know if I can explain."

He waited, watching her hands. She had long fingers and she moved them unconsciously and gracefully in the water.

"Awhile back, I came to Alaska for a visit," she said, looking away from him. "Took the ferry, stopped in Juneau, Petersburg, Ketchikan, Haines. You know, the whole loop. It's all beautiful, but there was something about Wrangell. I don't know. It just felt...comfortable, I guess. Like a pair of jeans you've worn for years until they're soft as flannel. I never forgot it. That feeling." Her gaze remained unfocused for a beat then she blinked and glanced at him. "Why did you choose Wrangell?"

He pictured the skeins of morning fog floating along the narrow length of Petersburg's harbor, the wooden walkways suspended over a Ketchikan slough, the quiet pace of the evening in Skagway after the tours had collected their passengers and departed. Then he'd arrived in Wrangell, and seeing the fishing boats tucked into the curve of Wrangell's tiny inner harbor, he had simply known.

"Roughly the same reason, I guess."

"And now it's home."

"Yes."

Clen swirled her hands in the water, watching the pattern of ripples. "Do you ever miss the other? The big city, the hustle and bustle, having a professional career?"

The question felt more personal than her others, and so he framed his answer carefully. "Sometimes I do. The further I move away from it, the easier it is to focus on the good and forget the not so good. I think the trick is to remember both."

She listened with a frown, staring at the patterns she was forming in the water.

"How about you?" he asked. "Do you miss Atlanta, your career?"

She gave her head a quick shake. "Good Lord, no."

Her sharp response puzzled him because her question about his past had sounded pensive, as if she were missing something, or someone.

"What about Wrangell?" he said, determined to keep her talking. "Is it what you expected?"

"Not exactly. But then I think most things turn out not to be what we expect."

"Yet we continue to be surprised by that. So what surprised you the most about Wrangell?"

Her expression went from a frown to a rueful look. "I guess I expected people to be friendly. Just not so..." Her hands stilled their restless movements.

"I think the word you're looking for is attentive?" Although

127

he suspected she was more likely thinking "pushy" or "nosy."

"More than. It's taken a bit of getting used to. A big city is so…impersonal."

He wanted to ask her about her marriage and the abbey then, to find out where they fit in, but he feared it might sever the tentative lines of communication they'd managed to string between them.

They continued to soak and chat, but he didn't learn anything more about her, unless he counted the fact she said so little about herself. He looked toward the meadow to see a moose emerge from the woods at the far end.

He pointed it out to Clen, and they watched until the animal turned and sauntered back into the trees. IIe got another smile for that.

A good day.

Chapter Fourteen

Hailey left word with Marian that another of Clen's pictures had sold, and Clen stopped by ZimoviArt to see which one.

"The one of Rolf Peterson's boat," Hailey said. "A young couple from Seattle bought it."

"Two down, two to go." Clen felt good about that, although the loss of Thomasina's portrait was still a sore point.

"I really owe you that lunch," Hailey said.

"That's okay. I won't hold you to it."

"Really, I'd like to. Thursday? And why don't you go ahead and frame another couple of harbor scenes. If you bring your portfolio by, I'll let you know the ones I prefer." Hailey fiddled with her checkbook. "Did you enjoy your day with Gerrum?"

Being an expert at offhand questions, Clen could recognize one, and she suddenly felt like she was treading on eggshells. "It was a pleasant day. I ended up with a lot of sketches."

"You sketched?" Hailey looked up, apparently surprised.

"Sure. That was the whole idea." And given the sketches, she didn't regret taking the trip, despite the increased teasing that followed. Gerrum had proven to be an easy companion, one who could be silent without fidgeting, and when he spoke, his comments were thoughtful and intelligent—a combination she'd always found appealing. Given different circumstances, they might easily become friends.

"That's good to know. Since I want more of your work to sell." Hailey handed Clen the check she'd written out. "Until Thursday, then."

When Clen walked out of ZimoviArt she found Elmer

Cantrell loitering by the display window. Kody had shifted to the other side of the doorway, away from Elmer.

"There's something you oughta know about that there Gerrum Kirsey," Elmer said, his lips lifting enough to show off a ragged row of brown teeth. "He's a half-breed."

Clen was angling to pass Elmer but, at those words, she paused and turned to face him. *Good grief, did people still use that term?* And look who was talking. "Half-breed?" she murmured, giving Elmer a cool stare and moving her eyes up and down the entire pudgy, unattractive length of him. In his case, a different genetic makeup could only be an improvement.

"Yeah. He's part Tlingit." Elmer spat out the word as if it tasted bad. "Best you don't mess with him. You can't trust them kind."

"Your concern for my welfare is touching." She felt her lip curling in disgust, but Elmer looked like she'd complimented him. So not only was the man repulsive, he was dumb as zucchini, not to speak ill of zucchini. "But you need to take the subject up with Gerrum." Who, she hoped, would knock every one of those nasty-looking stubs down Elmer's ugly throat.

"Hell, don't do no good. Nothing gets to that man. Acts like you ain't said or did nothing."

Something she'd already witnessed and, actually, it did have a certain elegance her tooth-removal plan lacked. Deciding, she turned and walked away from Elmer. Kody scrambled to join her.

"Hey, lady," Elmer yelled. "I'm doing you a good turn. So's you know what you're dealing with. Ain't like you're the only woman he's stringing along."

Kody turned and growled at Elmer's aggressive tone.

Clen bent and touched the dog's head. "It's okay, boy."

Kody licked her hand as if to reassure her he'd be happy to bite Elmer if she wanted him to, but she was now committed to Gerrum's nonviolent solution. She continued walking, tapping her thigh to encourage Kody to follow.

Elmer's odious comments had raised her hackles as well as Kody's, and her first impulse was to find Gerrum and invite him to a very public lunch. But while that might send the right message to Elmer Cantrell and his ilk, it might send the wrong message to Gerrum—something she didn't want to do.

She picked up her pace, leaving Elmer and his insinuations behind. Kody trotted at her side, whining to remind her to slow down. When they reached the lodge, she told the old dog to stay and lengthened her stride to a jog as she followed the road leading out of town.

After a fast mile, she still hadn't outpaced the restlessness released by the encounter with Elmer—a restlessness that intensified as the past swirled around her like one of Wrangell's frequent rain squalls.

Racism. Bigotry. It was perhaps the main reason she ended up married to Paul Douglas.

She turned onto a faint track leading to the water, found a rock to sit on, and let memory pull her under.

Paul had asked her to marry him, but she hadn't yet given him an answer the night they went to the Segovia for dinner. The Segovia, as lily white as its tablecloths, was one of Atlanta's most expensive and exclusive restaurants, the kind of place Paul liked. She'd considered it overpriced and pretentious.

After they ordered drinks, Paul excused himself to make a phone call. When he returned five minutes later, he was accompanied by an elegantly dressed young black couple. Behind them, the maitre d' motioned frantically at one of the waiters.

"Clen, I'd like you to meet Tom and Candy Smithson," Paul said. "I thought, if it's okay with you, they might join us? The maitre d' claims their reservation was lost, and he can't seem to find another table for them, even though the restaurant is half empty."

"It's very okay." Clen stood and held out her hand, first to Candy then Tom. "How lovely to meet you both."

The maitre d' hovered, wringing his hands and trying to get Paul's attention, which was focused on seating the Smithsons. "Mr Douglas, there's been a mistake. I found the reservation. I can seat Mr and Mrs Smithson."

"As you can see, they're already seated." When Paul used that tone, secretaries trembled, and the maitre d', despite his tuxedo, rose boutonniere, and highly polished shoes, was obviously a secretary at heart. He slunk away.

Candy turned a worried look toward Clen. "We don't want to impose on you."

"Nonsense," Paul said. "If that man had his way, he'd seat you by the kitchen and ignore you. Much better to sit out here in the middle, where they can't forget you."

As if responding to Paul's assessment, waiters appeared and, with a flurry, gave the Smithsons silverware and menus and took drink orders. When it arrived, the food was awful—the pasta mushy, the steaks tough.

Paul smiled at Tom and Candy. "In your honor, if I'm not mistaken."

They ate bread and salads and picked at the entrees, taking their time, because eating was really beside the point. At first, Tom and Candy had been visibly nervous but they were also determined. They'd come to the restaurant, they told Clen and Paul, as their way of furthering the cause of civil rights.

By the time the evening ended, the four of them were chatting comfortably, as if sitting in public, black and white together, was a commonplace occurrence, which it might one day be, thanks to people like the Smithsons.

After that dinner, Clen, thinking Paul's championing of the Smithson's right to eat at the Segovia was a sign of a loving and generous heart, had finally agreed to marry him. Except...if she were totally honest, she'd have to admit it wasn't the only reason. Perfect honesty required her to admit her mother had also had something to do with it.

Her parents had come to Atlanta for Thanksgiving, and Paul joined them for dinner. Her mother was smitten. In the kitchen after dinner, she asked Clen avid questions about Paul.

"My, he's attractive, Michelle."

And Clen knew what else her mother was thinking, even though she didn't say it: A woman with your looks doesn't usually attract a man as good-looking as this one.

"As a matter of fact, he asked me to marry him."

"Oh my goodness, Michelle! How wonderful. When is the wedding?"

"I haven't said yes."

"Why ever not? He's handsome, he's charming, and he has a good job with excellent prospects. What more do you want?"

Love. She wanted love. But she couldn't tell her mother she was no more sure of Paul's feelings than she was of her own. "He's been waiting a month. Another couple of weeks shouldn't be a big deal."

"A month? You mean he asked you to marry him a month ago, and you still haven't given him an answer?"

"I gave him an answer. I said I'd think about it."

"Good lord, Michelle. I've never seen you as a femme fatale, I'll admit it. But this is ridiculous. You're playing with him like a cat with a mouse. It isn't right for either one of you."

Her mother was correct in saying it wasn't a good situation, but only partly right in her cat and mouse analogy. She had that backwards. More like Paul was the cat and Clen the mouse.

She didn't believe, any more than her mother did, that he really wanted to marry her. She figured as soon as she said yes, he'd lose interest and move on, and she'd be left with the empty life she'd had before he entered it. "I just want to be sure."

"Well, you need to work on that."

Later, Clen walked Paul to the door, and as she returned to the living room, she could hear her parents talking.

"Well, I certainly never expected Michelle to end up with a man like that." Her mother.

"Our daughter has grown into a beautiful, accomplished woman, and she's lucky to have met a man with the intelligence to recognize it." Her father.

So was that it then? She'd married Paul because her mother thought he was too handsome for her gawky daughter, and the gawky daughter wanted to prove her mother wrong?

Maybe, although that didn't explain why she'd stayed married to him after the loss of delight and the deepening of indifference. After cross words became more than occasional and silences accumulated.

Had she been hoping it would work out?

No. Hope was one of the first casualties.

More likely it had been inertia, along with the belief her life wouldn't be any better without Paul. So why go through the upheaval of leaving him. At least, that was her thinking before she discovered he was unfaithful.

The sudden blast from a boat horn jerked her back to the present. The waters of Zimovia Strait were gray today under a low overcast. Summer in Alaska, indeed. For sure, nothing like Atlanta.

A splat of rain hit her cheek and another tapped her shoulder. She zipped her jacket against the chill and pulled out the waterproof poncho she'd begun carrying after she discovered how much it rained in Wrangell. Then she sat watching the rain pock the surface of the water, forming infinite, interlocking circles.

Everything affected everything else. It was never enough to take one thing in isolation without considering all that came before...and after.

Paul, only the tip of her personal iceberg.

Chapter Fifteen

1966 - 1982

ATLANTA, GEORGIA

After graduating from Marymead, Clen moved to Atlanta, because it was both a long way from Colorado Springs and it was where Maxine lived. She hoped to find a position where her degree in mathematics would be put to good use, but all she could manage was a secretarial position in a brokerage firm.

"Michelle, how wonderful. Administrative Assistant. It sounds very impressive."

"A secretary by any other name is still a secretary, Mom."

"But, you'll have opportunities, sweetie."

Oddly enough, her mother turned out to be correct, although not in quite the way she'd no doubt meant.

Clen was assigned to work for a man who drank too much at lunch and expected her to pick up the slack. At first, she thought she was being stupid to cover for Edward, until she realized he was providing her with more opportunities than most assistants were given.

And it was all going swimmingly until Edward passed out at the office Christmas party, attracting the attention of Paul Douglas, a higher up and the firm's most celebrated bachelor. In the New Year, Paul started dropping by Edward's office to ask probing questions.

When it became obvious Edward relied on Clen for more of the answers than he should, Paul's attention switched abruptly. "Miss McClendon, I believe I understand your reluctance in this affair. However, I assure you I intend to get to the bottom of it. With or without your help."

Clen employed her best silent stare. She didn't want to inform on Edward, although he richly deserved it for being stupid. But in her mind, the equation had been balanced by the experience she'd gained.

Paul grimaced and left. Shortly afterward, Clen was transferred to a position with a more abstemious executive and Edward was assigned a new assistant. Within three months of that change, Edward was gone, and Clen had begun training as a broker.

She enjoyed her new responsibilities, although the added responsibility gave her little time to think about whether she was on a career path that would satisfy her for the long haul.

Over the next year and a half, she saw Paul Douglas on a regular basis—at business meetings and at the firm's mandatory Fourth of July and Christmas parties. Females, single and married, spent those occasions hovering around Paul like anxious hummingbirds. Clen watched from a distance, relieved she felt no impulse to join them.

She never expected a man who had his pick of women like Paul did to be interested in her. So she was rendered speechless when he called and invited her to dinner.

"You can't give me the silent treatment over the phone, Clen. A simple yes, I'd love to, is all that's needed here."

"Okay. I'll have dinner with you."

"See. Was that so difficult? I'll pick you up at seven."

Paul was used to always getting his own way, and that was attractive at first, although she didn't let him know it. She wasn't playing hard to get, just making sure that when he moved on, and he would, he wouldn't take a piece of her heart with him. As she continued to accept his invitations, she worked to project an air of disinterested sophistication she copied from Audrey Hepburn films.

"How do I get to second base with you, Clen?" Paul finally asked as he kissed her goodnight.

"I need to feel there's more to it than you racking up a score."

"What can I do to convince you it's not?"

"I don't think there's anything you can do."

"How about this? Marry me."

"That's not funny."

"I'm not trying to be funny. This may be the most serious I've ever been. I want to marry you."

"But...I need to think about it."

"Meanwhile, about second base?"

"Not a chance."

He sighed, but he didn't withdraw his proposal, and in the days that followed he remained attentive and affectionate.

After Thanksgiving, she finally screwed up her courage to end the game. "You know that question you asked me to think about?"

"Which one?"

"The one that involved second base."

"Oh, that question." Paul sipped the last of his wine, set his glass down, and looked at her.

"Is the offer still open?"

"Let me think." He stared at her through the shimmer of candlelight.

That's that, she thought, surprised at the sudden stab of sorrow. She looked away from him, wishing she could take her words back.

"Hey, Clen. Don't go away." He took her hand in his, pulling it gently, pulling her attention with it back to a subject she no longer wished to pursue.

"I was teasing. The offer is still very much open." He reached into his pocket. "I was beginning to think I was going to have to return this." He opened his hand. A ring lay there, one with a large pear-cut diamond.

Looking at the ring, Clen wanted to push back her chair and run. Paul slipped the ring on her finger. It fit perfectly, but then Paul had a talent for that kind of thing.

The waiter returned with their desserts, and she pulled her hand out of Paul's and buried it in her lap until the coffee had been poured and they were alone again. She twisted the ring, wishing she could give it back, not because she'd changed her mind about marrying Paul, but because she wasn't sure how to handle such a fancy ring and the man who went with it.

Paul smiled at her. "Now, the important question. How soon can we get married?"

"I haven't thought about it yet."

"Well, you better start thinking. You're the bride. It's your show."

"What I'd really like to do is elope."

"Hey, works for me. The sooner the better."

"We can't. Mom would kill us."

"Well, I can't say that scenario appeals to me. I'd rather have a more formal do than have Stella McClendon on my case."

"I'll try to keep it small."

"That doesn't matter, Clen. Big wedding, small wedding, elopement—as long as you say 'I do' to being Mrs Paul Douglas, that's all I care about."

~ ~ ~

She knew by the time they'd been married a week it was a mistake. Well, perhaps that was a bit of an exaggeration, because it wasn't really until they returned from St. Thomas and started the day-to-day routine of their lives that she realized she shouldn't have married him. And the reasons were all petty.

Like, before the wedding, he'd lavishly praised her cooking, but after, he always suggested a possible alteration to the recipe. Before, he'd gone to art shows and the theater with her. After the ceremony, he made excuses to bow out, finally admitting he had neither the time nor the interest in socializing with anyone not associated with the investment business. He also refused to help around the house, telling her to hire a maid, something that might work for the big stuff but was no help with everyday tasks.

Those and other irritations all worked like sandpaper, rubbing away her feeling of newlywed happiness until that was gone. Finally, only the lackluster smoothness of duty and habit remained as her life settled into one of quiet resignation.

One day, several years into their marriage, Clen bought a sketch pad, some pencils, and an eraser. Paul fussed about her drawing but eventually ignored it, giving her the opportunity to sketch him when he was unaware—watching television or engrossed in a report or a book. With her pencil she tried to pry under his skin, to get to know the stranger sharing her life.

When he was away on a business trip, she laid all the drawings on the dining table and circled slowly, first one direction and then the opposite, seeking an answer to her question. *Who are you?*

The drawings looked blandly back.

~ ~ ~

Paul left Barringer and Hodges shortly after they married to a position that involved extensive travel. Clen kept expecting him to say he was going to look for something that allowed him to stay home more, especially when his trips began to take him away for several days at a time.

At first, she minded being left alone so much, but after awhile she realized how peaceful the time without him was. When he came home, his presence altered her internal harmonies like dissonant music.

For his part, the constant travel energized Paul, and he seemed happier than he'd been in years.

Chapter Sixteen

1985

WRANGELL, ALASKA

On Thursday, Hailey showed up for their lunch toting a grocery bag. "I thought it would be fun to have a picnic."

They walked over to Shakes Island, where a half dozen visitors wandered in and out of the tribal house. Hailey led the way to a spot near the water.

Clen spread the blanket she'd borrowed from Marian, and Hailey pulled food out of the bag. "I wasn't certain what you'd prefer, so I had them give me a selection of meats and cheeses. And I got éclairs for dessert, by the way, in case you like to plan ahead."

"If we eat all this, we'll either need a nap or a long hike."

"I guess I got carried away."

"It all looks delicious." Hoping to put Hailey at ease, Clen took one of the buns and added slices of ham and turkey. "Marian told me this is your second summer in Wrangell, and I've been wondering ever since, what made you decide to come here?"

Hailey, building her own sandwich, shrugged. "When I decided to open a summer gallery, Wrangell seemed like the best bet."

"It's a bit off the beaten path, though."

"That's why you like it, right?"

"You may be right." Not that Clen intended to admit how close to home the comment was.

"How about the fall. What are your plans?" Hailey said. "You aren't staying in Wrangell, are you?"

"No. I'll leave once the lodge closes for the season. I just haven't figured out where I'm going yet."

"How about next year. Are you coming back?"

"The Jeffers asked me to, but I don't know if I will."

"Well, be sure you stay in touch. I'd like to continue handling your work."

"Oh, I see. You're asking out of professional interest." Clen smiled at Hailey, who smiled back before taking a bite of her sandwich.

"So, why a summer gallery?" Among other things, Clen was wondering how someone so young had managed to finance it.

"I worked in the personnel department of a greeting card company. Part of the job was recruiting artists. I finally decided I could put my eye for talent to much better use."

"You're lucky to have made a success of it so quickly."

"Actually, I almost went under the first month." Hailey had a wry look.

"What saved you?"

"Not so much what, as who. After three weeks here, I'd sold only a couple of Tess's quilt squares, and I was feeling totally desperate. Then Bev Feeney showed up. She was carrying this huge purse with a major case of the uglies, and she pulled this thing out that looked like a small hairy dog. I thought, 'What in the world?' It was a fur parka, of course. After that, Dorothy Demetrioff came in and showed me these intricately knitted scarves that seem to float around your neck. 'Them's qiviut,' she told me, 'under wool of the musk ox.' Which explained why I'd never heard of it. Then Dorothy and Bev spread the word, and some local carvers stopped by. I've been in the black ever since."

"What do you do in the winter?"

"I spend it in Seattle. Last year I landed a job in a French restaurant. The tips were good, and it gave me the days free to scout out artists."

"Does your family live in Seattle?"

"Nope. There's just me. Well, I do have a brother, but I haven't heard from him in years. I don't even know if he's alive." Hailey spoke in a casual way, but there was something—a sudden desolate look in her eyes—that indicated she wasn't nearly as blasé as she pretended to be.

"I lost a brother." The words formed and were said before Clen could remind herself it wasn't a good idea to share too much of herself with anyone in Wrangell. "That is, he died."

"Oh, I'm sorry. Was it recent?"

Clen shook her head. "When I was nineteen. He was eleven. He had leukemia."

"I bet you miss him. I haven't seen my brother since I was thirteen, and I still miss him. One day he just went off. He left Grammie and me a note saying not to worry. We did, of course, but there wasn't much else we could do."

"Your grandmother raised you?"

Hailey nodded. "My mom died when I was ten. Dad couldn't take care of us, so we went to Grammie's. She lived in your basic log cabin on a small piece of land where she raised chickens and goats. She always said we were just like chickens, scratching to get by." Hailey smiled.

"You must have done a lot of scratching. To own a gallery, I mean."

"I guess." Hailey shrugged. "I left Edgington when I was fourteen, after I won a scholarship to a Catholic boarding school in Kansas City."

"That's where you lived with the nuns?"

"It was. When Grammie died, they let me stay with them in the summers. Then I went to Omaha for college. Another scholarship."

"You did all that on your own? And then you came to Wrangell, on your own, to open a shop. I'm impressed."

"Isn't it what you've done? Come to Wrangell on your own."

"I'm nearly forty. That's a big difference."

"I think you're tougher than you look," Hailey said.

"Well, for sure you're tougher than you look." Clen smiled, looking at Hailey's delicate features, silky bronze hair, and golden eyes.

A boat went by, and they watched it pass.

"Have you ever been married?" Hailey asked.

"I was. How about you?"

"No. Not even close."

"I find that hard to believe."

"I went to a Catholic women's college," Hailey said.

"So did I," Clen said. "And we certainly didn't lack male companionship."

Hailey's lips twitched. "Male companionship, huh? If your companions were anything like the guys who showed up to our mixers..." She shook her head and shuddered.

"That bad, huh?"

"I developed a very dim view of the entire gender." Hailey took another bite of her sandwich, then brushed away a persistent fly. "So, what do you think of Gerrum," she asked.

"Whoa. Where did that come from?"

Hailey gestured from the nearby boats toward the tribal house. "I consider it a natural segue."

"He's an interesting man."

"Oh, come on." Hailey said. "You could say the exact same thing about Elmer Cantrell."

"Elmer isn't interesting. He's a disgusting racist."

"Of course he is, and I didn't mean to divert you from the subject at hand, which is Gerrum, not Elmer." She circled a finger at Clen. "Proceed."

"He's intelligent. Pleasant. Very knowledgeable about the area."

Hailey frowned. "You could be describing a piece of furniture. Nice color, comfortable padding, fits the decor."

"How would you describe him?"

Hailey took a bite and chewed with a thoughtful look on her face. "Well, he made me rethink my position on the male gender."

"Did he now? That sounds extremely serious." Clen was teasing, but at the look that came over Hailey's face, she decided that wasn't the best idea.

"Too bad he's so much older," Hailey said, sounding mournful.

"How old are you?"

"Twenty-eight."

"How old is Gerrum?"

"Nearly forty."

"That's only twelve years. Not so many if you care for him."

"He's the perfect age for you."

"Me? No. Absolutely not. I did not come to Wrangell looking for a man."

"I think he likes you."

"I like him, too. Or at least I don't dislike him." Like she did Elmer.

While they talked about Gerrum, Hailey pulled off pieces of bread and rolled them between her fingers before tossing them toward the water.

"I've been wondering about something," Hailey said. "Do you ever draw portraits from photographs?" The words were quick and light, and she kept her face averted.

"Why do you ask?"

"It's just...the only picture I have of my mom is a photograph, and it's getting tatty. I thought you could..."

"Of course, I'd be happy to try. What about your dad?"

"Oh. No. I mean. I don't have any pictures of him." Hailey had that desolate look, again, so Clen didn't push.

~ ~ ~

Gerrum encountered Clen downtown and extended the dinner invitation he'd been debating for over a week.

"I really don't think—"

"Don't think. Say yes." Although he'd given it a lot of thought himself, now he'd taken the step, he was all in.

"It's not that simple."

"Sure it is."

"This is a small town. People talk. Having dinner with you, well it just isn't—"

Disappointed, he finished it for her. "A good idea."

She nodded, looking relieved.

"That working for you? Letting what others might think or say shape how you live?"

"Of course not."

"Prove it. Come to dinner with me."

"What about Hailey?"

It caught him off guard, as if he'd patted Kody and the dog had snapped at him.

He blew out a breath. "What about her?"

"I've heard the gossip about the two of you."

Damn and blast the old biddies who ran around town sticking their beaks into everyone else's business. "You should have figured out by now Wrangell gossips blow everything out of proportion."

Clen stood waiting, as if he hadn't yet spoken.

He sighed. "Hailey and I are friends." The truth, as far as it went. Lately, though, he'd seen little of her, and when they did meet, they seemed to have less and less to say to each other. He missed the ease they'd once shared and the opportunities to converse about something other than weather or fish.

It was also what he enjoyed about Clen, the conversation. "Sometimes dinner is just dinner."

She examined him for another moment. "Where were you thinking we might have this dinner?"

Given her lukewarm response so far, he figured he might as well go for broke. "My place. I happen to be a good cook."

Her head began to shake.

"Haven't I given ample proof I'm harmless?"

Her lips twitched, and it gave him hope for another attempt. "You can bring your sketchbook."

She examined him for a time, then firmed her lips. "What time?"

"How about six thirty?" He waited until she nodded in agreement, then he turned and walked quickly away, not wanting to give her any opportunity to change her mind.

~ ~ ~

Thursday evening, Gerrum opened the door to find both Clen and Kody on his porch.

"You've surely won that dog's heart. And Kody's pretty picky."

Kody gave the minuscule porch a sniff before flopping down. Clen smiled at the already dozing husky. "I'm a soft touch for treats."

Gerrum ushered her inside the small house he rented near the harbor and seated her at his kitchen table. She said yes to a glass of wine then, between sips, she sketched while he prepared the meal. At first he was self-conscious, knowing she was watching his every move, but as he put together a salad, warmed the bread, and washed a filet from the salmon he'd caught that day, he relaxed. When everything was done but the final cooking, he sat across from Clen while she continued to draw.

Eventually, he grilled the fish, and when Clen took her first bite she smiled. "Hey, you are a good cook. This is delicious."

"One of my least appreciated talents."

They finished eating, and she helped clear the table. Then she asked if he'd be willing to let her finish an earlier sketch. He poured another half glass of wine and, taking occasional sips, watched her draw.

"So, tell me about the winter," she said, as her glance moved between him and her sketch pad. "There aren't any tourists to take fishing or on Stikine trips, right?"

"No. No tourists. No fishermen."

She continued to draw. "So what's it like?"

"Similar to Seattle, except we get more snow and a bit less daylight."

"I wasn't asking for a weather report. I just wondered what you do."

"Come on, let me show you."

He led the way from the kitchen to the room he'd turned into his writing space. A computer, a recent addition that was having a positive impact on his productivity, occupied the table in front of the window, and a side wall was lined with bookcases. The books weren't in order but he knew what was there. Everything from politics and biography to cosmology and fiction. Good companions during the long winter.

Multiple copies of his own book sat on the top shelf between a set of polished granite bookends his sister gave him when the book came out. Clen wandered over to the bookcase. She tipped her head to read titles, and he leaned against the doorjamb watching her.

"You wrote this?" She sounded surprised. It meant she didn't know he was a writer. He'd wondered if she knew.

"What's it about?"

"It's a mystery."

"Well, if the author has no idea, who does?" She threw him a quick glance.

It was the second time he'd caught a hint of a puckish humor, and he grinned in response. "It's a private investigator story."

Instead of reaching for a copy, she stood like a child who'd been told not to touch, her hands in her pockets.

"I read a lot of mysteries, but I've never come across yours."

"Thousands of books out there. Some are bound to escape notice."

She turned from the shelves to face him. "Oh." Her eyes widened.

"What is it?" But he knew, of course. When she turned, she'd seen the portrait hanging on the wall next to him.

"I didn't realize..." Her posture stiffened and her voice had a toneless quality. "I thought Hailey sold that to a tourist."

"I call her my melancholy lady. I've been meaning to ask you her name."

"Thomasina." Clen continued to look like someone recovering from a shock.

He cast around for something to keep the conversation going. "Was she a friend?"

"More a beloved enemy."

He raised his eyebrows in question.

"In college. She was the dean of students. We fought over stupid things like dress codes and demerit systems." Her words were quick and jerky.

"And now?"

"We lost touch." She turned away, back to his books.

If it upset her that much, he'd drop it, although he would like to know more about his lady.

"Will you let me borrow your book, Gerrum?"

147

"Sure." He walked over, pulled out a copy, and handed it to her, realizing, as he did so, the last time he'd felt this uncertain was as a teenager working up the nerve to ask out some now-forgotten girl. It was discouraging to feel so tentative after thinking he'd reached a balance in his life. A place where the mistakes he'd made in the past no longer burdened him with regret. A place where he was...comfortable.

They returned to the kitchen, but Clen had reverted to the woman who kept everyone, including him, at arm's length.

"I have enough sketches for now," she said.

"May I see?"

She tore a sheet out of the book and laid it on top of the other sketches, then picked them up and tapped them into an orderly pile. "They're pretty rough." She sounded reluctant, but she handed them over.

He looked through them. One drawing was of his hands, large and blunt-fingered, with only an indication of an arm and torso. Several were quick studies of his face from different angles.

It was interesting, seeing himself through her eyes. As in the Stikine sketch, she'd used firm lines for nose and jaw, given his mouth a humorous tilt, and made his eyes look deep-set and calm. For the first time, he could see the Scandinavian as well as the Tlingit contributions to his appearance.

He pulled out the sketch that showed his resemblance to his father most clearly. "I wonder if I might have this one when you're finished with them. My mother would like it."

"Keep it. As a thank-you for dinner."

He considered it a poor thank-you when she turned down dessert, gathered her things, collected Kody, and left as if she were fleeing something unpleasant.

~ ~ ~

It thoroughly unsettled Clen to discover Hailey had misled her and Gerrum was the one who'd bought Thomasina's portrait.

Beloved enemy. Why had she said that? She couldn't still be grieving the ending of that relationship, could she? But apparently she was. Grieving in a quiet, steady way that had no correlate in the sharp regret she felt over the failure of her marriage.

148

The other surprise was the discovery Gerrum was an author. She'd asked to borrow his book in order to change the subject from Thomasina, but now she was stuck. She'd have to return the book, and that meant seeing him again when what she should be doing was cutting this off. Now.

Unbidden, a single moment from the evening replayed itself—when she'd turned to find Gerrum in the doorway, watching her. In the instant before she noticed Thomasina's portrait, she'd wondered what it would be like to give up worrying about either past or future and simply lean into that solid strength, although no way was she succumbing to such an impulse. Not given her history with relationships.

She laid the book on the dresser and stood looking out at Wrangell's tiny harbor. The windowpanes were crisscrossed with the lines of antennas, net booms, and masts, all lit softly by the lingering twilight of an Alaskan summer night. In the exact center was the single straight line she knew belonged to the radio mast of the *Ever Joyful*. She traced it with a finger then leaned her forehead against the window. Her breath fogged the pane, smudging the line that had become a companion of sorts on nights when the past kept her awake.

She rubbed the mist from the window to find a luminous night fog had begun to obscure the harbor.

~ ~ ~

The next time Clen encountered Gerrum, he invited her to join a tour group he was taking to Anan to see bears feasting on migrating salmon. She opened her mouth to decline, but found herself accepting instead. She offered to help with the galley. He said it wasn't necessary, but he'd appreciate it.

The group for that day included two elderly couples, two middle-aged women traveling together, and a young family with boys who looked to be about seven and nine. Even before they cast off, the two boys were jostling each other, and shortly after the *Joyful* cleared the harbor, the boys initiated a game of tag that ended abruptly when one of them knocked a cup of coffee out of another passenger's hand. Clen stepped in with a towel as Gerrum put the engine in neutral and gestured to the parents to join him in the wheelhouse. Clen maneuvered close enough to overhear what he had to say.

"Mr and Mrs Cole, this is a small boat, and your boys can't run around without knocking into other passengers. And when we get to Anan, it will be essential they behave with decorum, or they'll put themselves at risk. Bears are unpredictable, you know."

Clen watched the two think this over. Finally, they glanced at each other, then marched out on deck. Each grabbed a boy by the arm. Gerrum leaned in the doorway to watch as the parents escorted the boys to the stern where their dad made a number of emphatic points and their mom backed him up.

Clen shared a look of amused relief with Gerrum, who then walked over to the woman who'd had her coffee spilled. "Mrs Davis, I'm sorry you were inconvenienced. Ms McClendon," he nodded toward her, "will be serving you and Mr Davis at no charge today."

Clen took a sweater over to the woman. "I can lend you this if you'd like me to rinse the stain out of your jacket."

"That would be lovely, dear. Always best to rinse stains out immediately."

Gerrum got back underway, and once Clen served everyone coffee and rolls and dealt with the stain, she took him a cup of coffee. She stood next to him, braced against the slight movement of the boat. "Does that sort of thing happen often?"

"Often enough to keep things interesting."

"Would the boys be in danger?"

"We have to hike to the observatory. Nothing says the bears can't use the same trail."

"Well, they're behaving, at least for now. You handled it perfectly."

"You helped smooth the situation too. You've earned a trip to Anan any time you want to tag along." He pointed ahead. "We're almost there. Moment of truth. Now to see how Brandon and Billy do with the bears."

Brandon and Billy did very well indeed. They came back aboard chattering with excitement about what they'd seen, and Gerrum rewarded their good behavior with a brief, highly supervised opportunity to steer the boat.

~ ~ ~

Clen had left Gerrum's book sitting on her dresser, but after the Anan trip, she finally carried it over to the easy chair and curled up to read it. The writing was good and the plot intriguing, but what pulled her in was the emotional honesty of the main character, Gabe Skyler. His vulnerabilities and his willingness to admit when he was hurting rubbed at her sore places.

When hours later she turned the last page, there were tears on her cheeks. She had no idea how she was going to face Gerrum and hand back this book. No matter what words she used, it would be awkward. Because reading about Gabe Skyler, part Tlingit and ex-attorney, disoriented her. What else in the story was autobiographical? That horrible scene with the girlfriend?

The nastiness in Elmer's tone whenever he spoke of Gerrum disturbed Clen, but the words Gerrum put in that woman's mouth—calling Gabe an Eskimo in a three-piece suit. Words that were both vicious and cruel. The thought someone might have said it to Gerrum made her furious.

And what about the rest? Was it Gabe who mourned the loss of his father, or Gerrum? Was Gerrum beaten by bullies at school or was that Gabe? Yet, even if the specifics weren't pulled from Gerrum's life, the clarity and vigor of his fictional character made it clear Gerrum was deeply aware of others and attuned to what they might be thinking and feeling.

So how much had he seen of what she was trying to hide?

She snapped off the light and looked out the window. The mast of the *Ever Joyful* was missing from its usual place. She stared at that blankness, thinking of other nights she'd stood tracing that delicate line with her finger.

Damn the man, anyway. Wrangell was a rest stop. One didn't establish relationships at rest stops. No point to it.

Chapter Seventeen

Clen was an enigma Gerrum spent a considerable amount of time thinking about. In spite of their time together, he still had no hint of why she'd shucked career along with husband, and she hadn't dropped a single clue about where the abbey fit in. Clearly, he needed to see more of her to get those details, but since the Anan trip, she seemed to be avoiding him.

Then one evening as he walked by Bear Lodge from the marina, Clen stepped outside pulling on a jacket. "Oh. Hello, Gerrum."

He had the distinct impression she wasn't happy to see him and was hoping he'd walk on by, something he had no intention of doing. "Looks like you're going for a walk. Would you like company?"

She stood in place, fiddling with her zipper before finally stepping off the porch and walking toward him. Kody raised his head, but when he saw Gerrum, he yawned and went back to sleep.

"Were you planning to walk somewhere specific?" he asked.

She shook her head. "I just need to stretch my legs."

"Mount Dewey's good for that."

She seemed more solemn than usual, but as they walked, he introduced everyday topics and got her talking. She told him she'd had a dozen for dinner that night—eight tourists and four locals. She'd served pork ribs and dumplings with brownies for dessert. He said he was sorry he'd missed that. In turn, he talked about the group he'd taken up the Stikine that day—a couple and their three children—and that tomorrow he'd be taking a group of four fishermen on a two-day trip.

"Do you do many of those?"

"Terry, my business partner, does most of the longer trips on *Joyful*, but I usually do several a season. Gives us both a break when we switch off."

They reached the top of Mount Dewey, and Clen walked over to the edge. He stood next to her, but left plenty of space because he could tell she preferred that.

"They talked about the *Marjean* at dinner," she said.

The *Marjean* had been found drifting west of Port Alexander after being reported missing two days earlier.

Clen stared at the boats carving lines into the navy blue of the strait below. "They said the life raft and the crew's survival suits were still on board. It means they're all dead." She shivered. "Does it happen often, that a whole crew is lost?"

"More in winter when the crabbers go out. Seas are rougher. Boats ice up." But the real truth was commercial fishing was a dangerous profession and accidents happened all the time. The possibility something might go wrong was a fact of life when one relied on a boat. He lived with it the way millions lived with the risks involved in driving automobiles. He was as careful as he knew how to be, and he didn't think about it much.

"One of the men said the *Marjean* may have been hit by a freak wave."

He heard the question in her voice, one she wasn't asking out loud. "That wouldn't happen in this area, not with the islands serving as breakwaters. Our biggest concern here is tidal rips."

"There are accidents, though."

"We realize this is an unforgiving environment. We treat it with respect."

"Three of the crew have families. Five children in all."

There was no good response to that.

Clen gave him a distracted look. "Sorry I'm being such a gloomy Gus tonight. It got to me. The way they talked about it. As if it were no big deal."

"I think it's their version of whistling in the dark. They're not unfeeling, but they can't let it in if they want to keep on doing their jobs. You'll see. John will start a fund for the families, and everyone will pitch in."

"I read somewhere that the deadliest animals are usually the ones with the brightest colors. Frogs, caterpillars, fish. It's a warning to predators. Don't eat me, because I'll kill you. I think Alaska is like that. Beautiful but deadly."

"All part of its charm." He liked the bit about poisonous animals. He'd have to use it sometime.

After that, knowing when she was likely to go for a walk, he managed occasional encounters. Not often enough to cause her to change her routine to avoid him, but often enough to keep a conversation going.

~ ~ ~

Clen was clearing up after dinner when Gerrum walked in. "Humpbacks have been sighted near here," he said. "I'm going to take a look. Thought it might be something you'd enjoy seeing."

"You mean right now?"

"The sooner the better. Word is the whales are hanging around, but they might move on any time."

She pointed at the sink full of pots and pans. "I need to finish washing up."

"Tell you what. Come with me now, and I'll help you clean up afterward."

She stood frowning for a moment, then shrugged. "Hey, what am I thinking? I've never seen a humpback, and the dishes aren't going anywhere."

"That's the spirit."

~ ~ ~

As they neared the area where the whales had been reported, Gerrum told her to be on the lookout for blows that would appear like puffs of smoke and last about a second.

It was fifteen minutes before he spotted the first one. He pointed, and a moment later, another puff appeared that she saw. "What do we do now?"

"We move closer, and then we wait. If we're lucky, they may come over and check us out."

When they neared the whales, he slipped the engine into neutral. The boat slowed then moved gently with the current as they waited to see what the whales would do. When they began swimming in a decreasing arc around the *Joyful*, Clen and Gerrum smiled at each other. One whale moved in close and exhaled loudly, blowing up a smoky spray that drifted across their stern.

"Good grief, they're bigger than this boat!"

"Yep. They could take us out with a flip of their tails or a good nose bump."

That startled her, but she was too fascinated to let it stop her from stepping outside. Gerrum stayed at the helm as the whales continued to move around the boat, popping up periodically as if checking to see if the humans were still watching. Clen clapped her hands in appreciation as one sounded, its tail flukes outlined against the sky.

After a time, the whales moved off, and Gerrum put the engine in gear, turning in a wide, slow arc back to the east. Behind them, their wake glittered in the setting sun.

Clen came back inside. "That was am-m-azing."

"You're cold."

"F-freezing, but it was worth it."

He offered his jacket but she refused. "I'll make tea."

"I have a better idea." He held out a hand. "Come here."

She'd watched those hands, calm and competent, handling a boat, patting Kody, pointing out a moose. After a brief hesitation, she placed her hand in his and felt the smooth softness of palm, the rougher slide of callus. He pulled her close then snugged her into his side, wrapping his arm around her waist. The in and out of his breath pushed gently against her back, and the steady beat of the engine pulsed under her feet. Warmth radiated from him, turning her flesh and bones warm and liquid.

She turned her head. "Ger— "

His lips on hers.

Her mouth moved in surprised response. As if dreaming it, she turned to face him and his arm curved around her. The engine note changed as the *Joyful's* momentum bled off. His mouth shifted against hers as slowly, slowly the gentle swell rocking the boat nudged her into his arms. Closer, closer.

Dear God, how could she have forgotten how good this felt. A man's arms. A man's lips on hers. She trembled, but no longer with cold. A pulse of desire caught her by surprise, swinging, spinning her through space, past moons and planets. To this man, this moment, this blessed moment.

Her hands cupped his face holding on, her fingertips brushing through black satin hair, thumbs grazing over the firmness of cheekbones and jaw. If she were blind, this would be how she would know him. From the angle and plane of forehead. From the way his nose felt nestled next to hers, from the clean taste of his mouth.

A surprise, how familiar his arms felt. Yet brand new, his mouth against hers. His kiss releasing a spring of emotion that flowed cool and fresh inside her, washing away, at least for the moment, the debris of her past. Breathless, she rested her head on his shoulder, her lips against his neck, knowing she needed to step out of his arms before it was too late.

But, really, it was already too late. Too late to pretend seeing him didn't make her feel a shivering of promise. Too late to pretend she didn't want him. And much too late to walk away from him and from Wrangell without consequences.

"We need to get back." His words were rough with desire and a mute question.

"Yes." Not the yes he wanted, but more would be madness. She could so easily lose herself in him. She took a breath and raised her eyes to his. "I need—"

He touched her lips with a finger, holding in the rest of the words. Then he reached past her to put the engine back in gear.

~ ~ ~

Funny how something like that could sneak up on a person. Gerrum thought the simple reason he enjoyed being with Clen was because she provided intelligent companionship. But holding Clen, kissing her, he knew what he really wanted was anything but simple.

Was that the reason he hadn't pushed for more? Or was it the surprise? Surprise at the strength of his emotions as he held Clen. Was stepping away an acknowledgment those feelings were more than physical desire?

Backing off hadn't been easy. Especially since the next step with Clen would have to wait. He had a three-day fishing charter starting in the morning.

As he maneuvered *Joyful* into the slip, Clen jumped onto the dock to tie up, then she stood waiting for him, her hands tucked in her pockets. "Thank you for taking me."

"My pleasure."

She turned and began walking, and he fell into step beside her.

"Hard to imagine hunting one from a canoe, isn't it? Or for that matter, killing one for any reason. Moby Dick aside, they seemed so gentle."

Her frenetic speech worried him and chipped away at the pleasure he'd felt kissing her. Gone, as well, any sense of the intimacy they'd shared. An intimacy not measured in inches or millimeters.

"Of course, if they weren't gentle, it would be very scary to be near one, wouldn't it," she said, her voice quick and uneven.

"That it would."

"Do they always come that close?"

"Rarely."

She'd set a fast pace, and this last remark took them to the back door of the lodge. Kody loomed, ghostly in the dimness of the porch. He stretched, then strolled over to meet Clen who knelt and buried her hands in the thick fur of his neck. The old dog whined softly, trying to lick her face.

Gerrum watched the two, knowing Clen had just reestablished her distance from him. A light year or two. "About those dishes," he said.

"Oh, I'm not holding you to that. It won't take me more than a few minutes." Clen stood, keeping Kody between them, obviously wanting him to leave. "Thank you, Gerrum. The whales...I'll never forget seeing them."

And letting me hold you. Kiss you. Will you never forget that, as well?

He suspected she was going to try.

It was more like taming a wild thing than courting a woman, this back and forth with Clen. And what an odd, old-fashioned word that was—courting.

Until tonight, he didn't realize it was what he was doing.

~ ~ ~

Clen stepped inside the lodge then closed the door and stood leaning against it, breathing quickly as if she'd run all the way from the marina. And from the moment she felt the dock beneath her feet, she'd struggled not to do just that, run. Instead, she'd walked at a reasonable pace, talking with Gerrum, hoping to get things back to where they'd been before the whales. Before he kissed her.

It had been a perfect experience, seeing the whales. A sense of the sacred drawing near. She'd last felt that when awakening to the nuns chanting Vigils at Resurrection. In the predawn darkness, she'd listened to that wordless vibration until it seemed, after a time, to be more than sound.

Before leaving the abbey, she arose one morning and made her way to the dimly lit chapel. She'd sat in the back, and the chant had swept past like a procession of medieval ladies in long gowns. She'd listened to the words only after she had absorbed the rhythm and sweetness of the sound itself.

And what about being kissed by Gerrum? Was that sacred? A shimmer of longing, as surprising as it was upsetting, made her tremble. No, perhaps not sacred, but an experience she would remember to the end of her days.

For that brief span of time, kissing Gerrum, she'd forgotten her reluctance to accept the friendship he offered. Forgotten as well her regrets over her wasted life, her guilt, her worries about the future. It had all slipped away as effortlessly as a bird skimming the surface of a sun-bright sea.

But now she was back on solid ground.

With quick resolution, she stepped into the lodge's kitchen to find the dishes were put away. A note was left on the counter.

> *Clen, Heard you had a chance to see humpbacks with Gerrum. Definitely not an experience that should be followed by dirty dishes! Marian*

Trembling, Clen wrapped her arms around herself. She needed those dishes. Needed the ordinariness of soapy water and a mess put to rights. Without that transition, likely she would face a long, restless night.

Chapter Eighteen

Clen was finishing up her breakfast duties when John Jeffers came downstairs. "Terry just called. It's probably just a minor glitch of some sort. Nothing to worry about, but the *Ever Joyful* didn't come in as scheduled last night. More than likely, Gerrum decided to anchor somewhere, but Terry's been trying to raise him on the radio, and there's no answer. Weather's been good except for the fog this morning, so they should be fine. No reason to think they aren't okay." John's worried expression contradicted his meandering reassurances, sending a cold swoop of dread through Clen.

"We'll need to check it out, though. Probably a bunch will show up to search. You up to making coffee and sandwiches for anyone who wants them?"

"Of course."

John left after filling a thermos with the last of the coffee and taking two sandwiches Clen quickly assembled. She refilled both coffeepots. Marian finished calling to spread the word and came downstairs to help prepare more sandwiches from pork roast and meat loaf leftovers and the lunch meat one of the men thought to pick up.

One after another, the men came in, picked up two or three sandwiches, and filled their thermoses with coffee. They touched their caps with fingertips and uttered soft, deep, "Thank you, ma'ams," on their way out.

Clen nodded in reply, her throat too dry for speech.

"Good luck and Godspeed," Marian said.

As soon as the provisioning was finished, Clen went to her room and stared out at the inner harbor. The enveloping mist turned the masts and antennas of the remaining boats to light pencil marks against the glass.

When not knowing what was happening became unbearable, she grabbed a jacket and walked over to the marina. As usual, Kody accompanied her. A group was gathered around the harbormaster's office. The volume on the marine radio was turned up so everyone could hear the searchers reporting their positions with quick, terse words interspersed with the crackle and hiss of static.

"North of Wrangell Island, fog is thick as a fricking blizzard."

From the muttered conversation of the people around her, Clen learned that fog throughout the area had grounded search aircraft. Fog also made the water search more difficult. Boats had to circle coves that in clear weather could be checked with a quick glance, and searchers had to take care not to run into rocks or each other.

She found a place to sit on an upturned crate, near enough to hear but far enough from the others to discourage anyone from striking up a conversation. Kody settled at her side and she rested a hand on his head, grateful today, more than ever, for the old dog's presence.

Time dragged, with no sign of the missing boat. Clen's body ached from being clenched like a fist, but every time she managed to relax, after a minute or two, her muscles tensed again. She gnawed on a knuckle until the sudden metallic taste of blood startled her into stopping.

She reminded herself of what Mary John once said about worry. That it was nothing more than a misuse of the imagination. But would Mary John be able to quell her worries if she were sitting where Clen was?

The nun would pray of course, but in Clen's view, it wasn't honorable, after ignoring God for so many years, to turn to Him only when she needed something. She and God may have begun, with Mary John's help, a rapprochement of sorts but they were not yet on speaking terms.

Instead of praying she tried to empty her mind, but her thoughts kept spinning out of control, bringing her images of Gerrum—maneuvering the *Joyful* into her berth, watching a moose, talking calmly about the dangers he faced. Those images alternated with ones of his body drifting amidst broken planking, his hair swaying like black sea grass in the current.

160

Hours passed, and the frustration in the voices of the searchers and the worry on the faces of those waiting for news, chipped steadily away at her. The mist caught in her hair and condensed into droplets that slid down her cheeks, pseudo tears in place of the ones she refused to shed. She hugged her knees, rocking, trying to ease the tightness in her chest and stomach. Kody whined softly. His tongue swiped at her cheek, and she leaned her forehead against his wet ruff.

Late in the day, boats came in to gas up and the men ate in quick shifts before using the rest of the daylight to continue searching. Clen stood at the stove in the lodge's kitchen, her back to the room, scrambling eggs with onions and cheese while Marian made more sandwiches.

While they ate, the men talked.

"Damn, if it ain't as thick as I ever seen it."

"Couldn't see an effing oil tanker in this soup. Damn good thing I hear real fine."

"I was back side of Deer Island. Come round the corner real slow and easy. Almost bashed old Hank coming the other way. Scared me shitless."

"Sure wouldn't want to get lost with no tourists. Gerrum's likely got his hands full."

"Odd that radio of his ain't working. Terry said it's new. I don't like it. Maybe we need to be looking for green planks on the shore."

"Hell, you think he got hit?"

"Or got caught in a rip. Sure ain't good we ain't hearing nothin'."

By the time the men shuffled out, Clen was so nauseated she barely made it to her room where she hung over the toilet, heaving without effect. She hadn't yet eaten breakfast when John gave her the news, and she'd been unable to eat since.

She washed her face and walked into the bedroom. Gerrum's book lay where she'd left it after reading it. She picked it up, turned it over, and looked at the man pictured there. A man whose quiet eyes asked questions she didn't want to answer. A man with a quick mind and a slow, thoughtful tongue. A gentle man. It would matter to her if he wasn't found.

She put the book down and returned to her silent vigil on the dock. Most of the people who'd waited during the long day had gone home. As she sat in the steadily increasing gloom, random memories flicked through her mind until one snagged and caught—the day Mary John asked her, "What do you want people to say about you at your funeral?"

"Hey, she moved!"

With a quick gesture, Mary John had waved away the impudent comment and waited for Clen to come up with a serious answer.

"I guess I'd want someone to say I made a difference."

"Hitler made a difference."

That was the difficulty with Mary John. Unconsidered answers didn't satisfy her.

"Well, obviously not that kind of difference. I...want to leave the world a better place."

"Better in what way?"

"When I figure it out, you'll be the first one I'll tell."

Mary John had continued to assess her with a grave expression. "Every action we take or fail to take changes the world, Clen."

She closed her eyes, willing the memory away, but it refused to go.

"Do you realize you never speak of your family?" Mary John said.

"I've told you all about Paul."

"But not the rest of your family."

"Well, there's Mom and Dad, Jason, and Joshua. And me, of course. Mom and Dad live in Colorado Springs and Jason lives in Denver. Oh, and he got married. So I have a sister-in-law. Nancy's her name."

"And Joshua?"

She hadn't meant to mention Josh but his name and Jason's were so linked in her memory she sometimes forgot to separate them. "He's...he died. A long time ago."

"Do you want to tell me about it?"

No. She didn't, even though that was what these meetings with Mary John were supposed to be about—the events that led to her abandonment of her marriage and her Atlanta life. Not just her husband's infidelity. That discovery only the tipping point.

Mary John walked her over to one of the garden benches, and they sat side by side in silence while Clen ordered her thoughts and got her voice to work. "When I was eighteen and Joshua and Jason were ten, Josh got sick. Leukemia. At first we were hopeful he'd get better, but by the end of my sophomore year in college we knew he wouldn't." She realized she was rubbing her hands together in a desperate washing movement. In order to stop, she sat on them.

"I spent most of the summer reading to him. Sometimes I'd look up to see the pain in his eyes. When it got bad, he whimpered softly and repetitively, like a newborn kitten. It was unbearable, but none of us had any choice but to bear it."

Memory had tightened in a band around her chest, shutting off her breath, and a high-pitched ringing filled her ears. Black spots danced and expanded in her vision and the bench melted away from under her. Such a relief to slide into the dark.

"Okay, Clen, deep breath. Now another one."

She had been lying on the ground and Mary John was kneeling next to her, rubbing one of her hands. A pale sky arched above and a leaf crackled under her cheek.

"Don't try to get up yet."

No, much better to lie here, eyes closed. What must it be like under the earth? Dark, of course. She relaxed against the ground, breathing when Mary John commanded it. After a time, the nun helped her back onto the bench and sat next to her. Without Mary John's hand holding hers, it would have been a simple matter to simply float off into the pale sky.

"Watching someone die of a terrible disease." Mary John's words tugged her firmly back. "Seeing their pain, not being able to stop it—it's the most difficult thing we ever have to bear."

As Mary John spoke, the images returned like smoke condensing back into ash—the dim room with its too-large hospital bed. A plaid blanket covering a small boy, pale and bruised, all bones and translucent skin—like a baby bird before it got any feathers. The cover on the bed perfectly smooth, as if when their mother tucked Josh in, he was already dead.

Clen pulled in a breath that coated her lungs with ice. So cold. "I was with him when he died."

Mary John was silent. She was praying, of course. Prayer didn't do any good but it might be comforting to believe it did. Too bad Clen couldn't manage it. Mary John's arm came around her and brought with it warmth. What was that saying? Warm as houses? Or was it safe as houses? Not that either made any sense.

The past. As ephemeral as the glimmer from a star, light years from Earth. Starlight thousands of years old. And if the night were clear and she looked up, it would fall on her and, in less than a heartbeat, be extinguished.

~ ~ ~

The fog continued into the second day, and waiting on the dock became unbearable. Instead, Clen walked. Where didn't matter. In the fog, everything was obscured—buildings, trees, water, people. Sounds were muffled, distant. No birds sang, no voices called.

Moving through downtown Wrangell, she felt like the last person left on the island. She paused so Kody could rest, and the quiet came and pressed heavily on her shoulders. A quiet that should be a relief, but wasn't.

For wrapped in silence and blinded by fog, she saw clearly—leaving Wrangell at the end of the season was a retreat, a giving up. A trading of the messiness of choice for a life as dull and featureless as the fog. A muffled life where only in memory would she watch a moose meander out of the trees or a whale break the surface of the sea to examine her with a large, calm eye.

A life without Gerrum.

Had he not gone missing, what would it have taken for her to admit she loved him?

Chapter Nineteen

The morning after the whales, Gerrum set off on a three-day trip with two Canadians. They were ideal clients—pleasant, undemanding, competent fishermen who needed very little hand-holding.

After they anchored the first night, Gerrum discovered the radio was receiving but wasn't sending. He wasn't really worried, though, until the next morning, when the engine wouldn't start, and he discovered the cable to the alternator was cut. It meant they were stuck until someone found them, and when the fog settled in, he knew that might be awhile.

The clients fished off the side of the boat or played cards, Gerrum cooked the meals, and everyone had plenty of time to rest. Throughout, Gerrum thought about who might be responsible for the sabotage, but his speculations went nowhere. He simply didn't have enough information.

His thoughts then turned to Clen, trying to figure out why she got to him the way she did. And why he would rather spend time with her instead of Hailey, who was clearly more available. Was it a matter of craving something he couldn't have? Would "having" Clen eliminate his growing desire for her?

He didn't think so. After weeks of slow discoveries, he suspected he'd never get to the end of what he wanted to know about her and share with her. Although it was unclear how anyone ever did know for certain one person would be sufficient to engage mind, heart, and body for a year, let alone a lifetime.

Perhaps it was unknowable.

One thing he did know. If he didn't make it back to Wrangell, what he'd regret most was never having made love to Clen.

~ ~ ~

Late in the afternoon of the second day, the fog lifted, and a Coast Guard plane spotted the *Ever Joyful* in a remote cove on Kupreanof Island. The nearest searcher was dispatched to check. Waiting for his report, the people around Clen stood or sat without speaking, most of them with their arms clutched around themselves as if to ward off a chill. Even the little girl who'd been restless and whiny stopped fussing and allowed her mother to hold her tightly.

"Rescue Base, this is the *Betty Sue*. I have *Ever Joyful* in view." A long pause filled with the hiss of empty air. "Rescue Base, we see three aboard...all waving at us. Everyone looking just—" A cheer broke out, overriding the rest of the transmission.

Clen's eyes welled with tears. She stood, but when her vision filled with black dots, she sat back down and took a deep breath. As the faintness receded, she became aware that she ached all over as if she'd just spent days clinging to a rock face. Something that might have been easier than what she had been doing.

She stood slowly. Everyone was laughing, talking, hugging. She turned and walked unsteadily back to the lodge. In the kitchen, hands shaking, she poured milk and unwrapped a leftover sandwich. She ate quickly, stopping to wipe away tears of relief only when they threatened to drip onto the food.

Marian snapped on a light. "Oh, Clen, you okay?"

Clen, sitting, staring at nothing, an empty glass and plate in front of her, looked up, startled. "Oh. Fine. You want a sandwich?"

"Right now, I don't care if I never see another one. You heard the news?"

"Yes."

"They'll be here about midnight."

~ ~ ~

Given the hour, Gerrum was surprised by the number of people standing on the dock as the *Joyful* was towed into Reliance Harbor. Seeing that gathering of friends, neighbors, and even strangers, he knew he'd been wise to suggest to his clients they let him do the talking.

He waded into the crowd, shaking hands and thanking everyone, looking for Clen. Although distracted, he answered the questions being tossed at him with care.

"Yeah, engine trouble...nope, not a sound from her. Must have been a bad area for the radio. Appreciate everyone coming out to look for us...yeah, good thing the fog lifted or we'd still be out there."

He reached the edge of the crowd without seeing Clen, but Hailey was there, standing apart. He walked over to her, and she lifted eyes filled with tears to his. Then she threw her arms around him and hugged him fiercely before releasing him. As if to reassure herself he was real, she gave his arm one last pat before she turned and walked quickly away. John, who'd been watching, cleared his throat, then apparently thought better of it, and said nothing.

Gradually the crowd dispersed until Terry, the two clients, John, and Gerrum, stifling a disappointment that felt bone-deep, were left to walk back to the lodge. Clen was there, sitting on the porch with Kody. Gerrum stayed behind while the others went inside.

Clen stood. "It's good to see you, Gerrum."

"It's good to see you as well."

To his relief, she stepped into his arms, and as her lips pressed against his, any puzzlement over why this woman filled his heart dissipated. She just did.

He pulled away with difficulty. "There are some things I need to tell the Jeffers. Do you want to come in or wait here?"

"I'll wait here."

Reluctantly, he left her and went upstairs to the Jeffers' private quarters.

Marian hugged him. "Oh, Gerrum, we were so worried." She stepped back still holding onto his shoulders. "You okay?"

"I could use a shower."

She wrinkled her nose and smiled. "True. I'm so glad you're okay." She patted his cheek, blinking rapidly.

"Yeah. Me too."

"Grab a cold one and tell us what the hell happened," John said as Marian pulled a fresh pizza from the oven. "And it better be good. You scared the begeesus out of us."

"Alternator wire was cut, the radio disabled." Gerrum took a long swallow of beer, then rolled the icy can across his forehead, remembering how he'd felt when he discovered the damage was deliberate. Good thing he'd had time to cool off.

Terry blanched. "God, Gerr. You're saying someone messed with the boat?"

"That's exactly what I'm saying." He waved away the offer of pizza.

"Going to be some mighty angry fisherman if it gets out you were sabotaged," John said. "Any idea who?"

Gerrum shook his head. "And it's hard knowing someone dislikes me enough for something like this."

"Maybe it was aimed at Terry." Marian nodded at his partner. "Don't you usually do the multi-day trips?"

"Yep."

"You riled anybody lately?" Gerrum asked even though he'd gone through that scenario and dismissed it. Easygoing Terry seemed to be a universal favorite around the harbor.

"Gosh, Gerrum. I don't think so."

"Another possibility is a kid, playing a trick," John said.

"Seemed a bit too involved for that." Gerrum shook his head in frustration. "For sure it's someone who knows engines."

"What about your clients? Maybe somebody was trying to give them a scare," Marian said.

"Doesn't look like it. We went through their enemy lists while they were wiping me out at poker."

"Well, there is one person in Wrangell who doesn't seem to like you much, Gerr," John said.

"Elmer Cantrell," Marian said.

"I thought of him, but I wasn't sure he was smart enough for this."

It was, after all, a neat, clever trick. With the alternator cable cut, there was enough juice to start the engine to begin the trip, and once started, it ran fine. But after he shut it off, it wasn't going to start again until the batteries were recharged. The job on the radio was almost as slick. Enough damage to prevent transmissions while leaving reception intact. They'd actually listened in while the search progressed.

The main danger had been getting caught in a tidal rip with a dead engine. Or not being found. And if Elmer wasn't responsible, it meant someone else must be hating him from the shadows, a thought that made him feel wretched.

"Elmer may not be too intellectual, but the sonofabitch knows engines," John said.

"Does he still think I'm here to get Wrangell Island turned over to the Tlingits?"

"Naw. Nobody'd listen. Finally gave up on it. Come to think of it, man's had a change of focus lately." John's tone changed to a nasal twang. "Regular lady-killer, that there Gerrum. Moving in slick as snot, taking all the women for hisself."

What the...?

"Always having morning coffee with Hailey, or going off to see bears and what have you with Clen," John continued. "Fair sticks in a man's craw. Makes him think it's high time a certain someone was taught a lesson, not to mention, them there ladies could sure use protecting."

"You quoting directly?" The words, although spoken by John, sent a pulse of unease up Gerrum's spine.

"More or less. Fact is, Elmer does have a flair for language I can't quite match. But that's the gist."

"He's a sneaky little weasel," Marian said. "I wouldn't put it past him to kick a kitten if he thought no one was watching."

"Nobody ever lost, betting on Elmer being mean and stupid," John said.

"Did he really say I needed to be taught a lesson?"

John frowned. "I was running my mouth, but come to think of it, he did say something like that, six, seven days ago. Mostly, I ignore the man. Nobody's good as Elmer at poisoning a person's outlook on a perfectly fine day."

"Has he been around?" Gerrum asked.

"He helped search yesterday," Terry said. "Part of today too, seems to me. Or at least he pretended to."

"He wasn't at the harbor when we came in." Gerrum had

looked because, despite doubting Elmer's competence, the man was still at the top of his suspect list. "You know, if it is Elmer, that gives me an idea or two."

By the time he finished telling the others what those ideas were, Terry was grinning. "Hot damn, Gerr. We're going to have us some fun."

Gerrum made his excuses then and went to Clen.

~ ~ ~

How strange that it would turn out to be so simple. With her hand tucked in Gerrum's, her worries, questions, and doubts faded to insignificance. She felt, suddenly, as young and hopeful as she had going off to Marymead the first time.

In Gerrum's kitchen, she leaned against the counter while he chopped onions, and sizzled butter in a skillet. While he worked, he told her about the sabotage and what he'd done while they were stranded. In turn, she told him what she'd done: the sandwiches and coffee, the endless waiting, the worry.

He lifted the skillet off the burner and slid the omelet onto a plate, cut it, and transferred half to a second plate he then handed her. Clen had eaten dinner, but she was still hungry enough from her two-day fast to eat her share.

When they finished, Gerrum got out bowls and a scoop. "I have homemade peach or Rocky Road?"

"An omelet and ice cream. Are you trying for a heart attack, Gerrum Kirsey?"

"I think I recently proved my heart's in pretty good shape." He met her gaze, making her heart jump.

"Peach. Just a small scoop."

He pulled a Tupperware container out of the freezer. So, was that how he spent his evenings? Churning exotic flavors of ice cream? It was only one of the things she didn't yet know about him—ordinary, everyday things—whether he squeezed the toothpaste in the middle, did the daily crossword, was a morning or an evening person. All unknown. All waiting to be known...but only if she had the courage.

She curled a bit of pale orange onto her spoon. Gerrum took a small scoop as well. It wouldn't take either of them long to eat. She shivered, telling herself it was because of the ice cream.

Gerrum picked up his empty bowl and carried it to the sink. She watched him, trying to decide what she wanted to happen next. Easier, to know what she didn't want. She didn't want the evening to end, not without discovering if kissing her meant as much to him as kissing him did to her. "I-uh...I read your book."

He turned toward her with a questioning look.

"And I liked it. A lot." She felt the heat of a blush start at her toes and travel up her torso until it emerged at her neck. "That was inane, wasn't it."

"Oh, I don't know." He sat across from her. "It's certainly preferable to a more erudite slice and dice."

"I thought only crudités were sliced and diced, not books."

"Shows you're not an author."

No, she was a woman alone with a man who'd kissed her with more than friendly intent.

As suddenly as it gusted through her, the giddiness retreated, and the past came to crouch beside her. She clenched her hands, then twisted them together until Gerrum reached out and took the nearest hand between his. She looked at their hands, Gerrum's blunt and sun-darkened, hers pale and delicate in comparison. Gradually, the steadiness of his grip calmed her frantically scurrying thoughts.

"You want to know what I did, while we waited to be rescued?" he said.

"Didn't you already tell me?"

He shook his head and waved his free hand as if to dismiss his earlier words. "I thought how nice it would be to just...talk to you."

She forced herself to meet his eyes. "I'd like that, too."

"If you're willing to try, I think we'll be more comfortable in the other room."

In the soft dark of the living room, they sat on the sofa and he settled an arm around her. After a moment, she relaxed against him. "While you were missing, I thought about you," she said. "How if you weren't found, it would make a difference to me. I regretted I never told you—" She struggled to steady her voice. "I care about you, and I'm so thankful...so relieved I got this chance."

"Me, too." Then, once again, he was kissing her.

For a time, she gave in to emotion and sensation, relishing a growing desire, but as that desire gathered momentum, she forced herself to pull away. "When we're kissing, I have trouble thinking straight."

"Is that a bad thing?" He traced her eyebrow and ran a finger down her cheek and under her chin, tipping her face to meet his gaze.

She gazed back, knowing that before this went any further, it was only fair to give him a hint of what he was dealing with. "I've never been much good at relationships."

He cocked his head, examining her. "They're works in progress for all of us, Clen. I've lived alone a long time. That might make a person think I don't do such a great job, either."

Okay, he wasn't going to be easy to warn off, but she already knew that. Hadn't she made it as clear as she knew how he shouldn't bother getting to know her? Did he pay attention? No. He just kept at her, like Saint did, like Paul, until she forgot to be always on guard.

Paul. The thought transformed desire into unease, and she pushed away from Gerrum's touch. "My ex-husband would be happy to tell you how inadequate I am." She closed her eyes against the hot burn of tears. She'd tried to believe Paul's adultery was all due to a lack in him and not her. Unsuccessfully, it seemed.

Gerrum pulled her back into his arms and settled her head on his shoulder. "Did this husband of yours ever concern himself with your needs, Clen?" The soft words might have been posed by her thoughts rather than by the man whose arms encircled her. Gerrum continued to hold her, letting his question simmer, and that gentleness calmed and comforted her in a way nothing else likely could.

He rubbed his cheek on her hair. "You know, we don't have to figure it all out tonight."

She nestled into him, too exhausted not to let it be. It was enough, for the moment, to have Gerrum's arms around her. A comfort after the stress of the last two days that she wanted to savor. He shifted, and she realized she'd come close to dozing off.

"Sorry, Clen. My arm was going numb." He wiggled it as she sat up and ran fingers through her hair.

"It's time we get you back to the lodge. Although I want

you to know it's not my first choice."

She stilled and turned to look at him. If she wasn't so exhausted, she might have weighed her reply, thought it over, but sometime tonight she'd stopped hiding from this man. "It's not my choice either." She took a breath and said the rest. "But it's best. At least for now."

She stood to find she was weaving with weariness. He helped her with her jacket, then walked her back to the lodge on the quiet streets. At the back door, he turned her and placed his hands on her arms. When she met his eyes, his expression made her knees go weak. "I'll be busy tomorrow morning, but I'll see you in the afternoon."

He didn't kiss her again. She was sorry about that, but also relieved.

Chapter Twenty

In the morning, before leaving for the marina, Gerrum called Anders Tolliff. The policeman came ambling along the wharf in plain view of everyone getting ready to head out for the day.

"This about you apologizing for running out of gas and causing a hell of an uproar?" he asked, coming aboard the *Joyful* where Gerrum and Terry were having coffee.

Gerrum poured a cup for Anders. "Didn't run out of gas. Need to show you a couple of things."

Anders set the cup down with a sigh. "Nobody ever invites me just for coffee."

Gerrum led Anders below and showed him the cut wire, then back topside to see the inoperative mike.

Anders sat down and picked up his coffee. "You got any ideas?"

"Got an idea. Nothing I can prove. Yet."

Anders stared at him a moment, then nodded. "Best you let us deal with it. I'll have a deputy stop by, see if he can pick up any prints."

"Doubt you'll find much, what with the mucking about I did trying to figure things out."

"Always worth a shot. I'll send someone over right away."

Anders left, and a half hour later his deputy came, dusted, and departed. John arrived, and while he and Terry cleaned up the mess left by the dusting powder, Gerrum repaired the alternator.

"It ain't going to be easy, nailing Elmer on this, you think?" Terry said.

"Expect not."

"All this fingerprinting. Won't do no good if he wore gloves. Besides, they probably don't have any of Elmer's prints to check against."

"When you're at the bar these next couple of nights, stand old Elmer a drink and collect the can."

"Hey. I saw that in a movie once. That works, huh?"

"Can't hurt to try."

Gerrum left to put in motion his part of the plan to nudge Elmer into the open.

His first stop was Maude's Café, because if there was one thing a person in Wrangell could count on, it was Maude's love of gossip and her talent and dedication to spreading it around. His plan had a chance only if John was correct—that no one ever lost betting on Cantrell's stupidity.

Gerrum was counting on it.

~ ~ ~

Clen snapped awake with tears on her cheeks and lay still trying to remember why she'd been crying. But the dream slipped away, leaving only the wetness on her face and a tightness in her chest. Then she remembered. Gerrum had been found. He was safe.

She climbed out of bed and went to the window to find the *Joyful*'s mast was right where it belonged.

After breakfast, to pass the time until she would see Gerrum, Clen grabbed her sketchbook and headed into the morning with Kody. She decided to walk to the petroglyph beach where black boulders etched with ancient graffiti lay. With the sun dodging in and out of clouds, the play of light and shadow would keep her hands and mind occupied for a time. Besides, the carvings were Alaskan and drawings of them might please Hailey and the odd tourist or two.

When they reached the beach, Kody found a sunny spot and lay down while Clen went in search of a carving. She located one and sat drawing it. After a time, her pencil lifted off the paper, and she sat staring at the water lapping among the rocks, sliding and rippling—now a dark tea color, now the shine of liquid gold. She thought about seeing Gerrum later and felt something she hadn't felt since those heady days at Marymead when a call on the intercom meant Saint was downstairs waiting for her. She shook her head, irritated with herself. It was well past time for her to stop dwelling on the past.

Something, incidentally, with which Sister Mary John at Resurrection concurred. "Sometimes, Clen, it's best to let go. Not try to remember. Unless..."

Ah yes. Always the other shoe dropping in her conversations with Mary John. That time the *unless* had been, "unless the past is distorting the present."

But the past always distorted the present. It had, after all, led to the present. Clen sighed. With a sudden rumble, her stomach reminded her of the meals she'd missed while Gerrum was lost. She collected Kody and walked back as far as Maude's Café. Usually she avoided Maude, who was a snoop and a gossip, but today, hunger overruled reticence.

When her hamburger came, she set aside a bite for Kody, who was waiting by the front door, then ate the rest quickly, before Maude could come at her with a coffee refill and prying remarks. At the moment, Maude was busy, talking to a man sitting at the counter. Clen glanced over to see Maude give the man an arch look.

"It ain't no surprise, you ask me. Terry and Gerrum just ain't the same kind. Word is Terry ain't a bit happy about the changes Gerrum's proposing. Didn't expect he'd resort to sabotage, though. But then, I'm no psychic."

Astonished, Clen stared at Maude. Well, the woman had part of the story right. As for the rest, was Maude flapping her mouth as usual, or did she really believe Terry and Gerrum were having problems?

The man said something Clen couldn't make out, but she had no difficulty hearing Maude's response. "Sat right there and told me hisself, he did."

Clen strained to make out the man's response but all she heard was the deep rumble of his voice.

Maude bristled. "Well, course he didn't come right out and say it. He's Native, ain't he? Said the person what done it should have knowed better. Clear as the nose on your face who he's talking about."

Funny. Maude seemed to be implying her information came directly from Gerrum. But why would he lead her to think he and Terry were having problems?

Clen left money on the table, picked up Kody's treat, and walked thoughtfully back to the lodge.

~ ~ ~

By afternoon, snippets of gossip about Gerrum and Terry being close to a break-up floated around Wrangell like drifts of fog. An hour before diners were due to begin showing up, the screen door squeaked open and Gerrum came into the lodge's kitchen. Clen barely had the presence of mind to turn off the burner before throwing her arms around him. He pulled away first, his eyes filled with merriment.

"Well now, if that's the greeting I can expect, guess I'll have to stop by more often."

"Do you think you will?"

He nuzzled her neck. "Will what?"

It tickled and she chuckled. "Stop by."

"Oh indeed, I shall."

He kissed her again then stepped back taking her hands in his. "I'm going to be tied up tonight, and I have a trip tomorrow. But tomorrow evening is for us. I'll come by after dinner, if that's okay?"

"I think that's a marvelous plan."

He cupped her face. "I'll see you then."

He left, and she looked after him, feeling surprise at the way she'd stepped into his arms—as if it was where she belonged.

~ ~ ~

When Clen opened the back door after dinner, Kody lifted his head to quiz her with a soft whine. She patted him and told him to stay. He licked her hand then put his head back down.

The sun was low in the sky and hidden by clouds, but a narrow band of clear tangerine lined the horizon. The calm waters of the harbor gathered that illumination and reflected it back. She stood for a time breathing slowly and deeply, focusing on the soft sound of boats rubbing against fenders, water lapping against pilings, and the random slap of a fish. Then she began walking toward the marina and its forest of masts and antennas, unmoving against the darkening vault of the sky.

177

When she walked up to the *Joyful*, reached out, and stroked a finger along the railing, Gerrum stepped out of the shadows on the deck.

She jerked her hand off the rail and pressed it to her heart. "I didn't know you'd be here. I just..." Her hand made a vague movement.

"I'm waiting for Elmer to show up."

"You think he's the saboteur?"

"I do."

"You're waiting on your own?"

"Terry's at the bar, grousing about me asking him to stay on board tonight, saying he's not going to do it. We're hoping Elmer will see it as a golden opportunity. If he does head this way, Terry and John will be right behind him."

"Do you think it'll work?"

"John said nobody ever lost betting on Elmer's stupidity. I hope he's right because I'd like to get this settled."

"I better go, then."

He stretched out a hand and stroked her cheek. "Tomorrow night. That's ours, no matter what happens tonight with Elmer."

"I'll hold you to it." Then she turned and walked away, while she still could.

~ ~ ~

Gerrum awoke and stretched. Sleeping on the *Joyful* always left him feeling stiff in the morning, which was one reason he was glad to leave most of the overnight trips to Terry.

The tin can alarm he'd strung when he finally decided to lie down was undisturbed. It meant the attempt to lure Elmer into action had been unsuccessful. Yawning, he stepped onto the dock and looked around. It was quiet. No people and no boats getting underway, although that was hardly a surprise, given the early hour.

Judging it unlikely Elmer would bother the boat in broad daylight, Gerrum headed home for a shower and breakfast. When he returned to the marina, he met Elmer coming toward him along the dock. If they'd been on a Wrangell street, Elmer would no doubt have made his usual big show of crossing to the other side, but that was problematic on the narrow dock.

Gerrum moved to the middle to make it even more difficult for the other man. Cantrell's stride hitched, but then he continued toward Gerrum, his mouth working. Gerrum didn't realize what Elmer was planning until a gob of spit hit his boot. He stopped and looked from it to the other man.

Elmer, who'd also stopped, glared at him. "And there's more where that come from."

Gerrum gave it a beat, then nodded pleasantly. "Yeah. I figured that out awhile ago. You're just full of shit."

Elmer looked startled, then his expression settled into contempt.

"I also hear you're good with engines," Gerrum said, his tone conversational.

"Sure am. Everbody knows it." Elmer managed to sound both disdainful and proud at the same time.

"Seems my engine had some recent attention from an expert."

Elmer's face went through a series of expressions that were interesting to watch. He'd be a real gift to anyone playing poker with him. Gerrum waited until finally the other man's expression settled into a smirk.

"I say what happened was a pansy Tlingit lawyer don't know enough not to get hisself stranded."

Gerrum noticed, although Elmer hadn't, that two heads had popped up on nearby boats, and wasn't it nice the way sound carried so clearly over water?

"I doubt most folks are thinking that," Gerrum said, raising his voice slightly so the listeners didn't need to strain. "But they might be thinking about the fact you don't like me, and some of them heard you say you'd like to teach me a lesson. Add in someone messing with my boat, and it doesn't take a law degree to put it together and come up with some pretty strong conclusions."

Elmer reared back slightly, as if Gerrum had delivered a light punch. "You can't go round saying shit like that with no evidence."

"Sure I can."

"'Sides, everbody thinks Terry done it."

Gerrum smiled and shook his head. "Now why would Terry do that, given his livelihood is tied up with mine?"

"He don't like you no more. Told me hisself last night."

"Naw. Terry was messing with you in order to get hold of something with your fingerprints on it. You know the police dusted my boat yesterday. Turns out they found some nice clear prints right where it counted most, and that beer can Terry picked up last night will give them something to compare to."

All the fingerprints had been smudged, but from the look on Elmer's face, Gerrum saw that he'd scored.

It didn't hold Cantrell down for long, though. "Hell, nobody's goin to believe a damn half-breed over me."

"Don't be too sure of that." The speaker was Rog Remington, who'd been taking it all in from his boat. Elmer spun around as Rog stepped onto the dock. A second man joined him and the two sauntered up to Gerrum and Elmer. "Mighty interesting conversation you two are having," Rog said.

Elmer's face turned red. "Ain't none of your affair."

"Sure it is. Didn't I just spend two days looking for Gerrum here? Seems to me I got gas money and about twenty hours of boat time tied into this here conversation."

"Me too," the other man pitched in.

"Let's just make sure I got this straight," Rog continued. "You have reason to believe Elmer here might be responsible for the sabotage?"

Gerrum nodded, beginning to enjoy himself. "Got to tell you, it was a slick piece of work. At first I didn't think Elmer had the smarts for it, but I hear he's good with engines, and he just confirmed it."

"Didn't confirm nothing."

Gerrum shrugged. "If it looks like a slug and leaves a slimy trail everywhere it goes, chances are good it's a slug."

"What the hell's that sposed to mean?" Cantrell's expression was close to a snarl.

"You want to confirm for us you ain't involved, Elmer?" Rog's voice was quiet, but menacing.

"Damn right, I didn't cut no alternator cable. Gerrum here can take his suspicions and shove them up his ass."

"That's funny," Gerrum said.

"What?" Elmer's face was nearly purple.

"About you knowing the alternator cable was cut. Did you

know that, Rog? Mike?"

Both men shook their heads.

"Is that what happened?" Rog asked.

"That's exactly what happened. Seems to me the only way Elmer here would know it would be if he did the cutting."

"Now, listen here. T'weren't nothing but a good guess. That's how I'd do it, if I was planning something with that kind of engine. Don't mean I done it." As he spoke, Elmer tried to sidle away from Rog and Mike.

Gerrum saw Rog exchange a look with Mike and a nod, then the two linked hands under Cantrell's ass and heaved him off the dock. Elmer surfaced spluttering and cursing, then swam to the edge of the dock and began to haul himself out of the water. The two fishermen stood watching, with arms folded. Elmer finally made it onto the dock where he collapsed into a shivering puddle.

Rog nudged at him with the toe of his boot. "Before you head off to get out of them wet clothes, Mike and I just want to get a couple of things real clear. One, we'll be sharing the gist of what happened here with every fisherman in the harbor. Expect any of us ever see you within fifty feet of either of Gerrum's boats, you'll get another chance to snort up sea water."

He paused. Elmer was shivering violently, but he didn't attempt to stand.

"Second, I want to hear you made a real nice contribution to the rescue fund. What do you think, Mike? Couple thousand sound about right to you?"

"Yep. That's the number I was thinking." Mike nodded, looking thoughtful.

"Okay. Anything else? Gerrum, you got any conditions for our boy here before he gets him some dry clothes?"

"I think you've got it covered." Anything he pushed would just make Elmer more resentful.

Rog reached down, grabbed Cantrell by the arm, and lifted him to his feet. "It occurs to me there's one other thing. I'd sure like to hear an apology both to those of us did the searching as well as to Gerrum here. Sure hope that don't require another dip in the drink."

"No. Don't got no call to do that. I'm sorry. Real sorry."

No question, Elmer was telling the truth. He *was* sorry. But his sorry was all about being caught and punished.

"You get going then, before you shake the damn dock to pieces. Mighty careless of you, falling in that way." Rog gave Elmer a little push and Cantrell scurried up the dock without looking back.

"Almost worth that twenty hours," Rog said thoughtfully, watching Elmer go. Then he chuckled. "Can't remember the last time something felt that good."

~ ~ ~

Dinner seemed interminable, but Clen finally finished and stepped outside. Gerrum was sitting on the step next to Kody, scratching the old dog's ears.

She pulled in a breath to steady herself and sat next to him. "Hello there."

He turned his head and smiled. "Hello there, yourself." He slid an arm around her, pulling her close.

So where had the feeling that danced through her all day gone? The anticipation of just this: being back in Gerrum's arms. But in this moment, anticipation was replaced with uncertainty.

She dropped her head on his shoulder. "I'm kind of nervous about what comes next." It was odd, though. She didn't have any difficulty admitting it to Gerrum.

He removed his arm and took one of her hands between his. "Moving a bit too fast for you, is it?"

"Yes." She breathed out in relief that he understood even if she couldn't explain. "I'm sorry. It's just, I haven't had much experience with this sort of thing."

"I know a way to fix that."

"Just jump in, right? None of that toe-in-the-water stuff."

He shook his head, still bent over her hand. "A toe in the water may be exactly what's needed." He looked up and held her gaze with his, his thumb gently smoothing over the inside of her wrist, making her breath catch. "There's no need for us to rush, Clen."

Her confidence seeped back. Determined, she pulled in another breath, stood, and held out a hand to him. "Come," she commanded, not caring if everyone in Wrangell saw them.

When they reached his house and stepped inside, she turned to face him. "I want to know how we are together. Slow or fast."

His lips curved, and his eyes gleamed.

"So how about it, Gerrum Kirsey?" Her voice shook as did her knees, but she held herself still, waiting for his answer.

"Come here."

He walked her into the living room, sat on the sofa, and pulled her onto his lap. Then he cupped her face with his hands and began kissing her in lingering exploration. Her nerves steadied, and she settled comfortably against him, enjoying the touch of his lips. There was passion in Gerrum's kisses that was all the more intriguing because it was held in such careful check.

But as they continued to kiss, Clen's left brain insistently pushed its way into her awareness, eroding the certainty she'd begun to feel. She pulled back and took a deep breath.

"What is it, Clen?"

"We need to talk." Words that were no easier to say than they'd ever been to hear. She slid off his lap, and he let her go, but he kept his arm around her. "I think something important is happening here," she said. "At least it is for me. But I need you to know, sex isn't a game for me."

Gerrum shifted until he was facing her, which only made talking more difficult. She swallowed and stared at her hands. She'd clenched them without realizing it. "And, there are things we need to take care of before...well before..."

"We make love?"

Startled she glanced at him.

"That is what you're talking about," he said. "Isn't it? Not just sex."

She looked back at her hands which were still clenched. She stretched her fingers out, noticing the bare spot where her wedding ring used to be. "I was brought up to believe I shouldn't have sex outside marriage. If I did, civilization might disintegrate. The seas run dry." She shifted. "I didn't believe it, of course, but something stuck. Because I never...I mean...you'll think I'm a terrible prude, but I can't..."

"Just hop into bed with anybody who comes along?"

"More or less."

"And you're wondering if I do?"

"I don't think most men would turn down an opportunity for sex if the woman was halfway attractive."

"You have a pretty low opinion of us."

"Not without reason."

It took a moment for her comment to register. "Your husband?"

She nodded.

"He was unfaithful?"

She nodded again.

"Then he was a blithering idiot."

She blinked at his vehemence.

"I won't tell you I've never slept with a woman, but I can tell you, I've never slept with one opportunistically. Women aren't the only ones who believe in true love, Clen."

"Still, look around at all the unhappy people who once thought they were in love."

"And yet we keep taking a chance on loving," Gerrum said. "Perhaps we're designed to be optimists in even the most hopeless situations."

"You think love is hopeless?"

"No. I think a life without love would be hopeless." He touched her cheek. "You and me, Clen, we're looking at the possibility of something amazing here. And sex is only part of it."

"I wish I could just…"

"Shh, I know, Clen. It's okay. Some of the best things take their sweet time."

"You're not just trying to make me feel better."

"Of course I am, but that doesn't mean it isn't true."

"We also need to talk about…birth control."

He smoothed the hair off her face. "Of course we do."

"If I go on the pill, it will mean waiting."

"Which won't be easy."

"But you're okay with it?"

"I'm okay with it."

~ ~ ~

And when the waiting was finally over, Gerrum undressed Clen, giving it the same comprehensive attention he'd always given to kissing her. The contrast to Paul's approach to sex couldn't have been more stark. Paul, a main event kind of guy, never bothered much with caresses.

Clen pushed those thoughts aside and gave herself up to Gerrum, whom she wanted to touch in return. Following his example, she moved slowly and deliberately, removing his shirt and unsnapping his jeans. Clothed, he looked solid, weighty. Naked, that solidity was revealed as muscle and sinew.

Running her palms over his chest, she paused to check the beat of his heart and smiled to herself at its rapid pace that matched her own. She touched his cheek and ran a finger down his breastbone and across his abdomen, circling his belly button—an innie. Meeting his quiet gaze, her own passion surged and her doubts slipped away.

He lowered her to the bed and when he moved inside her, his rhythm deepened and quickened, filling her with a pulsation as steady as a heartbeat, as deep, dark, and lovely as a star-filled sky, until together they tipped over the top in a slow, delicious slide.

Afterward, she lay beside him, breathing deeply, smiling.

So that was what it felt like to make love.

Chapter Twenty-One

Clen tucked herself into Gerrum's heart and his life as if there were an empty spot just waiting for her. He knew women thought they were the romantic ones, and it was probably true not many men cared about flowers, candlelight, and the other trappings that spelled romance for most women.

For him, the romance was in kissing Clen and rubbing his hand in her hair, feeling it spring soft and silky against the roughness of his palm. It was walking by the harbor on a clear night and holding her hand while they looked up to watch the stars come out one by one. It was looking into Clen's eyes, like quiet waters, reflecting that light.

On one of her evenings off, as they cooked a meal together, Clen told him the story of how she went off to college wearing a frilly dress her mother picked out.

"I've never known anyone less suited to frills than you, my love."

"I ditched it at the dinner stop, along with my name."

"What's the name you ditched?"

"Michelle Marie."

"Hmm. Euphonious."

She snorted. "It shows a complete lack of attention. Do I look like a Michelle Marie to you?"

"A good name is rather to be chosen than great riches."

"Shakespeare?"

"Proverbs."

"I didn't know you were into quoting the Bible, Gerrum."

"Not a Bible fan?" he asked, although it was clear she wasn't from the distaste in her tone.

"Sorry. Unconscious reaction. What I'm not a fan of is religion."

He started the burner under a skillet before he spoke again. He wanted to hear the story, but he knew not to push too hard. "That's an interesting position." *Especially for someone who'd spent time in an abbey.*

"About that quote," she said. "One of many?"

"Not really. When I was six, a teacher wrote it out for me after she heard some kids teasing me about my name. It seemed to fit your situation." At times like this he felt like he was walking on eggshells in conversations with Clen—maneuvering around an obstacle he couldn't see but which was clearly there.

"Did you beat up the kids who teased you?"

"Didn't need to. Most bullies are cowards, you know. Once I developed some muscles and stood up to them, they backed off."

"Like in your book. So that did happen to you."

"Not exactly. But it's where the idea came from."

"Do we ever escape our pasts?"

"Probably not. But for me it's a good thing. Without a checkered past, I'd be hard-pressed to have anything to write about."

~ ~ ~

"I've been thinking," Gerrum said, as he and Clen soaked in the Stikine hot tub.

She stretched out a foot and ran it delicately up and down his leg. "Deep thoughts or shallow ones?" Contentment flowed through her, as warm and encompassing as the hot spring water.

"I want you to move in with me."

Startled, she withdrew her foot. Although for today she'd put the future out of her mind, that detail had begun to niggle like a pebble caught in a shoe—the question of what she would do when the lodge closed for the season. Gerrum's intent expression meant he'd wait as long as it took for her to answer, but it wasn't a simple proposition he was making, even if it could be answered with a single word.

"Maude will have a field day," she said, testing his resolve.

"She will." He looked serious, but amusement glinted in those dark eyes.

"This is your place, Gerrum. I don't want to make it uncomfortable for you."

"Nobody with the slightest spark of intelligence pays any attention to Maude. And what would make me uncomfortable, in the extreme, would be to spend the winter sleeping alone."

The teasing words were a welcome break from the weight of the decision, and she grabbed it. "Such a romantic."

"Come here, woman, and let me show you just how romantic I can be."

"Uh-oh. You never know when a moose might drop by."

He hooked an arm around her and pulled her onto his lap with a splash. "A moose, huh?" He held her without kissing her, and she knew that although he was willing to be playful, he was still waiting for the answer to his question.

"Living with someone is...it can be difficult. It requires compromise. Unselfishness. I don't know if I can do it." Not the real reason for her unease, but at least it sounded plausible.

Gerrum held her for a time before speaking. "Compromise and acting unselfishly aren't difficult when you care for someone and want to make it work." He shifted slightly, and she settled more firmly against him. "All either of us can promise is to try, and that we'll talk about anything that bothers us."

"What if we fail?" She already cared enough for Gerrum that failing would be dreadful.

"What if we succeed?"

They met each other's eyes, in silence. And into that quiet whispered a memory of the desperate pain she'd felt when Gerrum was missing. If they cut short what they'd begun to share without discovering where it might lead, it would hurt. Horribly.

For a moment longer she let herself imagine her life without this man, and her heart clenched with a certainty of agony. "I'm about parboiled." She nibbled on his ear then rested her forehead against his. "Maybe we can go home and you can show me that romantic side?"

"You're not using the term home loosely are you? Because I'm real delicate, you know. I can be hurt easy by careless talk."

She shifted in order to look him in the eye, making her expression a solemn one. "I never use the word home loosely."

He stood, setting her on her feet. "Good. I'm glad we got that settled. I'm ready to go home, too."

But first he pulled her back into his arms. The warmth from Gerrum and the hot spring water mixed with the cool of a breeze that tickled her neck and flowed over her back. "Hey, don't forget that moose," she said, breaking off the kiss.

He laughed. "Better a moose than Maude." He let her go, and she climbed out of the tub, sprinkling bright diamonds of water in his hair.

They grinned at each other the whole way back to Wrangell.

~ ~ ~

The night Clen finally told Gerrum about what happened with Paul, he listened silently as the story poured out, then he folded her against his chest.

"I ended up at an abbey, and Sister Mary John tried to help me change."

He leaned away and looked her directly in the eye. "I think you're wonderful exactly the way you are."

It was so easy loving Gerrum. Like free-falling through space without any fear of the landing. Sometimes she felt so light, it was hard to remember she was made of flesh and bones, until they made love. Then she was grateful for that flesh and those bones. For their delightful, delirious collision.

~ ~ ~

Clen was laying out the ingredients to make lasagna for the dozen expected for dinner when Marian came in from her sewing circle. "Has Gerrum said anything to you lately about Hailey?" Marian asked, shedding her jacket and the tote bag containing her latest project.

"Hmm. Like what?"

"Doreen said Hailey just hasn't been herself lately. Twice in the past week, she didn't open the gallery, which is a first.

Then someone else said they'd seen her a couple of times having serious discussions with Gerrum. I thought he might have said something."

"No. Afraid not."

"Yeah, I should have figured. Gerrum's a man of few words, isn't he?"

"Oh, I wouldn't say that. Although compared to Maude, he's a clam."

"Everyone compared to Maude is a clam."

"If you're so worried about Hailey, why not just ask her if she's okay?"

"Doreen did. Hailey brushed her off. Said she had a bug. Hadn't been feeling well."

"That could be it, you know."

"No. Somehow I don't think so."

As Marian had intended, Clen asked Gerrum about Hailey while they were taking their evening walk.

"As far as I know, she's in perfect health."

His vague answer meant Clen was going to have to do her own investigation, but when she arrived at ZimoviArt the next morning, she found it closed and Doreen from the Visitors' Center next door fussing about it. "Gerrum was here awhile ago asking about Hailey. Said if she comes in to let her know he'd be at the marina."

Clen decided to walk over to the marina to surprise Gerrum herself. She found *Ever Joyful* was right where it was supposed to be, but both the jet boat and Gerrum were missing.

She didn't see him until she arrived at his house after dinner. He was sitting at the computer when she came in, and he stopped writing to greet her with a big smile and a kiss.

"How was your day?" she asked.

"Busy. We did some work on the *Joyful*."

"Didn't you take the jet boat out?"

"Oh...yeah. I had a couple show up who wanted to do a quick run over to the garnet reef."

She wouldn't have noticed his hesitation if she hadn't been looking for it. "I stopped by ZimoviArt today," she said, watching him closely. "It was closed. Doreen said you'd stopped by. Did you and Hailey ever get together?"

"We must have missed each other. I'll have to check in with her tomorrow."

No question, the man was squirming. But why? If he was willing to leave a message for Hailey with Doreen, it must be innocent.

"Say, I'm hungry," Gerrum said. "How about I make popcorn."

It felt like he was deliberately changing the subject. Perplexed, Clen let him get away with it.

~ ~ ~

The next day, Clen went back to ZimoviArt. The gallery was open and Hailey was sitting behind the counter staring out the window. As always, Hailey was beautifully dressed and her lovely hair was smoothed into a sophisticated French braid. She looked, Clen judged, exactly the way Stella McClendon wished her daughter would look. Clen cleared her throat.

"Oh. Clen. Sorry, I guess I was woolgathering. It's a nice day, isn't it."

"It is. Are you feeling better?"

Hailey appeared puzzled.

"Marian came home from sewing circle with a report you've been ill."

"Oh. No. Well, just a touch of summer flu. Left me feeling tired, so I took time off. But I'm fine, now."

"Did you know Gerrum was looking for you yesterday?"

Hailey turned away, blushing. "Hey, I sold another one of your paintings. End of last week. You're turning into one of my best sellers."

"Maybe we can squeeze in another picnic to celebrate?" Clen said.

"Sure. Absolutely. Let me check the ferry and cruise schedules and let you know."

Hailey always had the schedules memorized. And what about that blush and the trouble she was having meeting Clen's eyes? Something was definitely going on, but it beat Clen what it might be. Baffled, she walked to the grocery store to check on the shipment of strawberries two people had stopped her in the street to tell her had arrived.

Maude was already picking through the pile of berries. Clen preferred to avoid the woman, but fresh strawberries were a rare treat in Wrangell.

Maude looked up. "Oh, Clen, just the person I was hoping to run into. You really need to make sure of that man of yours, dearie."

Clen favored Maude with a blank stare.

"So you know about Gerrum and Hailey?" Maude said.

Clen continued to stare. Maude, undeterred, shuffled her feet as she continued to talk. *Polka, two-step, gossip gallop.*

"He and Hailey come regular to the café. Together. And when they think nobody's looking, they hold hands. I thought you and he were an item, so I remarked it as being awful strange."

The image of a woman wearing a tight red dress with Paul's hand resting on her back blanked Clen's vision. When it cleared, she realized Maude was giving her a triumphant look.

How dare the old biddy insinuate such a thing about Gerrum. Besides, didn't she realize anyone having an affair in Wrangell would know enough not to conduct it in the full morning light of her voracious scrutiny? Clen turned and walked away.

But in the days that followed that encounter with Maude, others also began to make teasing remarks about her keeping an eye on Gerrum.

"Hey, I was you, I'd make sure my claim was staked real good," was how one of them put it.

"I seen him going into her house. Evening time it were," another said.

She brushed the remarks off. Gerrum had every right to meet with friends, when and how he wished, even if the friend in question was a beautiful young woman. Clen had friends, too. In fact, most mornings, after the guests left for the day, she had coffee with John Jeffers. Sometimes Marian or someone from town joined them, and sometimes it was just the two of them. For all she knew, not only was she being regaled with stories of Gerrum's coffee breaks with Hailey, Gerrum might be hearing tales of her morning coffees with John.

Except...she and John didn't hold hands.

Annoyed with herself, she pushed the thought away. Planting doubt was what Maude and her cohorts were hoping to accomplish. Clen was not falling for it.

~ ~ ~

"The jet boat's been running a bit rough lately," Gerrum told Clen as they finished lunch. "I plan to spend the afternoon doing maintenance. May take awhile. Doubt I'll make it to dinner."

She tried out a come-hither look that made him grin. "I'm serving fried chicken. Sure you don't want to change your mind?"

He swooped her into an embrace. "Of course I do, but I've been putting this job off, and I need to get it done."

"The old *carpe diem* approach, hmm?"

He kissed her neck, waking up nerve endings that responded only to him. She knew she could do it. Derail his plans, and hers for that matter. But it was even better when they waited. Anticipation. She would think about him as she cooked, and it would make her mouth water.

"Don't get too tired this afternoon." Her voice was hoarse. "I have plans for later."

"Umm. Dare I hope they include me?" he asked.

They laughed together until he stopped it with a kiss.

She pulled away and smiled. "You're very tempting today, Mr Kirsey. But I need to go." Thank God for tonight.

She left for the lodge to start dinner preparations, but halfway there, she realized she'd forgotten the sketch of John she'd done for Marian. She turned and walked back. Stepping onto Gerrum's porch, she glanced through the window beside the door and froze.

When they think nobody's looking, they hold hands.

Hey, I was you, I'd make sure my claim was staked real good.

Don't think you're the only woman he's stringing along.

I seen him going into her house. Evening time, it were.

Clen had been so certain of Gerrum and the love growing between them, she'd refused to consider the gossip and teasing remarks could be rooted in any sort of reality. But that reality was now right in front of her.

Hailey. In Gerrum's arms.

"Hailey and I are friends," he'd said the one time she'd asked him about Hailey directly, but the question had made him uncomfortable. And he never did define what he meant by friend.

Numbness. Thank God for numbness. But it never lasted, and then pain replaced it, stabbing, spreading. No blood, although it hurt so much there ought to be blood.

Dammit, Gerrum. This time, I held nothing back. This time, I believed in happiness...in you. How could I have been so blind? So stupid.

A frenetic giggle threatened to break free. No need to step back on the porch she couldn't remember abandoning. No need to look again. The image of those two embracing was seared into her memory.

Strange, but her legs seemed to be working normally, in spite of the rest of her being so frozen she had to remind herself to breathe. She walked past large trees and small houses with blank facades and dripping shrubbery, the street solid beneath her feet, although she felt as if she were inching along a high wire hundreds of feet above the ground. But if she was doing that, she would simply step off into space and end it.

Kody stood and stretched as Clen stepped on the lodge's porch. He rubbed against her, whining a greeting, and she knelt and took his head between her hands, sinking icy fingers into his warm coat. He licked her cheek, a brief touch of warmth, then cold again.

Too bad she couldn't take Kody with her. She bent her head, blinking away tears, then went inside.

Chapter Twenty-Two

Clen entered the lodge's kitchen after seeing Gerrum embracing Hailey and found it as deserted as the street. Automatically, she began pulling together ingredients for dinner. If she was forgetting anything, it didn't matter. Nothing mattered. She was simply filling time. Doing whatever it took to keep herself from thinking.

"Oh, Clen, there you are," Marian said.

After a moment to arrange her face, she turned around.

"Clen? Are you okay?"

She clamped tight on a sob, agony spreading through her chest into her head. An excuse. She needed an excuse...her head, throbbing with a steady pain. "Migraine. I need to lie down."

"You go right ahead. I can finish this up."

Thank God she hadn't yet moved out of her room at the lodge, although she rarely slept there anymore. In that room, she tipped two acetaminophen tablets into her hand, swallowed them with a gulp of water, then stood with her forehead against the cool of the windowpane.

Dear God, what am I going to do?

She undressed and lay down, pulling a pillow over her face to block out the light, but it couldn't block the images in her mind. Gerrum and Hailey locked in each other's arms, Gerrum's hand smoothing Hailey's hair which was loose and wild. Hailey's hair, the color of amber...Amber, the woman Paul took to St. Thomas. The four figures twined together, Amber and Paul, Hailey and Gerrum, their faces staring, their mouths open, laughing at her. Except Gerrum wasn't like

Paul. She would have bet her life on it.

Good thing she hadn't.

She stopped trying to hold back the sobs, just muffled them with the pillow. Eventually, she drifted into exhausted slumber and awoke to the weight of the pillow on her face. She pulled it tight against her nose and mouth, an older, darker memory taking hold.

Eventually, she slept again and had a dream, one where she felt wide awake. She couldn't be, though, because Thomasina was sitting in the corner by the window.

"I remember the first time I met you, Clen. Your hair was sticking up in random cowlicks and, of all the horrors, you were wearing slacks."

No question, Thomasina was in one of her tongue-in-cheek moods.

"Why did we stop talking?" In the disembodied way of dreams, Clen felt she could say anything to Thomasina and the nun would answer.

"Oh, I don't know. I suppose I was busy. You weren't getting demerits anymore. Perhaps that was why." Thomasina spoke quietly, her voice calm and uninflected, the kind of voice one might use to pray routine prayers.

"It was after the garden sister died."

"Garden sister?"

"I called her Sister Gladiolus."

"Ah. Sister Gladys...Glad. Yes. You may be right." A faint thread of sorrow began to color Thomasina's even tones.

"You loved her more than you loved me."

"Was it a competition, Clen?"

"Of course. It always is." She wished she could see Thomasina's face, but she couldn't seem to raise her head off the pillow.

"I did love Glad. We were supposed to love without holding on." Thomasina sighed softly. "Glad was the only one who understood why I picked the name Thomasina."

"Not because of the cat?"

If this weren't a dream, Thomasina would snort. Instead, her voice remained pensive. "Of course not."

"Then why?"

"For Thomas, the apostle. Doubting Thomas."

"You had doubts?"

"Oh my, yes."

"I thought you had all the answers."

"You were so young, my dear."

For a time, Clen lay silent, the night quiet bestowing its gift of peace. She knew without turning her head, Thomasina was still there. "I have to leave Wrangell."

"Why?"

"It hurts too much to stay."

"Will leaving make it hurt less?"

"It's a start."

"You should know by now, Clen, it doesn't work that way. Our past always comes with us. It shakes us up, no matter where we try to hide."

"I can't believe it shook you up, Thomasina."

"Then you didn't know me at all."

"I tried to know you. But I was just one of the girls."

"Of course you weren't. You were much more. The daughter I once hoped for. Ah, but that's all so long ago."

"It still hurts, what happened to us."

"It hurts me too." Thomasina fell silent, and after a time Clen knew she was gone.

Quiet lapped around her then, like water touching gently along the *Ever Joyful*'s hull, and when morning came she awakened to the sound of birds and a cool breeze lifting the curtains. She lay for a time, thinking about her night visitor. She looked at the spot where Thomasina sat last night. Nothing there, not even a chair. Yet what they'd said to each other...all of it true. Clen had thought she was competing for Thomasina's love and approval, and she'd acted no better than a two-year-old and with the same degree of understanding of how love worked. For when it seemed Thomasina was rejecting her, Clen turned her back, firmly and finally, on the nun.

It all happened years ago. By now, she should no longer miss Thomasina. Odd that she did, while she could barely remember Paul or what it was like to be married to him. Of course, she had been another person married to Paul. A person encased by duty and habit. Numb to both grief and joy.

Mummified until Gerrum set her free.

Gerrum. God, how that loss hurt.

At the reminder, something essential inside of her clenched with misery.

Chapter Twenty-Three

Earlier

Gerrum bumped into Hailey as he came out of the Visitors' Center. Hailey's face tightened as she stepped back and saw whom she'd run into.

He dropped the hands he'd automatically placed on her arms to steady her. "Hailey. Hey, where's the fire?"

She blinked rapidly, without speaking, and his gut contracted with guilt. Since he and Clen had gotten together, he hadn't talked to Hailey. "How about coffee? I'm just on my way."

Her head moved in a quick shake. "No. Oh. I...yes. I could use coffee."

She could use more than that. She didn't look a bit good. Her eyes shadowed, her hair, usually carefully arranged, shoved back in a careless ponytail.

At Maude's Café, they settled across from each other in one of the booths and Hailey asked him a question about the aftermath of the sabotage. She wasn't paying attention to his answers, though. He stopped talking and waited until she looked up.

"What's wrong, Hailey?"

At first, he didn't think she was going to respond. Then, "I'm...well...I guess I need to ask you something."

His mind scuttled in search of what topic could be making her look so strained, wishing he didn't have a good idea what it might be. "Won't hurt to ask. I can always refuse to answer."

"Since you aren't practicing law anymore, does that mean you don't have to keep information confidential, like questions people ask you?"

That had to mean it was a legal rather than personal issue, and he was enough of a coward it was a relief. "I don't spread around information people don't want spread around."

"Not even to Clen?" Hailey gave him an intent look.

He met her gaze, wondering at the oddity of the request, then nodded in agreement. "Not even to Clen."

"Promise?"

He had no intention of sharing Hailey's business with anyone else, with or without going through a song and dance about it. "I promise."

She picked up one of the empty sugar packets and began pleating and unpleating it. Finally, she looked up and gave him another searching appraisal. He sat back, sipping coffee, allowing her whatever time she needed to make up her mind.

When she finally spoke it was with obvious reluctance. "I need to know how to get hold of a trial transcript."

"What type of trial?"

"Murder."

With the one word, her reluctance began to make sense.

"Was it first degree murder?"

She lifted her coffee cup and hid behind it. "Yes."

"And the verdict?"

"Guilty."

"How long ago was the trial?"

"Eighteen years."

"That's a long time."

She put the cup down, lips tightening, and in that instant, he saw what she would look like as an old woman.

"Would you be willing to help me get the transcript, Gerrum?"

"I'll need more information."

She pulled out a pen, picked up a spare place mat, turned it over, and started writing. When she finished, she turned the mat around and pushed it toward him. He glanced at her then began to read.

    Defendant: Kenneth Connelly

    Defense attorney: Mr Dillon

    Trial Date: February 1968

    Trial Location: Olathe (Kansas City), Kansas

His thoughts spun, quickly offering up the most likely explanation for the desperation and grief he read in the lines of Hailey's face. Kenneth Connelly had to be someone close to her, perhaps her father, because eighteen years ago she would have been a young child.

"Does Kenneth have a middle name."

"It's James."

"Do you know his birth date?"

"I'm not sure of the year, but his birthday is April sixth."

"Do you know the date the murder occurred?"

"September eighth, 1967." Her tone was bleak.

"And the victim's name?"

"Rose Connelly."

"What was her relationship to Kenneth?"

"His wife."

Damn. He glanced up from his notes to find Hailey was barely holding it together. Her hands desperately pleated a sugar packet. He took those restless hands in his, held on for a moment, then squeezed lightly before releasing her and asking the last of the necessary questions.

"How about Connelly's address in sixty-seven?"

She closed her eyes briefly and pulled in a deep breath, and when she spoke, she'd regained most of her composure. "Martha Street, in Kansas City. I don't know the number."

From her reactions, it was clear he didn't dare ask the two questions he most wanted to ask. Were Kenny and Rose Connelly her parents? And why did she want to see the trial transcript now, so many years after the fact? Instead, he kept the interaction as businesslike as possible, given the subject was murder.

"I'll need to find out from the appropriate district court how long they hold transcripts and how to go about getting a copy. Might take awhile."

"It's already been awhile." She sounded resigned. "I guess

it's no biggie if it takes more time."

~ ~ ~

It required a day and a half of phone tag with his contact in the Seattle prosecutor's office for Gerrum to come up with the name and number for the clerk of courts for the Johnson County Kansas District Court. The morning after he spoke to that individual, Gerrum stuck his head in ZimoviArt and invited Hailey for coffee. She put up the back-in-fifteen-minutes sign, locked the door, and walked with him over to Maude's. Once they had mugs of coffee in front of them, he outlined what he'd learned.

"Bottom line, while the county should still have the transcript, they might not be willing to go looking for it, but if they do, they'll charge you for a copy. A one-week trial could run you several hundred dollars."

Hailey's face fell at the news.

"However, since it was first degree murder, there's another possibility. The verdict was likely appealed. That means the defense attorney may have a copy of the transcript."

"But he might be retired." Hailey wrinkled her brow. "Or dead. He was old."

Adults all look old to children the age Hailey had been. At least Gerrum hoped that was true, or he'd have little chance of getting his hands on the transcript, and he wanted to be able to do that for her.

"You have to decide. If you go ahead, it's going to take time and effort to track this down."

She was silent a long time, looking past him out the window. Finally she sighed. "I want to try. Will you help me? I'll pay you for your time."

"I'm happy to help, but only as a friend."

"You're a good man, Gerrum Kirsey. If Clen didn't have a firm hold on your heart, I'd be tempted to hang in there." She smiled.

It wasn't much of a smile, but he smiled back, feeling uncomfortable and at a total loss for a more appropriate response.

~ ~ ~

A helpful clerk at the Kansas Bar Association helped him locate Mr Dillon.

"Kenny Connelly trial, sixty-eight?" Dillon said. "Sure, I remember it. My first murder one case. Got trounced. Figured on a second degree guilty. Jury surprised me. Recollect that little gal, too. Sweet little gal. Held it together real well. Did better than most of the grownups. Give her my regards, will you. Be happy to send the transcript. Only kept it because it was my first."

When it arrived, the transcript was the size of War and Peace. Gerrum delivered it to Hailey's house, and she invited him in for a cup of coffee. While he sipped, she removed the stack of onion skin pages from the box and piled them on her kitchen table. The last thing she took from the box was a large brown envelope, its flap secured with red twine. She opened it, glanced inside, then re-fastened the twine and dropped the envelope back into the box.

Gerrum knew she eventually began to read it, because at intervals over the next several days, she waylaid him to ask questions. The first was about jury selection. She told him the twelve people originally called were retained, despite one of them being acquainted with a prosecution witness.

"Does that make any sense, Gerrum? Why didn't Mr Dillon challenge her?" she asked.

"Well, you usually go by your gut instincts on a jury, Hailey. Attorneys also have some information about potential jury members. But a juror acquainted with a prosecution witness..." He trailed off as Maude arrived to top off his cup. He waited until she moved out of earshot before continuing. "If it was my case, I'd remove that person. Take my chances on the rest of the pool."

"So why do you think Mr Dillon kept her?"

"It could have been an attempt to bluff the jurors into believing he was confident his client wasn't guilty. But it might have been inexperience. He told me he remembered the case because it was his first murder trial. And he did say the jury surprised him."

"Surprised him how?"

"He said he expected a guilty verdict but on a lesser charge."

Hailey bit her lip so hard it turned white.

He laid a hand on her arm. "Are you okay?"

She ducked her head, blinking fast.

"Kenny Connelly's your father, isn't he?"

She hitched in a breath. "Of course. Stupid of me to think you wouldn't figure that out."

He picked up her hand, which was icy, and chafed it between his.

"S-so you're saying Dillon thought he was g-guilty."

"Or, he knew he had a weak case."

"But if a person is innocent, it shouldn't matter." She looked up briefly, her eyes swimming with tears.

"You're thinking in moral terms, Hailey. The law deals with what can be proven beyond a reasonable doubt. It's why defendants are found not guilty instead of innocent." He held her hand until her breathing smoothed out, then he let go.

She brushed at the dampness in her eyes. "There's something else I need to ask you. Every time a witness starts to tell the jury something my mom said, the defense objects, and the judge always sustains the objection. Why is that?"

"Judges follow rules of evidence to ensure fundamental fairness. It means they usually exclude testimony relating a one-on-one conversation with the deceased since it would be impossible to corroborate."

Hailey took a careful breath. "Sometimes it seems more like a chess game than justice."

"Hey, why do you think I'm now a grubby Alaskan fisherman?" He looked at her over the rim of his mug.

"I thought it was because you know how good you look in flannel shirts."

That startled him, but then he decided she was teasing, a sign she'd caught her emotional balance. At least for the moment.

~ ~ ~

"Can you come by my place this afternoon, Gerrum?" Hailey said two days later. "I have more questions, but I hate asking them in front of Maude."

By then, he was spending most of his free time with Clen, so he suggested meeting Hailey in the early evening while Clen was busy with dinner at the lodge. At Hailey's, he found the transcript now sat divided into two unequal piles.

Hailey poured him a beer without asking and sat kitty-corner from him, sipping a glass of iced tea. "I'd forgotten a lot of it, but as I read, I keep remembering things."

"Is that what this is about? You trying to remember?"

"God no. I wish I never had to think about any of it again, but my brother left me no choice."

Gerrum raised his eyebrows in question and Hailey sighed. "It's a long story, but the gist is after Mom was killed, Adam and I went to live with our grandmother. Adam left Edgington when he was sixteen, and we never heard from him or about him again. Until a couple of weeks ago. I got a letter. From Adam's...widow." She stopped and chewed on her lip. "For years, I had no idea if Adam was even alive." She took a deep breath. "It surprised me how much it hurt to find out he isn't. His...Sally found me through Tess. She's the one who does the quilt squares. Sally wrote because she and Adam have a son and she wants him to know his dad's family. It made me realize I don't know for sure what happened to my mom, and I need to know. I thought the transcript would help."

"Has it?"

"Sometimes I feel like I'm reading about two strangers who just happen to have the same names as my parents. And I'm discovering things I didn't know. Like my dad's IQ is seventy-six. Borderline retarded. My IQ is nearly twice his. How can that be?"

"Maybe your mom was really smart."

"If she was so smart, why did she marry him and let him abuse her?" She rubbed her forehead. "Although, I don't really remember that, but after I read about it, I had a dream. I don't know. Maybe none of it's real, what I think I remember." She stopped and shuddered. "How do people do it? Make it their life's work to deal with this sort of thing? And then to talk about it as if it's a picture in a book, a setting on a stage."

"I don't know."

"Mom was shot in our apartment. In the bedroom. After it happened, Dad kept the door closed. One afternoon, I snuck in to get Mom's photograph out of the drawer where it was kept. I tried not to look, but as I turned to leave, I saw the bed. It had a huge brown stain. And there was this smell...unlike anything I'd smelled before. Dark, moldy, sweet. It made my stomach heave. I got out and pulled the door shut, but I couldn't get away from the smell." She stared at her hands, clenched in her lap.

Gerrum sat without moving, waiting to see if there was anything else she needed to say.

"A month after it happened, the police came. They brought Mom's sister with them, and they took Dad away. Aunt Iris helped us put our clothes and toys in grocery bags. She was rushing us, and I almost forgot the photo of Mom." Hailey propped her head on her hands.

"She took us to Grammie's with our stuff still in those paper bags. Grammie lived in a house that wasn't much more than a cabin. Edgington wasn't much of a place, either, but it was such a relief to get away from Kansas City, I didn't care.

"The first thing Grammie did was hug us and pat us and murmur sounds that weren't even words, but they were so much better than any of the words we'd heard since Mom died. Then she fed us a big meal. I ate so much I thought I'd burst.

"After dinner, she had us bathe, and while our hair was still wet, she sat us in the middle of the kitchen. First, she cut Adam's hair short. When she finished, she gave Adam's head a rub, and he ducked and smiled. When I saw that, something tight inside me started to loosen."

Gerrum didn't try to comment on what Hailey was saying. He thought what she mostly needed was to know someone was listening.

"Grammie combed my hair and I leaned back against her, and she told me, 'You know, Hailey darling, I used to do the same thing for your momma when she wasn't no bigger than you are. My, your momma had pretty hair. Just like yours.'"

Hailey's gaze was unfocused. Her words slowed and took on that Southern lilt, and she had just a hint of a smile on her face. "Grammie made us feel safe. She fed us and kept us clothed and warm. Every day we went to school and did chores and our homework, ate, and slept. And then we repeated it the next day. Eventually, we put away the memories of that time, just like Grammie put away our toys when we weren't playing with them anymore. Or at least I thought we did."

She stopped and blew her nose. "God, I'm sorry. I don't know what got into me."

"It's okay. Sounds like your grandmother was a wonderful woman."

"She was. I miss her a lot."

He pointed with the nearly full beer at the transcript. "You said you had some more questions?"

"Actually...I want you to look and tell me what's in here." She handed him the brown envelope that came with the transcript.

He undid the twine and pulled out the contents, a series of photographs. He glanced at Hailey who was focused on her glass of tea.

The first photo was of a bed with a huge dark stain in the middle and a gun lying to the side like a question mark. He turned it over without showing it to Hailey.

The second photo was worse—taken from above and to the side by a photographer looking through a small lens, framing and focusing carefully, so no detail would be lost. The same bed, but with Hailey's mother lying there, hair in a cloud, obscuring the source of the blood that had formed a dark pool under her head.

It wasn't a picture Hailey should see.

"Do you ever notice," Hailey said, "how this time of day the sun slants through the window and the dust motes look like tiny specks of gold. Dancing like angels are supposed to dance on the head of a pin." Her voice was dreamy. "Do you believe in angels, Gerrum?"

"I believe people can play that role."

She shook herself. "Yeah, I don't believe in them either."

The next photo had to be Hailey's dad. He was a small, almost frail-looking man with hair pulled into a wispy ponytail. He was wearing a T-shirt with a logo Gerrum didn't recognize. It had several dark smudges on the front and one sleeve. His face was smudged as well, and he had a startled look, as if the camera flash awakened him from a nightmare.

Gerrum turned the photo toward Hailey. "Is this your dad?"

She stared at it, then she nodded. "I'd mostly forgotten what he looked like. The last time I saw him was after the trial. Neither of us could think of anything to say."

"Is he still in prison?"

"I don't even know if he's alive. Although someone would have told me, right? If he wasn't."

"I expect so."

She looked again at the picture of her dad. "You know, there's something wrong with that picture."

"What?"

She shook her head, looking frustrated. "It's like when you know a word is misspelled because it looks odd, but you don't know how to change it to make it right."

"Is something missing? Or is something there that shouldn't be?"

"I don't know."

"Maybe you'll figure it out if you sleep on it."

"Maybe." She set the photo down. "I need to let you go. I've imposed on you long enough."

"Hey, isn't that what friends are for? To help when they can. I'm happy to do it." He slipped the two crime scene photos back in the envelope. "I don't think you should look at these."

"Could you just...dispose of them for me?"

"Of course."

They both stood. At the door, she put her arms around him in a brief hug. "Thank you, Gerrum. I don't know how I'd manage this without your help."

~ ~ ~

Gerrum began stopping by Hailey's house every couple of days. Often she asked him questions about how the trial was being conducted, or she would give him a section of the transcript and ask him to read it and tell her what he thought.

Tonight she answered the door, looking wan.

"Are you okay?" he asked.

"I'm not sleeping very well. I really just need to finish the transcript."

"How much more do you have to go?"

"About a hundred pages. There's something else I want you to read."

"Sure, be happy to."

In the kitchen, Hailey handed him a cluster of pages. He

started to read, then looked up at her in surprise. "Mr Dillon called you to testify?"

She nodded. "That's another reason I wanted to see the transcript."

Gerrum began reading the back and forth between Dillon and Hailey.

Q: Now, Hailey, you remember when I came to your grandma's and we talked about your dad and your mom?

A: Yes.

Q: Well, we're going to chat, just like we did then. I'll ask you questions, and all you have to do is tell me what you told me when we were sitting in your grandma's kitchen.

A: Okay.

Q: Hailey, did you ever see your dad threaten your mom in any way?

A: No.

Q: Did you ever see your dad hit your mom?

A: No.

Q: Did your mom and dad ever have fights?

A: Not exactly. Well, they yelled sometimes.

Q: Now, the week before your mom died, you two had a conversation about life and death, is that right?

A: Yes.

Q: Can you tell us what she said?

A: Mom told me it don't pay to fall in love with no man. She said she ain't happy and she don't know what she's going to do. And she started in to crying.

Q: Did your mom ever say she wanted to die?

A: Sometimes she said she wished she was dead. But I know she didn't mean it. She loved us.

Q: Did you love your mom, Hailey?

A: Yes.

Q: Do you love your daddy?

A: Yes.

Q: No more questions, Your Honor.

"When I read that, I was furious," Hailey said, nodding toward the pages he was holding. "I thought, what was Dillon thinking, putting a ten-year-old child on the witness stand. For what? I added nothing of substance. Nothing. The prosecutor didn't even bother to object when I told the jury what my mom said."

"I'm sure Mr Dillon did it to remind the jury you existed and would be affected by their verdict."

"Clearly. And just as clearly, I failed to be pitiful enough. You know, I cried myself to sleep for months afterwards, thinking I'd said something that hurt my dad, and I've hauled around a feeling of guilt ever since, all for nothing. He's guilty, isn't he?"

"I'd need to read the entire transcript before I could give you an opinion. But from the parts you've shown me, there are some loose ends. What do you remember about that day?"

"All I remember is getting called out of class. Aunt Iris, Mom's sister, was waiting for me in the office. She told me Mom was in the hospital. But once we were in the car she told me the truth." Hailey stopped, gulped. "After that, everything is confused. Lots of comings and goings. Clusters of people talking in whispers and shutting up if they noticed me watching them."

"What about your brother? Where was he through all this?"

Hailey frowned. "I don't think Adam was around until later, but I don't really remember."

"Did the police ever ask you any questions?"

She shook her head. "No. Adam and I went home with Iris the night it happened, and we stayed a couple of days. Until the funeral. Then we went back to our apartment."

"Was Adam questioned later?"

"Not that I remember."

"Did you and he ever talk about that day?"

"No. Why are you asking so many questions about Adam?"

"In the interview with the police you had me read, your dad said Adam got home from school before your mom was shot. So did you and Adam come home at different times?"

Hailey sat, chewing on her lip and slipping the rings off and on her fingers. "No. That's not right. We got out at the same time. And we didn't usually get home until after Mom left for work."

Gerrum picked up the pages, looking for the interview Hailey's father gave the police that he'd read on a previous visit. "Here. The way your dad tells it, he and your mom just finished lunch and she was getting dressed for work when Adam got home."

"He must have been suspended or maybe he skipped school. That happened a lot when he was older." She sat frowning over her thoughts and Gerrum waited to see what else she remembered.

"I thought I'd read the transcript and find all the answers. Instead it just feels more mysterious."

"Have you thought about talking to your dad?"

"I don't know if I can."

"It took guts for you to revisit this. It might be easier to put it behind you if you have the whole story."

"If I ask him about it, he might lie."

"You're smarter than he is. I think you'd recognize what was true."

He left her then, certain she was coping with what she'd learned, but he came home to questions from Clen that forced him to balance his need to be open with her and his promise to Hailey to keep private matters private.

It was one of the most uncomfortable positions he'd ever been in.

Chapter Twenty-Four

Clen had left for the lodge to start dinner, and Gerrum sat down to finish reading the newspaper before going to the harbor. There was a knock on the door and when he opened it, Hailey flung herself across the threshold and into his arms. He nudged the door shut and stood in his front hall holding her while she sobbed incoherently. When she was calm, he led her to the kitchen and made tea.

"I figured it out, Gerrum. What's wrong with Dad's picture. He smoked. And he always had a pack of cigarettes tucked in his sleeve."

"The police could have taken them away before they took the photo."

"But it was taken in our apartment, and I remembered something else. The shirt he was wearing. It was Adam's."

"You think Adam shot your mom?"

"I don't know. But he had terrible nightmares afterward. He'd wake up screaming, with his hands over his ears. And he acted funny about guns. Grammie had a twenty-two she used to shoot at foxes. Adam refused to touch it. And he was so...angry all the time. I just thought...oh, I don't know what I thought." She bit her lip, looking frustrated. "Sally said he was killed trying to beat a train at a crossing, but I think it may have been suicide." Hailey's eyes once again filled with tears. "I don't understand anything. Maybe Dad didn't do it. Maybe he's innocent. But if he didn't do it, it means Adam did."

"Maybe it was an accident. Remember your dad saying the gun needed to be cocked, and being shocked that it didn't?"

"He left the gun right by the bed. Who leaves a loaded gun

lying around when they have kids?"

"You told me he isn't very smart, Hailey. Maybe that's why."

Eventually, Hailey left, and not two minutes later, Terry called. "Gerr, real sorry to do this to you, but I got to dump a trip on you. I'm supposed to be at the harbor, meeting the clients, matter of fact. But Jenny's in labor. We're on the way to the hospital soon as she gets her bag packed. Clients are good ones. Brothers. They like the area around Thorne Bay. Booked for two days. Names are...yeah, hon, give me a minute here..."

"That's okay. I've got it. You take care of Jenny."

"Thanks, Gerr. Make it up to you once the little guy gets here."

"Just go."

Gerrum grabbed his own kit and a change of clothes. On the way to the marina, he stopped at the lodge to tell Clen what was happening. When no one responded to his hello, he scribbled a quick note and left it on the counter.

The first thing he did after returning from that trip was to stop at the lodge to see Clen. He found John and Marian working on dinner.

"Hey, where's Clen?"

"She had to go home. Her mom's in the hospital." John dried his hands on a towel. "Here's the number where she can be reached." He pulled a piece of paper out of his pocket. "I expect she's probably called and left you a message by now telling you what's happening."

"We heard about the baby," Marian said. "They finally had a boy. Terry's ecstatic."

"Yeah. I better get cleaned up." He backed through the screen door which he was careful not to bang, because Marian hated when it banged. Walking to his house, knowing he wouldn't be seeing Clen, it felt like he was carrying something much heavier than an overnight bag.

He went directly to the phone to check his messages. There was only one—Marian from two days ago saying Clen wasn't feeling well and went to lie down.

How could there be no message from Clen? Maybe she didn't have time before she left, but by now she would have. Feeling uneasy, he dialed the number Clen left with the

Jeffers.

"Could I speak to Clen please?"

"Clen? Oh, you mean Michelle. I don't know why she insists on that name."

"Could I speak to Michelle, then."

"I'm afraid she isn't here."

"Will she be back soon?"

"Now why would you think that? Michelle hasn't been home in over a year."

"Are you Mrs McClendon?"

"Yes. And you are?"

"You aren't sick?"

"Excuse me?"

He took a deep breath. "Clen, that is Michelle, is a friend of mine. Two days ago she left Wrangell, suddenly. To go home because her mother was in the hospital."

"How odd. I'm perfectly fine."

"Do you have any idea where she might be?"

"What did you say your name was?"

"Gerrum Kirsey."

"Oh yes. I believe Michelle has mentioned you. You're the author?"

"That's right. About Clen? I mean Michelle. Do you know where she is?"

"I suppose she could be at that abbey. She seemed so attached to it, we were beginning to think she might become a nun."

"Could you tell me the abbey's name and location?"

"Let me see. It's on the tip of my tongue. Oh, I know...Resurrection, that's it. It's somewhere in Vermont. Or she may be visiting her brother. Just like her not to tell us her plans."

He got the brother's number and gave Mrs McClendon his number and asked her to call if she heard from Clen. The brother, Jason, didn't answer his phone, and he still wasn't answering in the morning. Frustrated and beginning to feel deeply worried, Gerrum filled the time between attempted calls with a trip downtown to pick up groceries.

Outside the IGA, he encountered Maude, who reached out a pudgy hand to grab his sleeve. "I heard Clen left. Is it true?"

He stared at the hand crumpling his shirt without permission until, with a sniff, she released him. "Well, all I can say is, it serves you right, Gerrum Kirsey."

What did?

"Don't you try that innocent act with me. I seen what you and Hailey was up to."

Maude in full cry, going after the dirt, like one of those dogs, some kind of terrier, weren't they? The ones that dig out badgers. Maude badgering. Then she and her cohorts would morph into hyenas, chewing on the bones of everybody's lives.

He'd always laughed Maude off, but not this time. "What is it you thought you saw Hailey and me up to?" His teeth were gritted, chopping the words into tight, brittle bits.

Maude took a half step away.

"What did you do?"

Maude shook her head, preening like a ratty old hen. "Well I never. I didn't do nothing. Just made sure Clen knew what you were doing. Seems to me a man ought to stick with one woman at a time, and I'm sure Clen agrees with me. Not that you and she aren't already a scandal."

The bright sun reflected in the gleam in Maude's eyes. Eyes as pitiless as those of a dead fish. Gerrum clenched his hands into fists to keep from slapping her silly. Right in the middle of downtown Wrangell with God knew who watching. And if she'd been a man, he wouldn't have hesitated. Maude took another shuffling step away from him. In her place, he would have taken more than a step.

"You, Maude Tillotson, are a nasty, useless old gossip. Get out of my face and stay out." Cold, his voice was, like snowmelt water.

Maude gave him one more glance, a peculiar combination of satisfaction and fear, and scurried away. He stood for a moment, breathing deeply, trying to still the flare of rage she'd ignited. Rage hot enough to set something ablaze.

After talking to Clen's mother, his mind had spun like an unattached flywheel, not coming up with a single useful thought about Clen's leaving, until Maude's words engaged a gear. Marian. He needed to speak with her. After all, she was the last person to talk to Clen.

"What do you hear from Clen, Gerrum?" Marian asked when he arrived at the lodge.

He shook his head. "Nothing. Her mother's fine, so that isn't the reason she left. I've been wracking my brain trying to come up with another explanation, but I've been drawing a blank, until I ran into Maude. She said the most amazing thing."

"Yeah, I'll bet. You and Hailey. Sitting right there, in front of God and man, holding hands. And you going to her house when Clen was tied up at the lodge."

"What?"

"Lord, Gerrum, it can't be a surprise. Maude's told everyone in Wrangell. The old witch isn't happy unless she's stirring in someone's pot besides her own. Clen didn't pay any more attention to her than the rest of us do."

Of course, he knew that. And yet... "Tell me about the last time you talked to Clen. The way she looked, acted."

Marian frowned. "Well, let me see. I came in and found her starting dinner. When I spoke to her, she turned around looking like she'd just lost her best friend, but when she said she had a migraine, I figured that explained it."

"That was Tuesday, right?"

"Right. I sent her off to bed. The next morning she said she was still feeling lousy, but she'd gotten a call her mom was ill. I drove her to the airport and that was that."

"Did she take all her stuff with her?"

"I'm not sure."

"Could I take a look?"

Marian nodded and fetched a key. Together they walked down the hall to Clen's room. They found the bed stripped and the sheets folded on the bedspread. Closets and drawers were uniformly empty. The only personal items were large bottles of shampoo and lotion and an easel and a stack of blank canvases, all things easily replaced.

"It doesn't look like she expects to come back," Marian said, looking around.

Gerrum walked slowly back to his house, trying to arrange the bits and pieces of evidence into a coherence that might explain something that felt inexplicable. He came up with only one possibility. On Tuesday, shortly after Clen left, Hailey had shown up. He'd stood in the hallway holding Hailey at least two, three minutes. During that time, Clen must have come back and seen them.

How long did she stand watching? A few seconds? Longer? And then what? According to Marian, she went to the lodge, started dinner, then complained of a headache. If not for the unexpected trip, when Marian called to tell him Clen wasn't feeling well, he would have gone to check on her. If she'd refused to see him, he would have insisted. Would have held her until she gentled. Until she realized she'd been mistaken in thinking him capable of betrayal.

A day of strong emotion. Blinding anger at Maude. Anger at Clen too, although he needed to cut her some slack since she'd been betrayed before. But it was still agonizing to know that when Clen was faced with the choice to trust or to doubt, she'd chosen doubt.

The thought brought bottomless, fathomless grief. Enough to drown in.

~ ~ ~

"Hell, Gerr," John said. "You're like a bear just out of hibernation, and winter hasn't started. When are you going after her?"

"Not sure I am."

"Now you know that's pride speaking. If she did see you with Hailey, you've got to admit she didn't up and leave for no reason. And what you two have, isn't it worth the effort to see if you can save it?"

"If what we had was so great, how could one small thing smash it?"

"That was no small thing. If Marian caught me with a beautiful young woman in my arms, she'd want an explanation, and it would have to be a good one. I trust yours is. Go find her. Have it out with her, at least. You'll regret it the rest of your life if you don't."

John was right. If he went after Clen and she believed him, the happiness they'd shared might return. If he did nothing, any chance at happiness would be lost.

But whether to go after Clen was a moot point. He didn't know where she'd gone. Her brother finally answered his phone and said he'd neither heard from Clen nor did he have any idea where she might be. It meant her mother's suggestion, Resurrection Abbey, was the only place left to look.

He asked John if he knew where Resurrection was located, and John dug out the letter Clen sent. There was no phone number, but the address enabled him to get the number from Information.

He asked the woman who answered the abbey's phone if he could speak to Clen.

"Oh, we never disturb our retreatants. Not unless there's a family emergency. Is this a family emergency?"

"Not exactly." But of course that's exactly what it was.

"I'm so sorry. I'm afraid I can't disturb Clen." Although the voice was light and wavering, the click disconnecting them was decisive. Still, he'd found her.

Going after her would be neither easy, nor would it be cheap, but what the hell. If money couldn't be used to secure one's heart's desire, what good was it?

Chapter Twenty-Five

RESURRECTION ABBEY STOWE, VERMONT

When Clen's headlong flight from Wrangell landed her on Resurrection's doorstep, the portress, Sister Kevin, opened the door, gave a happy cry, and hugged her. "Mary John will be so glad to see you, dear."

"I'll be glad to see her too. You'll tell her I'm here?"

"Of course. You're staying with us?"

"If I can?"

Kevin smiled. "Your old room is free. Now isn't that lucky?"

~ ~ ~

The small room welcomed Clen as if she'd been gone five minutes rather than nearly five months. The narrow bed with its white coverlet, the straight-backed chair, the fresh flowers in the vase on the simple desk—a stem of chrysanthemums signaling autumn was on the way. In winter, flowers would be replaced by sprigs of ivy or holly, and her sitting here, waiting through that season until daffodils, the first heralds of spring, appeared. Woven through it all, the nuns' chanting, the routine, the quiet days. With no emotions, no drama, no more losses.

Still, this time, peace would be harder to come by.

She'd had only a few weeks with Gerrum, but it would be a long time before she managed to banish the memory of his hands touching her, his lips kissing her, his body moving in synchrony with hers. An even longer time until she forgot the comfort of knowing Gerrum was nearby. Solid, steady. A foundation upon which she'd begun to rebuild her life.

She shook her head, trying to shake free of the memories. Memories she intended to push away until, eventually, a day might come when she wouldn't think of him at all.

~ ~ ~

The Vigils chant awakened Clen at three fifteen. She lay listening as the peaceful notes faded and the silence returned.

After breakfast, she walked into the garden. With a faint rustling of skirts, Sister Mary John joined her. "The Lord be with you, Clen."

"And also with you, Mary John."

The nun, solid. Like Gerrum in that way. With eyes that saw inside you—discovering a speck of memory here, an old worn-out theory that should be discarded there.

"Come, Clen. We'd better sit." Her hand settled on Clen's arm, steering her firmly.

Funny how they always chose the same bench. People as territorial as any animal. Or was it just a habit...sitting in this spot with Mary John, who rubbed her hands to warm them that other time, too.

"I c-can't bear it." So cold.

"Can't bear what?" Mary John, determined, calm.

"He... they." She stopped, took a breath. "You see, I...I fell in love with a man. And I thought he loved me. But he...and another woman..." There hadn't been enough time yet. It was still impossible to say it.

"He was unfaithful."

It wasn't a question, but Clen answered anyway. "Yes."

"You'd better tell me about it."

It took awhile to pull together the words. While she did, Mary John waited.

"His name is Gerrum Kirsey. He used to be an attorney. In Seattle. Now he's a fishing guide in Alaska, and he writes mysteries." All the surface, unimportant bits, but they were all she could manage.

Someday none of this would matter. Not today, though. "A

few weeks ago, his boat was sabotaged, and he was missing for two days. That's when I knew...I loved him." She was like an engine winding down. Pretty soon she would stop, and maybe she wouldn't be able to start again. "Being with him was..." But if she stopped, Mary John would just start rubbing again. "Until three days ago, I thought he was the most loyal, honest, and loving person I'd ever met, and that I could trust him with my heart as well as my life. And I thought Hailey—" Clen never cried. Well, hardly ever. Which was why it was hard to stop once she started.

Mary John didn't seem to mind, though. "That's the other woman. This Hailey? You know her?"

The calm in Mary John's voice steadied Clen. Propped her up. "She runs an art gallery in Wrangell, and she's so...beautiful." A completely inadequate word to describe Hailey, with her perfect skin and tawny hair. Her poise and elegance. Her intelligence and wit. Why would any man choose her if he could be with Hailey? "I liked her, but she was always..."

"What?" Mary John prompted.

"I don't know. Doesn't matter." Nothing mattered beyond the one fact. The fact of Hailey and Gerrum.

"How did you find out about them?"

"I went to his house, unexpectedly, and they were there. In the hall. In each other's arms."

"Did you ask Gerrum to explain?"

"He doesn't know I saw them."

More quiet after that. Mary John used quiet the way most people used words. In that quiet, the thought drifted in. She should have had it out with him. Right then. Or at least the next morning.

But he could have made an effort, too. To come to see her. To explain what was going on. But he hadn't...

"Please, stay here." Mary John released Clen's hand. "I want to say a prayer." She walked over to the nearby statue and stood before it with head bowed.

Prayer wasn't going to help. Besides, Clen had gone a long time without it, the words dried up and blown away with Josh. Even when Gerrum was missing, she hadn't prayed. And she especially disliked praying to statues. What did people see in them anyway? All exposed hearts, insipid expressions, and garishly painted robes.

Not this one, though. Not garishly painted. In fact, not painted at all, its curves likely as cool and smooth to the touch as the snow they resembled. She'd forgotten until this moment she'd stared at this particular statue before, while talking about Josh. Did she notice then the way light glanced off a cheek and shadows pooled under the eyes of the two figures depicted—a woman holding a man's body on her lap? Pain frozen in stone.

Mary John finished her prayer and came to sit beside Clen. "I want you to think about something, Clen. I want you to consider other explanations for what you saw."

"What I saw was clear."

Mary John patted her arm and nodded toward the statue. "What do you see?"

Easy enough to figure out what Mary John was suggesting. That there were many kinds of embraces. But Mary John hadn't seen what Clen saw. Mary John gave her shoulder a squeeze, then went inside. Restless, Clen wandered from the organized tidiness of the garden into the green and gold disorder of the woods surrounding Resurrection. Anger accompanied her. Anger at Gerrum and Hailey but also anger at herself.

For running away. Again.

~ ~ ~

The word "abbey" had evoked an image of a stone castle-like building, perhaps with ivy-covered walls, so the simple brick structure set among trees beginning to turn gold was not what Gerrum was expecting.

He stepped onto the porch and rang the bell. More than a minute passed without a response. He was about to ring again, when an elderly nun dressed in a traditional black and white habit opened the door and greeted him in the soft voice he'd last heard when he'd telephoned.

She bowed. "The Lord be with you. Can I help you?"

"I hope so. I'm here to see Clen McClendon."

The nun pursed her lips, examining him, then without speaking, motioned him to follow her to what they no doubt called their parlor. It was roughly the size of his Wrangell living room and furnished with several straight-backed chairs and two formal settees. Lounging not encouraged, apparently.

"Please, wait here. That is, if you wouldn't mind?"

He nodded and she backed out, pulling the door closed.

For fifteen minutes, he alternated pacing with staring out the window, his frustration growing. Finally, the door opened and another nun, also in traditional garb, walked in. This one was middle-aged and round-figured. A comfortable, motherly sort of person, or so he thought until he looked in her eyes. Those eyes were nothing like the gentle, inquiring eyes of the nun who'd answered the door. Instead, these were the eyes of the person one called when someone came to disturb a "retreatant" who was choosing not to be disturbed.

"I'm Sister Mary John." She extended a blunt hand almost as work-roughened as his.

"Gerrum Kirsey."

"Sister Kevin tells me you have asked to see Clen McClendon." She folded her hands into the wide sleeves of her habit and stood perfectly still, staring at him with careful eyes.

"Yes."

"And that it's not exactly a family emergency."

To counter his discomfort, he employed one of the tactics he'd found to be successful when he was practicing law. He nodded without speaking and waited for what she would say next.

She gestured toward the settees. "Please. Have a seat, Mr Kirsey."

Willing himself to patience, he waited for her to sit, then took the settee facing her across a small patch of faded rug.

"Clen was quite disturbed when she arrived here. Do you know why that might be?"

"I have an idea. But I don't know for certain."

"What is your idea?"

Ordinarily such a conversation would either annoy him or make him uncomfortable, but knowing Clen was nearby, he now felt calm. "I think Clen saw something she misinterpreted and it upset her."

"And there was no reason for her to be upset by what she saw?"

"No."

Mary John sat motionless and silent after his "no," and he had the impression she was prepared to continue to remain that way indefinitely. Further, he suspected she wasn't going to let him see Clen unless he did a better job of explaining himself.

"Clen may have seen me comforting a friend...a woman who's been going through a difficult time. What Clen saw...well, she could have thought...the woman and I...but it wasn't..."

He had no idea how long the silence lasted after he stumbled to a stop. Mary John continued to sit, her hands once again tucked into her sleeves.

"Please. You have to let me see her. I need to tell her—" His throat convulsed, cutting off speech. He swallowed, took a breath, then another, fighting his way back to control. Finally, he raised his eyes to the nun's face.

"I'm extremely sorry to tell you, Mr Kirsey. A short time ago, Clen left without saying where she was going."

"You put me through the third degree, and she's not even here?"

She had the grace to wince. "I do apologize. I wanted to assure myself of your sincerity in the event Clen was in touch."

He swallowed, trying to get his voice under control. He really needed to stop yelling at middle-aged women. "And you have no idea where she might have gone?"

"No. I'm sorry. But if she is in touch, I will urge her to contact you." She stood and bowed slightly. "The Lord be with you, Mr Kirsey."

There must be a set response to that, but he had no idea what it might be, although the habit of courtesy was strong enough he stood and bowed in return. Then he returned to Stowe where he rented a room for the night. Calls to Clen's parents and her brother went unanswered.

He had no idea what to do next.

Chapter Twenty-Six

MARYMEAD COLLEGE MEAD, KANSAS

From a distance, Marymead looked exactly as it had the first day Clen saw it twenty-three years ago. She pulled into the parking lot, puzzled that it was empty. Surely fall semester should have started? She stepped out of the car into the heat and humidity of a late summer Kansas day and walked up the steps of the Administration Building. There she found a NO TRESPASSING sign affixed to the door.

She turned to look over the campus, noticing for the first time that the grass surrounding the two dormitories and the Fine Arts Building was dry and overgrown and the flower beds were filled with weeds.

It looked desolate, and it made her feel like she'd been transported to some indefinite future time—a feeling so real, she glanced at her hands to see if they were gnarled and spotted with age. Maxine would know what happened, of course, and would no doubt have shared that information if Clen had bothered keeping in touch.

A spasm shivered through her, reminding her of the horrible shaking attacks she'd suffered through most of her junior year. She'd known they'd been caused by grief and guilt and had only stopped because, eventually, she'd been too worn out to feel anything.

If Thomasina hadn't gone away, Clen would have confessed to her, but by the time the nun returned, Clen had buried that time so deeply, she thought she could live her life as if it never occurred. But the last few days had made it clear that was folly.

~ ~ ~

Clen drove downtown and parked near Mead's tiny library. Inside, a young woman who looked about twelve sat at the main desk chewing gum and reading a magazine. She looked up with a bright smile when Clen entered.

"I wonder if you can tell me what happened to Marymead College?"

"Oh, it was closed a year ago."

"But why?"

"Bishop decided it cost too much."

"Just like that?"

"Pretty much. Bummer. I was hoping to go to school there."

"What about the sisters?"

"Hmm. Well, I don't know much about that. There's a nun who comes in here occasionally. She should know. She lives right over there." She pointed out the door. "You could see if she's home."

Clen thanked the girl and walked across the street to the small apartment building the girl had indicated. The mailbox for apartment 1B was labeled, Sr. S. Moriarity. Clen found the right door and knocked.

The woman who answered was a sturdy redhead with freckles across her nose.

"Sister Moriarity?"

"Yes?"

"I'm Clen McClendon. I was a student at Marymead. I came to visit and discovered it's been closed."

"Ah, yes. A terrible thing for the entire town." Her voice carried a hint of the brogue promised by her name and her coloring. "Would you like to come in?" She gestured for Clen to take one of two chairs in the sparsely furnished front room. "When did you graduate, dear?"

"Nineteen sixty-six."

"Ah, before my time, I'm afraid. I didn't arrive until seventy-three."

"Do you know Sister Thomasina?"

"Oh, my goodness. Of course. Marymead's last president.

Installed right before the bishop decided to shut us down. She fought the good fight. Well, you know what a fighter she was. But only a miracle would have saved us." She sighed.

"Where is she now?"

"Oh dear. Is that who you came to visit?"

Clen nodded.

"I'm so sorry. She died, you see. Last spring." Her brogue thickened and her eyes welled. "She was a great favorite of mine. Such a bonny person."

"How...what happened?"

"A heart attack. I saw her afterward. She said it should be no surprise since her heart had been giving her great difficulties for years. She was speaking metaphorically, of course. We thought she was going to be fine, then..."

"Where..." Clen stopped to clear her throat. "Could you tell me where she's buried?"

"Why at the Motherhouse in Lawrence. Do you think you might go there?"

"I...I don't know. Maybe."

"If you go, would you put a rose on her grave for me? Thomasina loved roses. Said they brought her comfort on her darkest days. There was a bush at Marymead she was partial to. She told me once it was a Gladys rose." Sr. Moriarity went over to the small desk, pulled something out, then turned and handed Clen a five-dollar bill.

Clen waived the money away. "I'd be happy to put a rose on Thomasina's grave for you, but I won't take money for it."

"It's a great kindness you do me. I loved her, and I can see you did, too."

"I...I need to get going." Clen stumbled to her feet.

"Are you okay? I'm so sorry I didn't have better news for you."

"Thank you for talking to me." She was done. She couldn't handle any more. With the barest civility, she nodded at the nun then got out of there.

She'd come back to Marymead looking for Thomasina, expecting the nun to somehow magically help her to deal with all that had gone wrong in her life—Josh, Saint, Paul, Gerrum. The litany of mistakes and estrangements that shaped her. But now that possibility was yet another dead end.

~ ~ ~

In the morning, Clen drove back to the college and parked behind the main building. The rose bush was still there, next to the trellis that no longer needed to be in good repair.

Clen snipped off three buds just beginning to open and placed them in the water she'd brought, then she sat back on her heels and listened to the buzz of insects as the dawn coolness began to give way to another hot day.

Nearby, the lilac bush that once shielded her was drooping, probably because it wasn't getting enough water. Next to it, the patch of earth where Thomasina and Gladiolus planted the yellow tulips that long-ago day was choked with weeds and leaf litter.

It felt like she could close her eyes and Thomasina and Gladiolus would be there, digging and talking about their lives. Clen wiped at her tears, then she pulled the weeds away from the Gladys rose. She cut back some of the canes, and stepped away, sucking the thumb a thorn pierced. She considered it rather shabby treatment since she'd just ensured the bush would be okay for a couple more years.

She brushed away the seed and leaf debris on her jeans, then took the roses to the car, and settled them in a cool spot for the drive to Lawrence.

~ ~ ~

LAWRENCE, KANSAS

At the cemetery at the Motherhouse, Clen walked in the direction of the newest-looking stones, relieved she'd managed to arrive at a time when nobody was on the grounds.

Thomasina's stone, like all the others, was white and plain: Sister Thomasina Moreland. 1917- 1984. Worry not. As the Father cares for the lilies and the sparrows, He cares for you.

Clen recognized the inscription. They were the words Gladiolus spoke to comfort Thomasina that time in the garden, and in this moment, Clen felt as if Thomasina was passing that assurance on to her. She didn't try to stem her tears as she laid two of the roses on the ground by the marker.

Sister Gladys's grave was across from Thomasina's. Clen

placed the last rose there.

~ ~ ~

DENVER, COLORADO

In the early evening, Clen flew from Kansas City to Denver. She called Jason from the airport to let him know she'd arrived.

"Good grief, sis. About time you let us know where you were."

"What are you talking about?"

"Gerrum Kirsey?"

Her heart began to pound with a thick, heavy beat. "What about Gerrum?"

"Well, first he called the folks looking for you and was surprised to discover Mom wasn't in the hospital. Ringing any bells, yet?"

"I can explain."

"I certainly hope so."

"Just not this minute. I'll tell you about it when I get there. If you'd give me directions?"

Jason's irritation wasn't the mood she would have chosen for her first visit with her sister-in-law.

~ ~ ~

Jason and Nancy had bought a home in a neighborhood where huge trees shaded the uneven slate sidewalks. Yards were small, but they were beautifully landscaped. Clearly, the people who lived here were house and garden-proud.

Clen found a parking spot on the street, and by the time she was lifting her hand to knock on her brother's door, it opened.

Jason stood there, hair rumpled, tie askew. "Where the hell have you been, sis?"

"Not exactly the warmest welcome, Jase."

"We've been worried sick about you. Sure, I get that none of us wants to live in each other's pockets, except Mom, but damn it, we're family."

"Can I come in at least?"

He stepped aside and Clen walked past him to hug Nancy, who gave her a sympathetic look. After a nudge from Nancy, Jason went and fetched Clen's luggage.

"Are you hungry?" Nancy asked. "We'd just finished dinner when you called, but I'd be happy to heat something."

"Thanks. I ate at the airport. A glass of water would be nice, though."

She followed Nancy to the kitchen and had taken barely one sip from the water Nancy handed her before Jason was back, looming in the doorway.

"He's not really mad at you, you know," Nancy said smiling at her husband. "He was worried, is all."

"I'm sorry. It never occurred to me to report in. After all, I rarely did it the year I traveled around, and nobody seemed to mind."

"Because we weren't getting calls from strange men trying to find out where you were. So what's the story," Jason said, still blocking the doorway.

"Could we at least sit down?" Clen said.

"Try the living room," Nancy said. "I have lesson plans to finish, so I'll let you two talk."

Jason moved to the living room, and Clen followed.

"I like Nancy," she said.

"Yeah, I like her, too. And don't go trying to change the subject."

"I'm not. What exactly do you want to know?"

"Why don't you begin by telling me about this Gerrum person."

"What did he tell you?"

"So we're playing it that way, are we?" Jason sighed. As a prosecutor, he never surrendered the questioner's role with good grace. "Said he was a good friend who wanted to make sure you were okay, since you left Wrangell without saying goodbye. If you got in touch, he asked me to tell you he needs to talk to you about Hailey. That it wasn't what you may have thought. So who is he?"

"The man I've been living with."

Jason sat back, blinking. "What happened?"

"I saw him with Hailey...in his arms."

"Maybe she fainted?"

"In the front hall of his house, at a time they both knew I'd be tied up at the lodge getting dinner?"

"Okay. Maybe not. But he did say it wasn't what you thought it was." Jason frowned. "Didn't you ask him about it?"

Clen was tired of that particular question. "I knew something was going on between them. The whole town knew, and Gerrum refused to talk about it."

"They were spending time together, in public? And everybody knew? Not trying to be clandestine?"

"It's hard to be clandestine in Wrangell. There are people whose major goal in life is to observe who does what with whom and then report it to the rest."

Jason shook his head. "If Gerrum was so hot for Hailey, why was he living with you?"

"You might recall, it's happened to me before."

"Yeah. True. But Paul at least tried to sneak around. In my experience most men do, and then they aren't upset like this Gerrum is when the woman leaves."

"Are you sure he's upset?"

"Yeah. I'm sure."

"You haven't met him."

"Well, I did do some checking."

"You what?"

"I called the place you've been staying. Bear Lodge? Talked to a Marian Jeffers. She couldn't say enough nice things about the man. Mentioned he'd been an attorney in Seattle. That gave me a whole new avenue to explore. Seems he was very well thought of. I even bought his book."

"And you did this because?"

"I wanted to make sure he wasn't stalking you."

"I don't think I've ever met anyone less likely to be a stalker than Gerrum Kirsey."

Jason stared at her with narrowed eyes. "Okay. When you saw him with Hailey, was he kissing her?"

Clen looked away from Jason, trying to bring up the image she'd been avoiding for nearly a week. Gerrum, his head bent, his arms around Hailey. And Hailey, her face pressed tight against Gerrum's shoulder.

How long did she stand watching them? A few seconds, a minute? Had they kissed? She didn't think so. Which was peculiar. Shouldn't they have been kissing? And Gerrum's hand. He'd raised it and let it rest on Hailey's head. Patting? As one would to soothe. To calm.

Had Clen really seen that or was she making it up? And why was it, the more she examined her memories, the more shrouded in mystery they became? As if she were staring at them through a mist that was growing in density the longer she looked.

She shook her head. "I'm not sure."

"Don't you think you would have noticed?"

"I don't know, Jase. I suppose I should have, but I didn't. Could we talk about something else? How are you doing?"

"I'm doing just swell. Something you'd know if you ever bothered to be in touch."

"Mea culpa."

"Yeah. Yeah. I forgive you."

"Phone lines run both ways."

"Okay. So maybe I'm not so great in the keeping-in-touch department myself."

"You think?" Clen said, relieved the conversation had shifted from Gerrum.

"Josh would have made sure we all kept in touch," Jason said.

"How can you be so sure? He might have run off to the circus for all we know."

"He wanted to be a pilot," Jason said.

"Did he?"

"And a fireman, and a cowboy, and a—"

"But most of all, he wanted to be a regular kid." Clen could feel tears gathering. She curled her feet under her on the sofa, trying to get comfortable, although she knew that wasn't possible.

"I think about him all the time," Jason said. "But there's no one I can talk to about him."

"What about the folks?"

"It makes them sad when I mention him, so I don't. Do you remember what a joker he was?"

"Lord, yes. He played enough jokes on me."

"I remember one time he turned all your clothes inside out. You always ran late for school. He figured you'd grab something and not notice."

Okay, she could play this game. "What was he? Seven? It was third period before someone asked why I was wearing my sweater inside out. Everyone was laughing about it. I wanted to kill him." She clapped a hand over her mouth, but Jason either didn't pick up on her choice of words, or chose to ignore them.

"So is he the one who put the garter snake in the chocolate box, or did you?" she said.

"I was just an accomplice. The ideas were all Josh's."

"The two of you, always so angelic looking. Although I knew nobody was likely to send me chocolates, I still fell for it."

"You were a good sport. Most girls would have fainted or screamed, but you didn't even rat us out."

"More fun to pay you back."

"I don't remember what you did to us after the snake."

Clen swiped a hand to brush away the dampness in her eyes. "That was right when he got sick."

She wondered if Jason was remembering Josh plotting one of his tricks. As for her, she was fighting off the memory of him lying in bed, quivering with pain.

"You know, by the time he died, I was relieved," Jason said. "I couldn't stand it anymore, seeing him suffer that way."

"Me neither." She closed her eyes against the memories. She shouldn't have come here. "I'm exhausted. I think I'll call it a day."

"We get up early around here," Jason said. "If you're not up, we'll leave a key and our phone numbers on the counter. Just don't go running off without telling us where you're going. Okay?"

"Yeah. Okay." She was too tired to argue the point.

Chapter Twenty-Seven

Clen awoke to the smell of coffee brewing and the quiet sounds of Jason and Nancy getting ready for work. She stayed in bed until she heard them leave, then took her time getting up. In the kitchen, she found the promised key along with a note and a map.

> *Clen, We're only a couple of blocks from the botanical gardens. I've marked the location on the map. We're members, so I'm leaving you the card if you'd like to visit. Help yourself to anything you find in the fridge. I'll be home by four. Jason usually doesn't get home until after six. We'll see you then! It's supposed to be a nice day. Enjoy. N*

Clen could well imagine Jase standing at Nancy's shoulder insisting she add there would be dire consequences if Clen left before they got home. She was glad to know her brother married a woman who would stand up to him.

While she waited for her toast to pop up, she looked out the window to see there was a small deck with a table and chairs. When her tea and toast were ready, she carried them outside. If anything, Nancy had understated the weather report. It was a gorgeous day.

And Clen had no idea how she was going to fill it, let alone all the days to follow. She sat with the sun warming her, listening to the birds, until the memories she'd spent twenty years trying to escape blanked everything out.

You have to help me, Mickey La. I can't take it anymore. You have to help me die.

No, Josh. Don't...

You said it's like going to sleep. So I'm thinking, if I'm already asleep, it shouldn't even hurt.

Josh, please, don't ask me to do this.

You're the only one I can ask. I've figured out how to do it, so you won't get in trouble. After Mom gives me my shot at midnight, she goes back to bed for a while. That's when you smother me. With a pillow. I won't feel a thing.

Josh, I can't. I just can't.

I'm not getting better. You know I'm not. And it hurts bad. I'm ready, Mickey La, please, help me not to wake up. Don't make me do this anymore.

At first, she'd refused to consider it. But every day, whenever they were alone, Josh begged her to make it the last day he had to suffer. And every night, she'd lain awake listening as her mother checked on Josh. Finally, one night, she slipped out of bed after she heard her mother leave Josh's room.

Josh was lying curled on his side, his thumb in his mouth, looking the way he had as a baby. She stood watching him a long time before going back to bed.

The next day was bad. Josh could no longer be soothed by stories and the medications did less and less to dull the pain. When she tried to comfort him, he grabbed her hand. *Please, Mickey La. Tonight. You have to. Please.*

That night, she'd again waited until she heard her mother leave Josh's room, then she'd gone to him, carrying her pillow. The shot he'd just received had done what work it could, and he was unconscious, but restless. She reached out and pressed his shoulder to shift him onto his back without waking him. As he moved, a tiny moan escaped, and his thumb popped out of his mouth. She took his hand in hers, feeling bones barely covered with skin. His breathing was shallow, his chest moving only slightly.

She smoothed the few wisps of hair from his brow and then, finally, she lowered the pillow. Such a simple thing. A pillow. Usually a comfort, something sought to ease the ache of a broken heart. Josh stiffened, his hand fluttering briefly in hers, then he didn't move again. She held the pillow in place until the clock struck the quarter hour. In the faint light, the ravages of the disease were invisible, and Josh was once again beautiful.

She'd stayed with Josh, holding his hand, until her mother came to give him his next dose. As he'd predicted, nobody suspected a thing. Her parents didn't even ask how long she'd been with Josh, or why she hadn't awakened them. *I'm so glad he wasn't alone*, was all her mom said.

On this beautiful summer day, Clen sat on Jason's deck in Denver and finally cried for Josh, tears she'd refused to shed for more than twenty years.

Then she went inside, washed her face, and called Gerrum.

He wasn't home, although that was hardly surprising since it was midmorning in Wrangell. He was probably working on the boats, getting them ready for winter.

"I'm in Denver. At Jason's." She tried to think if there was anything else she needed to say, but there wasn't.

Eyewitnesses are notoriously inaccurate, Jason once told her. But juries still love them. If she were sworn in and asked to testify to what she'd witnessed at Gerrum's that day, could she do it? With complete certainty?

Probably not. The images were overlaid with too much emotion and reaction for her to remember precisely what she'd seen. Which was perhaps why she'd reached a place where she was ready to listen to what Gerrum had to say.

~ ~ ~

Waiting for Gerrum's call, Clen went to the bookcase in the living room, picked a book at random, and lay on the couch to read. The next thing she knew, she was startled awake, her heart hammering. She tried to work through what awakened her and, after a moment, she realized it must have been the doorbell.

She padded to the door and opened it to find Gerrum there, oddly formal in dark slacks and a blue dress shirt she'd not seen before. Book-signing clothes?

They made him appear foreign, not her Gerrum of the flannel shirts and jeans. Or maybe the strangeness was more in the way he stood, balanced, as if he was prepared to move either toward her or away. And his expression was wary. Even more disconcerting, his eyes held no gleam of humor. Instead, they were shadowed with an emotion she was afraid to name.

Seeing that, her throat dried out completely. "What...why, how did you get here?"

"I flew. From Boston."

"Boston?"

"I went to Resurrection. Jason called to tell me you were here."

"Oh." Her hands clutched the door frame and her body refused to stop trembling. She ached to touch him so she wouldn't feel so separate. Seeing him, she no longer doubted she'd misinterpreted what she'd seen. And with that certainty, she knew her response—that swift and sure belief he had betrayed her—had broken her connection to him.

"Can I come in?"

She gestured him inside, through the living room and kitchen and out to the deck.

"Would you like something to drink?" Her voice wobbled. She cleared her throat, trying to steady it. "Water? A beer?"

"Water would be good."

She poured two glasses and came and sat across from him. "I blew it, didn't I?"

A lift of his eyebrows was his only response. No change in that wary look that was frightening her so badly.

"I saw you and Hailey, and it hurt so much, I didn't stop—"

"No, you didn't."

The words made her wince.

"Hailey's been going through a difficult time. A family matter. That's all. I would never—" His tone. Controlled, cool. Not as cool as those eyes, though. "I thought you'd figure it out. Call me." His words held both pain and a question.

"I can't take back what I thought. Can you forgive me?"

He examined her, rolling the glass between his hands. She tried to read him, but he'd gone opaque.

"You stopped trusting in us, Clen. In yourself. Giving up like that? Without a fight? Too easy. I need to know you won't do it again. That you'll stick around. Yell at me, if necessary, but don't ever leave like that again."

"You'd give me another chance?"

"Only if you're willing to be more open about..." He stopped speaking and looked her in the eyes. "Sometimes it feels as if you're holding back. I don't know..." He shook his head, looking frustrated.

He was right. She'd always held something back. Not wanting him to see her too clearly. Who she was. What she'd done. Sins of omission and commission.

He leaned across the table, and took one of her hands in his. "Tell me, Clen. What were you thinking just then?"

She struggled to meet his eyes. She'd already tried to confess, first to Thomasina and then to Jason, but she'd been unable to manage either one. Thomasina being dead was the ultimate barrier, of course, but why hadn't she told Jason when they were speaking of Josh last night?

It would have been selfish.

The thought came fully formed, as if spoken aloud by Mary John...or Thomasina.

But what about Gerrum? Did she have to tell him?

It happened long before she met him, after all. Still, not telling was an omission, a lie of sorts. Lie, lye—she'd never noticed that pairing before, but it was true. A lie eroded everything it touched, just like lye.

She took a deep breath and willed her muscles to relax. "I need to tell you something...about the real reason I went to Resurrection the first time." With those words, the high wire was back, suspended this time over a thundering falls, and she was preparing to take her first step.

Gerrum sat waiting, his hand unmoving, cupping hers.

"You see, I had another brother. Joshua. Jason's twin. He...he had leukemia. It was awful. Those last months. He asked me...he begged me to help him die." A shiver ran through her body, and Gerrum's hand tightened on hers.

She waited for the black spots, the ringing in her ears. When they didn't come, she raised her eyes to Gerrum's face. He looked puzzled, and no wonder. Struggling with how to tell it, she'd merely confused him.

She pulled her hand away, distancing herself. "I did what Josh asked. I smothered him."

An expression flickered in his eyes. Too quick for her to

interpret. "How old were you?"

She shook her head, denying that absolution. "Old enough. Nineteen."

"Did you love him?"

"Yes." She swiped a hand at the tears sliding down her face. "Oh, yes. So much."

Gerrum recaptured her hands and closed his own over them. "And he asked you to do it?"

"He begged me for days. He'd worked it out. The best time. How to do it so nobody would suspect."

"Do you regret doing it?"

The act had cast a dark shadow over her life. And yet, if Josh were here today, in pain, dying, begging her to help him… "No. I don't." Her words faded into birdsong and the faint hum of traffic.

The two of them continued to sit, hands connected.

"Come home with me, Clen."

"You still want me despite—"

"God, yes. The past can go to hell and welcome to it."

He stood and opened his arms, offering her the shelter of his embrace, the steadiness of his love. What he'd always offered.

She stepped into his arms and tucked her head into the curve of his neck, holding on tight as his warmth flowed into her, calming, soothing like a benediction. He rubbed his cheek against her hair, and she pulled in a deep breath, feeling a looseness, an ease she hadn't felt in years.

She and Gerrum, finally, with nothing separating them.

Chapter Twenty-Eight

The day after Clen and Gerrum returned to Wrangell, Clen went to the lodge to see John and Marian. Gerrum offered to go with her, but this was something she needed to do for herself, by herself.

Kody dozed in his usual spot by the back door. She bent to greet the old dog, then stepped inside to find Marian clearing out the kitchen, preparing for winter now that the season had ended.

Marian looked up when she heard the door. "Clen. Oh, my goodness." She came around the counter and threw her arms around Clen. "I'm so glad you're back. We were so worried, and Gerrum was simply frantic."

The words made Clen wince, but Marian's voice held no reproach.

"It was an idiotic thing to do," Clen said. "You're not mad at me, are you?"

"Do you want me to be?"

"I'm hoping you won't be. And that you'll let me come back next summer to cook."

"What do you think, John?"

Clen hadn't seen John when she came in, but there he was, standing in the doorway to the guest lounge. "Let me see if I have this straight," he said. "We take back the best cook we've ever had. Or, we spend the winter trying to convince some kid coming here for a summer is a great resumé builder."

"Well, that's an easy one," Marian said.

"Yep." John nodded, smiled, then put on his jacket and went out the door.

Clen turned to Marian. "Would you like help cleaning up?"

"I'd love it," Marian said. "Besides, you don't think you can waltz in here and say you're back without giving me the gory details. Spill."

Clen pulled in a breath, let it out, and took her place next to Marian. "So what do you know?"

"All we know is Gerrum checked with your folks and discovered your mother wasn't sick. He finally tried the abbey. Is that where you went?"

This wasn't easy, deciding what to share after keeping it to herself so long. Most people probably didn't need to do that, not when they were talking to someone as kind as Marian. "I seem to have a habit of running off to Resurrection when I have a problem."

"I guess that's better than going to a bar and drinking yourself into oblivion."

"More inconvenient, though."

Marian chuckled. "Indeed." A serious look replaced her smile. "You and Gerrum. You are together, right?"

For a moment, the memory of how it felt being estranged from Gerrum was so strong, Clen couldn't reply. The body did that sometimes. The brain recalled, the body froze. Then everything loosened again. "Very together. I've moved in with him."

"About time." Marian grinned broadly and hugged her again.

How did one learn to be spontaneous and openly affectionate like that? Probably years of practice. And she'd barely begun. Only a short time with Gerrum and already it wasn't so difficult to lift her arms and return Marian's hug.

~ ~ ~

Clen had one more stop on her reconciliation rounds. ZimoviArt was closed for the season, but Hailey was there, packing up. Clen tapped on the door. With a startled glance, Hailey gestured for her to come in.

"I was surprised to hear you hadn't left for Seattle yet,"

Clen said.

"I have the house until the end of the month, so there's no rush."

"Well, it doesn't look like you have much left to do here. Must have been a good year." Not the most sensitive comment, she realized. "For the gallery, I mean," and she'd just made it worse.

"I...I suppose so. As usual, Tess's quilt squares were the biggest sellers, and all but one of your paintings sold." Hailey's gaze skittered about, and waves of distress filled the gallery with a slight discordant vibration. No question, the difficult news must have been really bad.

"That's the reason I'm here, to pick it up. Save you the trouble."

"I appreciate that. It's right over here." Hailey gave her another distracted look.

Clen had never before been aware of another person's upset in quite this way. At least, not that she could remember, but maybe when she locked up her own emotions, she gave up that awareness. She still would have noticed Hailey didn't look good and that her movements were stiff and jerky, as if her joints were mechanical and had gone too long without oil. And given Hailey's distress, Clen couldn't just pick up her painting and walk out.

Deciding, she set the painting down and turned to Hailey. "You know, we never did get around to celebrating my other sales. How about you come over, for lunch. Today. That is, if you'd like to?" And if that wasn't the most awkward invitation on record, it had to be close.

"Oh, I don't think...you and Gerrum will want—"

"Gerrum's out for the day." Finally, Clen's voice began to behave. "He and Terry are winterizing the boats. If you don't come, I'll have to eat by myself." *Well, that was certainly gracious.* "I'd like you to come." *Better.*

"I don't know. Are you sure?"

"I'm sure." Clen moved decisively to shift the picture over by the door while Hailey put on her jacket.

Together they walked to Gerrum's house, where they spent the first moments hanging their coats and dealing with the picture. Then they went to the kitchen, where Hailey sat at the small table while Clen heated soup and sliced bread to go with

242

it. With another glance at Hailey, Clen got out a bottle of wine and two glasses. She served the soup, poured the wine, and sat facing Hailey.

She lifted her glass. "To a successful season."

Hailey bit her lip but raised her glass in response.

"And to friendship."

Hailey looked startled, then nodded without speaking. Clen took a sip of wine, watching as Hailey picked up her spoon and stirred her soup.

"I need to ask you something," Hailey said, with a quick glance at Clen. "When you left. Afterward, I worried you...that you thought Gerrum was—"

"If you're trying to ask, did I see you in Gerrum's arms in this house, the answer is yes, I did."

Hailey continued to avoid Clen's gaze.

"And then I did one of the dumbest things I've ever done. I jumped to the wrong conclusion on the basis of a few seconds' observation after I'd spent months getting to know Gerrum."

"I'm sorry. I didn't stop to think. I didn't mean to hurt you, or Gerrum."

"My own fault, thinking what I did. Not that it's impossible to imagine Gerrum in love with you. It isn't. Too easy, actually. That's why, well...anyway, my mistake was believing he would go behind my back." Clen took a fortifying sip of wine.

"You don't have to worry, you know. Not about Gerrum and me." Hailey pulled at the rings on her fingers. "I fell in love with him, but when I let him know—" She chewed on her lip. "He said I was too young for him, but he hoped he could be my friend." Hailey grabbed her wineglass and took a quick gulp of wine. "I'm sorry. The day I came here. I can't explain what it's about."

"That's okay." Clen dipped bread into her soup. "You know, this reminds me a bit of the meals at Resurrection Abbey. I visited there for a while." She no longer doubted that was general knowledge. "No wine, of course." But thank goodness for the wine, today. Without it, she and Hailey would be too skittery to put three coherent words together. "Lunch was always soup and bread, and we were supposed to savor it while we listened to a reading from scripture. It was very peaceful."

"Do they allow non-Catholics to visit?"

"Aren't you Catholic?"

"I'm nothing, really."

"We often had non-Catholic visitors at Resurrection."

"I guess an abbey would be a good place to, well, to sort through problems?"

"It was for me. The silence helped, but I found it was also good to talk about things."

Hailey gave up on the soup and began fiddling with her knife. Clen poured more wine. Hailey looked up from the patterns she was pressing into the tablecloth with the knife to smile briefly. "If I drink any more, I won't get anything done the rest of the day."

"If you get behind, I'll come help."

Hailey put the knife down, picked up the wineglass, and looked out the window. "You say talk can help. Maybe you're right. Maybe it would help if I tell you why I came to see Gerrum that day."

If Hailey was willing, Clen wasn't going to put her hands over her ears.

Hailey's voice started out strong but began to tremble. "Gerrum helped me find something out. The answer to a question..." She shuddered. "When I had the answer, at first I couldn't bear it. Gerrum was the only one who knew anything about it, that's why I came here." Her eyes, huge and dark, gleamed with tears that overflowed and started down her cheeks. She looked so vulnerable, so young, so bereft, Clen understood exactly why Gerrum had ended up with her in his arms.

"It's okay. You don't have to do this, Hailey."

"Yes. I think I do." Hailey took a deep, shaky breath. "Gerrum was helping me find out what happened to my mother. She was killed...shot. My father was convicted, but I figured out my brother had something to do with it." Her teeth clamped on her lip, turning it pale from the pressure. "I'd heard from my brother's widow, you see. She told me he was hit by a train, and they have a son..." Hailey bent her head, sobbing.

Clen went to her, putting an arm awkwardly around the other woman's hunched shoulders. The story was garbled, but Clen understood enough to know why Hailey asked Gerrum not to tell.

Hailey wiped her eyes and blew her nose. "I'm not making any sense, am I?"

"That's okay." Clen patted Hailey's shoulder and sat back down. "Take your time."

"It's all so confused, what happened. I don't think my dad shot her, but he bought the gun, loaded it, and left it sitting there. I hate him for that."

"You have every right to be angry."

For a time they sat without speaking, and Clen thought about her own anger. At God. As useless as Hailey's anger, but with a much less rational basis.

"Somehow, we have to figure out how to stop being angry and forgive," Clen said.

Hailey looked up, perhaps in response to the tone of Clen's voice. Clen stood and started water heating for tea. She turned back to the table to see Hailey had caught a beam of sunlight in the contents of her wineglass and was moving the small rainbow it produced in an arc on the table top.

"Do you think...that is, would you mind giving me the address for Resurrection? If I went there..." Hailey sighed. "Maybe I could find a way to forgive him."

Chapter Twenty-Nine

1986

During the winter, a FOR RENT sign appeared in ZimoviArt's window. When Clen saw it, she went looking for Doreen to ask about it.

"Oh, Hailey went off without renewing the lease. Afterward, she wrote Bill saying she ain't coming back. He just didn't get the sign put up till yesterday."

Clen was concerned about Hailey, and Doreen's news added to her unease. She asked for Hailey's address, but Bill had misplaced the letter.

~ ~ ~

In the spring, Clen's second in Wrangell, she and Gerrum were married in the tribal house of the Tlingit clan. Gerrum's mother and sister, Clen's family, and their Wrangell friends were in attendance.

When the season started, Clen went back to cooking at the lodge. It was a decision Gerrum encouraged, saying for him the busy summers made the quiet of the winters not just bearable, but something he looked forward to.

It wasn't until autumn, a year after Hailey left Wrangell, that she finally wrote. Clen scanned the contents of the letter, letting out a sigh of relief and beginning to smile as she reread.

Hailey was fine. She'd spent time with Sister Mary John at Resurrection, and then she'd met her brother's widow, and that had gone well. She hadn't yet contacted her father, who was still in prison, but she thought even that might be possible, eventually.

She wrote that she'd found a job in a gallery in Portland. The owner planned to retire in five years. If all went well, Hailey was going to buy her out. And last, but not least, she said she hoped Clen would send work for the gallery.

~ ~ ~

Winter tightened its grip with long, dark days of howling wind and sleet spitting against the windows. Clen countered the gloom by adding the absent sun to her paintings—a slant of light along the side of a boat, a reflection from a window, a shimmer in the water. While she painted, Gerrum worked on a new novel.

She'd once read about a scientific experiment where people were placed in a cave with no way to measure the passage of day and night. After a time, they began to eat, sleep, and live to a different rhythm. It was what she and Gerrum were learning to do.

Loving Gerrum was making up for all that had gone wrong in her life. The lost years with Paul—wiped away as if they were a story she could no longer remember clearly. The older pain—the loss of Saint—healed over as well. And the sorrow over Josh's death was no longer tinged with darkness. Her remaining regret was Thomasina, but perhaps a person wasn't meant to reconcile every estrangement.

"Thomasina was the first person to call me Clen," she told Gerrum as they cooked dinner together one night. "She told me once, I earned more demerits in six months than anyone else had in four years."

Gerrum humphed. "And you sound extremely proud of it. What did she do? Rap your knuckles."

"Of course not. And I *was* proud of it. To punish me, she made me think." Memories flashed and the winter dark receded. "She asked me once how I'd spend the day, if I knew it was my last. I said I'd spend it in the chapel on my knees, begging forgiveness for all my transgressions." The memory made Clen smile. "She told me I was being flipping flippant. And demanded I give an honest answer."

Gerrum chuckled. "You still are flipping flippant, love. But

247

how did you answer the question?"

"Oh, you mean the last day one? I didn't. There were too many things I wanted to do, and one day wasn't going to be enough to accomplish any of them."

Talking about Thomasina had brought tears to Clen's eyes. She sniffed and swiped at her cheeks. "I loved her, you know. But when she disappointed me, I pushed her out of my life."

"What did she do to disappoint you?"

"Shortly after I told her Joshua died, she went away. Without saying goodbye. She had her own troubles, but it didn't matter to me. All I knew was I wanted her to stay and fix me."

"What made you think she could do that?"

"I was young, remember. I figured if I could manage to tell her what I'd done, and she didn't reject me..." Suddenly, Clen was having trouble getting all the air she needed. "I went to see her last year, when I left Wrangell. But Marymead was closed. And she'd died. So I never had a chance to tell her how sorry I was. For acting the way I did."

Gerrum put his arms around her. "Don't you think she knows?"

"How could she? I refused to communicate with her. For years."

"You believe the spirit lives on, Clen. It means we're never finished. We can always say we're sorry."

"It's not the same."

"Maybe not, but it's still worth doing." He continued to hold her. "You do realize if you'd confessed to Thomasina way back then, we might never have found each other."

"You're saying I had to make a whole bunch of bad decisions before I was able to get it right?"

"Something like that. I've made bad decisions of my own, you know. But I like very much where they've led me."

"Is that a compliment, Mr Kirsey?"

"Definitely. So tell me. Now that you're older and wiser, would you have a different answer to how you'd spend your last day?"

"Fishing for a compliment, are we?"

"I take every bit of encouragement I can get." His tone was

light, but his expression was serious.

Her own sense of play evaporated as she looked at the man she'd married. "I'd spend it loving you," she said, laying the words like a gift before him, thinking how simple it had become. Questions about life, where she was going, what she was going to do. Her answer to all of them—Gerrum.

And could he be right about all those wrong turns being necessary for her to reach this right place? Or maybe they hadn't been wrong turns after all. Because now, looking back, she was beginning to see that her life, through all its twists and turnings, ups and downs, had been illuminated by grace. A grace she'd thought absent.

But now, in the gloom of an Alaskan winter, the gleam of that grace was visible, intertwined inextricably with the dark strands. The whole made more beautiful by that random shining.

A Note to Readers

Dear Reader,

Thank you for the gift of your time in reading *Absence of Grace*. I hope you enjoyed it and that you'll consider taking another few minutes to tell a friend about the book or to post a review. I'm so grateful for reviews, which are vital to my books' successes.

Reviews need not be elaborate. Even a brief statement of your opinion is a help to prospective readers.

I also hope you'll want to keep in touch with me by signing up for my mailing list. In addition to being informed of my new releases, you'll also receive a periodic newsletter.

I love hearing from readers. You can contact me through my website at ANNWARNER.NET

Acknowledgements

Many friends and relatives have been supportive of my career as a writer. It is the encouragement of these special people that has helped me through the many rough patches every writer encounters.

Evelyn Bowman, Shauna Buring, Jayne Close, Eugene Coats, Barbara DeSalvo, Elizabeth Eichel, Gary Grunewald, Kay Hartsel, Lois Kupferberg, Jean Nichols, Charles Pippenger, Rose Reifenberger, Kathy Steele, Andrea Wall, Delores Warner, Daphne Wedig, Dennis Worthen, Patti Worthen

And to all those who have written to comment on my stories, especially those of you who have told me my novels have been a source of comfort or distraction during tough times, thank you!

My gratitude as well to everyone who has posted a review of one of my books. Your kindness makes it easier for others to discover my novels.

I also wish to acknowledge and thank Jason Black, who saw more clearly than I did the story *Absence of Grace* needed to be and helped me to see it as well.

My heartfelt thanks!

About the Author

The books Ann loved most as a child were those about horses. After reading Mary O'Hara's Wyoming ranch stories, she decided she would one day marry a rancher and own a racehorse—not necessarily in that order.

Since it was abundantly clear to Ann, after reading *My Friend Flicka* and *Green Grass of Wyoming*, that money could be a sore point between husbands and wives, not to mention racehorses don't come cheap, she decided appropriate planning was needed. Thus she appended a "rich" to the rancher requirement.

But when she started dating, there were no ranchers in the offing, rich or otherwise. Instead, Ann fell in love with a fellow graduate student at the University of Kansas. Not only does her husband not share her love of horses, he doesn't even particularly like them, given that one stepped on him with deliberate intent when he was ten.

After years in academia, Ann took a turn down another road and began writing fiction. Her first novel, *Dreams for Stones*, was published by Samhain Publishing in 2007 and was re-released in 2015. The protagonist is both a university professor and part-time rancher—proof perhaps that dreams never truly go away, but continue to exert their influence in unexpected ways.

Those unexpected influences have continued to play a role in Ann's succeeding books, including this one.

I love hearing from readers. Questions and comments about my books are always welcome.

Visit me at AnnWarner.Net

Other Titles by Ann Warner
Similar to Absence of Grace

Dreams for Stones
Dreams TrilogyBook One

Indie Next Generation Book Award Finalist
Available as a free download.

Poignant and haunting, *Dreams for Stones* is a story of loss and second chances. Alan Francini, a man who has given up on love, and Kathy Jamison, a woman who has learned to let go of love too easily need all the magic of serendipity, old diaries, and a children's story to take another chance on love.

Persistence of Dreams
Dreams TrilogyBook Two

Alan, Kathy, and Charles's story continues. The ending of his love affair with Kathy and an arsonist seeking revenge are the catalysts that alter the shape and direction of deputy district attorney Charles Larimore's life. Forced to find both a new place to live and a way to ease his heartache, Charles finds much more as he reaches out to help his neighbor Luz Montalvo which eventually forces Charles to come to grips with his fractured friendships. He will also discover the source of his nightmares and the fragmented memories of his childhood.

Unexpected Dreams
Dreams TrilogyBook Three

Murder made to look like an accident, family secrets, interfering mothers, lovers in conflict. All combine in a satisfying mix in this contemporary romantic mystery.

Doubtful

Doubtful Sound, New Zealand - For Dr. Van Peters, Doubtful is a retreat after a false accusation all but ends her scientific career. For David Christianson, Doubtful is a place of respite after a personal tragedy is followed by an unwelcome notoriety.

Neither is looking for love or even friendship. Each wants only to make it through another day. But when violence comes to Doubtful, Van and David's only chance of survival will be each other.

Counterpointe

Art, science, love, and ambition collide as a dancer on the verge of achieving her dreams is shattered by an injury. Afterward, Clare Eliason rushes into a marriage with Rob Chapin, a scientist. The marriage falters, propelling Clare and Rob on journeys of self-discovery. Rob joins a scientific expedition to Peru, where he discovers how easy it is to die. Clare's journey, which takes her only a few blocks from the Boston apartment she shared with Rob, is no less profound. During their time apart, each will have a chance to save a life, one will succeed, one will not. Finally, they will face the most difficult quest of all, navigating the space that lies between them.

Love and Other Acts of Courage

A freighter collides with a yacht and abandons the survivors. A couple is left behind by a dive boat. These are the dramatic events that force changes in maritime attorney Max Gildea's carefully organized life where win, lose, or settle out of court he gets paid and paid handsomely. As he represents the only survivor of the yacht sinking and gets involved in the search for the couple missing from a dive trip, his reawakening emotions catapult him into the chaos of joy and sorrow that are the necessary ingredients of a fully lived life.

Ann's Cozy Mystery Series
The Babbling Brook Naked Poker Club

Books One - Four Now Available
Book One available as a free download

A painting worth millions, valuables gone missing, and a game that is more than a game. And that's just the beginning. These novels are set in a retirement community, but life for the residents is far from over. Colorful characters cope with both the mysteries and difficulties of life along with other more concrete dilemmas.

Made in the USA
Columbia, SC
12 July 2020